PENNY PRESTON
AND THE
SILVER
SCEPTER

• MISALIGNED BOOK II •

ARMEN POGHARIAN

PENNY PRESTON AND THE SILVER SCEPTER

· MISALIGNED BOOK II ·

CamCat
Books

CamCat Publishing, LLC
Brentwood, Tennessee 37027
camcatpublishing.com

Hardcover ISBN 9780744302172
Paperback ISBN 9780744301304
Large-Print Paperback ISBN 9780744304688
eBook ISBN 9780744304886
Audiobook ISBN 9780744302110

Library of Congress Control Number: 2020952099

Cover design/book design by Maryann Appel

5 3 1 2 4

For Anna, my own Penny and a dedicated Editor

WELSH AND CELTIC TRANSLATIONS

WITH PRONUNCIATION HELP FOR SELECT WORDS

General Notes about Pronunciations

Please note that while there are variations in Welsh pronunciation, for the most part, the suggested pronunciations follow the northern rules (at least for vowels). Also, there are no silent letters in Welsh, so everything is pronounced.

Vowel sounds are generally short for words with more than one syllable, a=*pat*; e=*pet*; i=*pit*; o=*pot*; u=*pit* (yes, u=i most of the time); w=oo as in the word *book* (yes, w is often a vowel); y=uh, like the a, in the word *above*.

Single syllable words typically use long vowel sounds [a=*father*; e=ae like *aerodynamic*; i=i in the word *machine*; o=aw like the word *hawk*; w=oo like the word pool; u & y are the same as i].

Ch sounds like the Scottish *loch*, not the English *church*. Not all words are Welsh in origin, for those without clear pronunciation rules, Welsh was used.

As for stresses, they typically fall on the second to last syllable. Also, while *Cait Sith* would typically be pronounced Ket Shee, I've left it as Kate Sith—call it writer's license if you must.

Below are definitions and pronunciations for the most common Welsh words.

Amddiffyniadau (am-thi-fuh-nia-dya): A Druid book of protections

Bedwyr (Bed-wir): One of Arthur's knights

Bodach (baw-dach): Entities from the fifth dimension trapped in the lower planes

Cait Sith (Kate Sith): Multi-dimensional cats native to our dimension

Caradog (Kair-ah-dog): One of Arthur's knights

Carchar enaid (kar-kar enide): Soul Prison—an object used by druids to control the power of others

Cei (Kay): One of Arthur's knights

Coch Coblyn (Koch Kob-luhn): Red Leprechaun

Conglfaen (Kongl-vyn): Keystone Talisman

Crom Dubh (Krom Doow): Powerful Bodach that takes an elemental form in the lower planes

Da bo ti fy ffrind (da bo ti vuh frind): Goodbye, my friend

Dawnus (dow-nis): Gifted, someone who can see spirits or has premonitions

Diafol Fragu (dia-vol fra-gi): Devil's brew, a Welsh curse

Derwyddon tân (dare-ooey-thon taan): Druid's Fire, used to control higher dimensional entities

Enaid (enide): Soul, a person's spiritual essence

Fomoire (vo-moy-ray): Demon/entity from a dark matter universe

Gwysio sianel (gwuh-sio sia-nel): Summoning channel from our universe into the upper dimensions

Hudoliaethau (Hid-oh-li-ee-sa): A druid book of incantations

Hysbrydion (Hes-bird-yun): Spirits/entities from the higher planes

Picau ar y maen (Pi-cair-uh-mine): Traditional Welsh cake flavored with cinnamon and nutmeg

Rhyfeddol (rhuh-veth-ool): Druid incantation of control

Teyrnwialen o Saith (teyrn-ialen aw syth): Scepter of Seven

PROLOGUE
LONDON IN 1666

I N A DIMLY LIT ROOM, THOMAS FARYNOR LIFTED THE NEARLY fifty-pound sack of flour from the floor onto the heavy wooden kneading table. He opened the sack and carefully poured the flour into a giant ceramic mixing bowl. Despite his care, a puff of fine, brown dust rose from the bowl enveloping his face. He stifled a sneeze and waited for the cloud of flour to settle. Flour dust and flames were an explosive mix that had destroyed more than a few bakeries. Satisfied it was safe, he retrieved the lantern from the outside windowsill. Using its flame, he lit small kindling fires at the back of each of his three open-hearth brick ovens. The glow from the ovens filled the room, revealing the all too small pile of wood next to the ovens.

He shook his head. "William!"

His son appeared from around the corner of the ovens.

"William, we need more wood."

"Are we baking cottage loaves tonight?" the young man asked.

"Of course. Tomorrow's the first Sunday of September, and you know what that means."

"Yes, the city will be full of people going to the Feast of the Farmer at St. Paul's."

"Hours of listening to the good Abbot lecturing against the sins of gluttony and lust hardly qualifies as a feast to me." Thomas chuckled. "But the important thing is, those people will be hungry. A lot of 'em are going to come down Fleet Street on their way to the bridge. And who are they going to pass at the corner of Fleet and Pudding Lane?"

"Us."

"That's right . . . hundreds of hungry souls walking right by our door. We'll sell as many loaves as we can bake. By stacking the dough into cottage loaves, we can make twice as many loaves and still sell 'em for the same price as regular ones," he said with a twinkle in his eye. "But we need a hotter oven. And for that, we need more wood."

"Father, it'll take me half the night to bring in that much wood. Who will help you knead the dough and stack the loaves?"

"Good point, son. Wake our boarder. As a journeyman carpenter, I'm sure he has plenty of experience hauling wood. Promise him an extra loaf for his help."

"Is it really necessary to offer him an extra loaf?"

"No, but he did a fine job repairing the cooling shelves; saved us half a shilling and several days of lost baking. Remember, any man can have a turn of bad luck. Someday, we may need the charity and grace of another." Thomas placed his hand on William's shoulder and smiled. "Now be quick about it so you have time to help me with the baking. I'll even let you make your own loaves."

William smiled back at his father, then disappeared around the corner. He hadn't been gone a minute when Thomas heard a loud banging at the door. He added some larger kindling to the fires and followed the sound. He opened it, expecting to find his son or the journeyman bearing an armload of firewood, but was surprised to see a small, disheveled man dressed in red, leaning on a gnarled walking stick.

"Pardon me, sir for the lateness of the hour, but there's a chill in the air and me bones are too tired to sleep on the street. Could ya see it in yer kind heart to spare a soul a warm place to pass the remaining hours of the night?"

"I've no time for beggars now. I've got baking to do. Come back after the morning crowd's been by, and I'll have a crust for you." He started to close the door.

"I'm no *beggar*. I'm merely a weary traveler denied the comfort of a warm fire in a strange place. Perhaps I'll have to teach the citizens of this unfriendly town a lesson in kindness." He banged his walking stick on the ground, spritely spun about, and walked away into the darkness.

Scratching his head at the odd spectacle, Thomas closed the door and turned back toward the hearth . . . just as William and the journeyman brought in their first load of wood.

"Father, what was that about?"

"Just a beggar."

"A strange time of night for a beggar."

"True, he was a strange beggar alright. A short, scruffy fellow dressed in red looking for a warm place to spend the night."

"Dressed in red?" the journeyman asked.

"Yes, all red, and he had a stout walking stick. No matter; he's gone. Now, why don't you two fetch some more wood while I add what you've brought to the fire."

The journeyman twisted a five-stoned ring on his finger and whispered, "*Coch Coblyn.*"

A WINTER'S DAY IN PIPER FALLS

P ENNY LEANED AGAINST ONE OF THE CENTURIES-OLD TREES IN Schoen Park. She nervously pulled her hat down over her ears. While a cold north wind blew through the park, she knew it wasn't the terrestrial weather that sent chills down her spine. It was the microfractures in the dimensional fabric. They signaled a pending temporal event when multiple timelines would coexist in the same physical space. Episodes of folded time were normally rare, but over the last several weeks, they had become quite common in Piper Falls.

Mr. Myrdin, who was *the* Merlin of Arthurian legend, and his companion Master Poe—a higher dimensional being trapped in a raven's body—tied the surge to their recent battle against the *Crom*

Dubh. It had taken the three of them and her best friend Duncan working together to defeat the icy extra-dimensional creature. While they had saved the universe from invasion, the monster's explosive death overloaded the dimensional fabrics with extra-dimensional energy. The resulting temporal aftershocks caused the increase in time folds.

Usually, time folds were short-lived phenomena that would fade away on their own. They might create a few paranormal incidents but were otherwise harmless. Unfortunately, the ones created by the aftershocks were more powerful. In addition to potentially trapping people on the wrong side of the fold they also attracted the shadow-like entities known as the *Bodach.*

The *Bodach's* connection to the fifth dimension had given them god-like powers in our universe. As teachers, they had helped establish early human civilizations. Eventually, they established themselves as deities reigning over the world. When Master Poe's arrival severed that connection, they lost their powers and began to slowly fade into nonexistence. Those who survived were drawn to extra-dimensional phenomena. If they successfully tapped into one of the powerful time folds, they could regain their powers.

To prevent that, Penny and Duncan had spent the month since the battle chasing and closing time folds. Penny's misalignment, which allowed her to interact with the higher dimensions, let her sense and close the time folds before they went critical. Using a talisman fashioned by Penny and Master Poe, Duncan was able to help her spot the folds.

He also made sure none of the "normal" townsfolk accidentally found themselves on the wrong side when Penny closed it. Tonight, they also had help from Simon, Penny's extra-dimensional cat known as a *Cait Sith.*

Time folds began as a singularity of extreme cold on the dimensional fabric. As they expanded, the fabric became thinner, creating small gaps. When the gaps became large enough, strands of time could leak through and weave an alternative timeline on top of the existing one. This singularity was the coldest and fastest-growing one Penny had ever encountered. Almost as soon as they had spotted it, the yellow time strands from the past began wriggling through.

"That's a big one," Duncan said.

"Yeah, it's also moving really fast. And someone was near the back entrance to the park. Can you run over there and make sure whoever it is doesn't get too close?"

"No problem," he said and took off down the snow-covered path.

What about me? Simon's familiar voice said in her mind.

I didn't forget about you. I haven't sensed any Bodach, but with a fold this powerful, it won't be long before they show up. Do you think you can keep them away?

Of course, I am Cait Sith.

Penny reached her hand down and scratched the large black cat across the star-shaped, white spot on his chest. A small purr emanated from the *Cait Sith* before he turned and left.

Confident that she wouldn't be disturbed, Penny turned her attention to the growing singularity. Seven yellow strands from the past had already slipped through and were interweaving themselves with the blue strands from the present. They were well on their way to forming an intermingled timeline.

Penny reached into the mass of yellow and blue time strands. Each strand was about five feet long and as thick as her pinkie. She grabbed the nearest yellow filament in her right hand. The cool sensation of interdimensional energy raced up her arm. She gave the strand a slight twist and a gentle tug. Its far end slipped through the incomplete weaving. She passed it to her left hand and grabbed a second, then a third strand. Despite her early concerns, closing this powerful singularity was going quite smoothly.

That changed the instant she turned back to reach for the fourth strand. Two new time filaments had emerged from the singularity. She had seen that once before, but these two filaments were unlike any she had ever encountered. They were intertwined like a tightly braided rope. The only way she could tell them apart was that instead of being yellow, one of them was blood red.

Even stranger, instead of working with the other strands to create a stable timeline, the new double strand followed a different pattern. It slipped in and out of the interdimensional tapestry the others were weaving.

Once its full length was enmeshed in their weaving, it began violently twisting and coiling itself. Within just a few seconds, the entire alternate timeline framework was ruined. All that remained was a roiling tangle of yellow and blue time strands with bits and pieces of the braided strand sticking out in odd places.

Penny glanced from the knot to the singularity, which was continuing to grow. While she couldn't see them yet, she sensed the approach of more yellow time strands. She needed to send the first set back through the singularity, but she couldn't do that until she separated them from the blue strands that belonged in this time.

She took a deep breath and studied the knot. She found a pair of yellow strands that looked promising, but when she pulled them nothing happened. She tried several more combinations of yellow strands but met the same result. If anything, the knot was now tighter and churning more rapidly. She began to wonder if this was an unsolvable puzzle like the one Alexander the Great faced with the Gordian knot. His solution was to cut the knot with his sword. She had no idea how to cut a time strand, much less what would happen if she did.

Penny, several of your friends are approaching the park.

Penny glanced toward the park gate. Gene Shoemaker, Eddie Macias, Mark Chapman, and the Anderson twins, Mary and Grace, had spotted her and were heading into the park. Besides Duncan, they were her closest friends, but none of them knew about misalignment, extra-dimensional beings, or that Mr. Myrdin was the real Merlin. There'd been a few close calls, but other than a few annoying rumors about a budding romance between her and Duncan, no one suspected anything.

Duncan will take care of them, Penny said.

He's at the other end of the park keeping that strange sign-waving man out.

Mr. Potter, the town's eccentric, sure seemed to have a gift for poor timing! *Can you keep them out?*

I am with them now. The girls are petting me, but the boys are less interested. I do not think they will wait much longer.

Master Poe's advice to her had been that once she started mending the fold, she needed to finish at all costs. He didn't say what would happen if she didn't, although she got the impression it wouldn't be good. If she couldn't untie the knot, all she could do was send all the strands through the singularity. If she did that, she would alter the fold and send some of the blue strands from the present into the past.

There was no telling what those strands would bring with them. While unlikely, Mr. Potter and her friends could get pulled into the past.

The boys have left and are only steps away from entering the park, Simon said.

She decided to give it one more try. She reached into the spinning maelstrom of time strands and grabbed one. As soon as she touched it, she knew it was the braided red and yellow strand. Besides being thicker than the others, the braided strand was strangely warm. Its temperature rose quickly, and in a few seconds, it became too hot to hold. She let go. As soon as she did a brilliant orange flash filled her vision. When it cleared, the roiling knot was gone. Even more astonishing, in her left hand, she held seven yellow time strands.

Simon's voice rang in her head. *The boys are at the gate.*

Faster than she thought possible, she opened a trans-dimensional rift, placed the yellow strands in it, and launched the rift through the singularity. It shrank to nothing and vanished, taking all signs of the time fold with it.

At that very instant, Gene Shoemaker crossed under the park's gate. As he did, the tassels on his wool hat floated through the air until they were standing up above his head.

With his eyes wide open, he said, "Hey! What's going on?"

"Dude, you look like a giant bug with antennae coming out of your head!" Eddie Macias said.

A spark jumped between the floating tassels, emitting an audible crack. They dipped down a bit but continued to float above Gene's head.

"Wow, that was wicked cool!" Eddie said.

"Awesome!" Mark Chapman said.

Grace Anderson rushed up to Gene. "Are you okay?"

Her twin sister, Mary, scowled at the other two boys. "This is nothing to laugh about. That was a powerful electrical shock. Gene could get seriously hurt."

Gene placed his hand on Grace's shoulder, looked her in the eyes, and shook his head. "Other than a slight ringing in my ears, I feel fine."

Duncan arched his eyebrows toward Penny as they both arrived on the scene. She pursed her lips and shrugged.

Mr. Potter, his fliers in hand, came to the gate a moment later and said, "I've seen this type of thing before. It's a buildup of static electricity. You know, kind of like what happens when you drag your feet on the carpet. Probably the combination of this dry winter air and passing under the wrought iron park gate."

"Are you sure?" Mark asked.

"Absolutely, we just need to give the charge a path to the ground and everything will be fine," Mr. Potter said.

"How do we do that?" Mary asked.

"One of us just has to touch one of the tassels," Mr. Potter said.

"I don't know. Did you see that spark?" Eddie asked.

Mark chimed in. "Yeah, that'll be one wicked shock."

"Nonsense," Mr. Potter reached out with a gloved hand and grabbed the left tassel. As soon as he touched it, there was a loud *crack*! Mr. Potter was knocked off his feet. If not for Duncan and Penny, he would've fallen to the ground.

"Are you okay, Mr. Potter?" Grace asked.

"Uh, yeah, I'm fine." He looked a little like Albert Einstein in that famous picture with his hair standing on end. Using his hands, he tried to force his hair back down onto his head. For the most part, it worked, but a few stragglers continued to resist gravity's pull. "It was a big static charge, but nothing more than a little shock," he smiled. Wiggling his fingers, he looked at his smoldering glove. "I guess I'll need a new pair of gloves."

2

ACROSS TOWN, A FEW HOURS LATER

NOT LONG AFTER THEY BUMPED INTO EACH OTHER AT LAST year's haunted Halloween party at the Bluebird Inn, Emily Robertson's secret crush on Ted Malone, her co-worker at the Monroe Institute, blossomed into a whirlwind romance. By December, they were a steady couple. They made it official when Ted spent Christmas at her parents' farm just outside of town. Ever the gentleman, he never complained about staying in the frigid, unheated guest room.

He spent a good portion of Christmas day with her father splitting wood for the stoves that heated the rest of the old farmhouse and helping her mother clean the dishes after their Christmas dinner.

In the few weeks since then, things had only gotten better. Emily wasn't sure what love was supposed to feel like, but she knew it couldn't possibly be better than what she felt for Ted.

She leaned across the car seat and playfully kissed him on the cheek.

"What was that for?"

Smiling, "Just for being you."

Ted momentarily took his eyes off the road to return Emily's smile.

Suddenly, Emily screamed, "Ahh! Ted, stop!"

Startled, Ted paused before looking up to see what looked like a gnarled dwarf version of Santa Claus standing in the road. He jerked the wheel. There was a loud *thump* and a *bump* as the pick-up truck swerved into the opposite lane. Ted quickly regained control and pulled off the road onto the shoulder.

"Do you think we hit him?" Emily asked.

"We hit something, but I don't know what it was." Visibly shaken, Ted unfastened his seatbelt and opened his door.

Emily followed him down the road. In the twilight, she could make out a small lump lying on the shoulder of the road. She ran to catch up to Ted, reaching him just as he stooped over the lump. "I think I might have hit this deer."

"Is it dead, and what do you mean you *think* you hit it?"

"It's dead, but it looks like it's been here for a while."

"What makes you say that?"

"Well, there are teeth marks on it like something's been eating it."

"Maybe you hit what was eating it?" she suggested.

"Maybe, but the only footprints besides ours and the deer's belong to another person. Someone wearing long, pointed shoes."

"Pointed shoes? Like high heels?"

"No, more like one of Santa's elves, albeit a very *heavy* elf," he chuckled.

"I don't mean to sound crazy," Emily said, she paused and bit her lip, "but when I screamed, I swear I saw a little man at the side of the road."

"Was he wearing red?"

"Uh-huh. How do you know?"

"I think I saw him, too. Help me look in the brush. Maybe we hit him and knocked him off the road. He might be unconscious."

Before they stepped off the road, they heard what sounded like an angry curse followed by several *pops* and a gentle hissing sound coming from Ted's pick-up. They ran back to the truck. Emily swore she heard a melodic laugh from somewhere in the woods.

She looked at Ted, but his attention was focused on his truck's tires. "Can I borrow your phone? I need to call a tow truck, and I should probably call the sheriff."

"Why? What's wrong?"

"All four tires are flat."

"That's strange."

"That's not the weirdest part. They all have identical puncture marks in them."

"Like they've been slashed?"

"No, more like they've been bitten."

KRIS JENKINS TOOK A DRINK OF WATER, SWISHED IT AROUND HER mouth, and spit the last remnants of toothpaste into her bathroom sink. She stared at her tear-streaked face in the mirror and wondered if she'd made a mistake in breaking things off with Randy.

To her reflection, she said, "He's a good guy, but there's no magic when he kisses me. A girl needs to feel a little magic from her man, doesn't she?"

As if in answer to her question, there was a loud knocking on her front door. She hesitated. She wasn't sure she had the strength to face Randy again. The knocking persisted. Unable to resist, she wiped away her tears, grabbed her robe, quickly looked in the mirror, and headed to the door. On the way, she promised herself she wouldn't take him back no matter what he said.

She opened the door, fully expecting to hear Randy's voice begging her to give him another chance. But instead, a strange, almost musical voice said, "Pardon me, ma'am, but it's a wee bit cold out this evenin'. Could ya see it in yer kind heart to spare some time by the fire for a down on his luck soul?"

She looked down and saw that the voice emanated from a stunted man with a long, ratty beard dressed in shabby red clothes. He held an oversized red cap in one hand and a gnarled wooden cane in the other. She noticed that his feet and hands were very long and out of proportion to his size. He reminded her of a grotesque cross between a troll and a garden gnome.

Despite his pleasant harmonious voice, the site of the twisted little man sent Kris's pulse racing. She wanted to scream. Her mouth dropped open, but nothing emerged. Not knowing what else to do, she slammed the door shut, bolted it, and ran back to her bedroom. She buried herself under her covers and drifted into a fitful, nightmare-filled sleep.

Kris woke up the next morning to the *ding-dong* of her doorbell. She looked at her clock. Who would come by at eight thirty in the morning on a Sunday in Piper Falls? Sure she'd imagined it, she fluffed her pillow and closed her eyes.

The doorbell rang again . . . and a few seconds later, yet again.

Randy or the gnome? she wondered but didn't want to see either.

Reluctantly, she got out of bed, slipped into yesterday's jeans and shirt, and headed to the front door. The ringing had become more insistent.

"All right, already. I'm coming!"

She opened the door to Deputy Sheriff Fred Barnes standing on her stoop.

"Good mornin', Ms. Jenkins," he said making sure to avoid direct eye contact.

"Good morning, Deputy." She knew the deputy had a crush on her. She always did her best to discourage him politely but coming to her house on a Sunday morning was a bit much. "To what do I owe the pleasure?"

"Well, uh, Ms. Jenkins, this ain't a pleasure call."

"Oh?"

"You see, there's been some, uh, complaints."

"Complaints . . . about me?"

The deputy nodded.

"About what?"

"About your laundry," he replied, returning his stare to the ground.

"Did someone steal my laundry?"

"Uh, no, someone stole Mr. Higgins's laundry, but yours ain't missing."

"Did I leave it out on the clothesline overnight again?" she asked in as innocent a tone as she could muster. "My dryer's on the fritz, and I keep forgetting to bring it in at night. Tell Mrs. Walsh I'll bring it in right after I've had my coffee and that it won't happen again."

When she finished, Deputy Barnes didn't say anything.

He just continued to stand on her doorstep.

"Deputy, I said I'd take care of it. Just as soon as I've had my coffee."

"Uh, I know, but I think you should come out here with me before you worry about your coffee."

Sensing he wouldn't take no for an answer, Kris Jenkins followed the deputy into her front yard where she was greeted by a spectacle she'd never imagined. She had indeed left her laundry out on the line, but it wasn't on the line any longer.

Her sheets shrouded the top of a thirty-foot maple. Socks and pants hung from the lower branches. Several bushes wore her favorite dresses. Worst of all, her underwear adorned not only her mailbox but those of her neighbors as well. Her panties dangled provocatively from the doors while her bras pointed suggestively upwards on the mailboxes.

Horrified, she turned back toward her house and noticed several scratches about waist-high on her front door.

PARANORMAL INVESTIGATOR DARIN KOLCHAK HAD JUST NODDED off, when a *ding* from his desktop computer on the far side of his Brooklyn apartment abruptly woke him. Groggily, he reached for the computer's mouse. The switch from power-saving mode to full-up screen flooded his face with light. He rubbed his eyes and blinked against the relative brightness. Once his eyes adjusted, he lowered his hand and saw that he had not one but three new emails.

The subject of the first email screamed that its contents were spam, but it was a slow night, so he opened it anyway. He shouldn't have bothered. Sarah Williams from London had won a $5 million sweepstakes in San Marino, but because the United Kingdom had never formally signed a peace treaty with San Marino after World War II, she couldn't claim her prize. Fortunately for him, the United States had signed a treaty. So, for the minor favor of sending the routing code of his American bank account to her, she'd happily pay him $100,000.

Kolchak chuckled at the scammer's creativity and audacity. He doubted most recipients even knew that San Marino was a real country, much less the false reports and rumors that it had been anything but neutral in the war. He whimsically contemplated replying with a brief history lesson but decided against it. No point in validating his email address for the spammer. Instead, he deleted the email and made a note to upgrade his anti-spam software.

The second email looked more promising. The subject simply read "Champy." The writer claimed to have unambiguous proof that Champy, Lake Champlain's cousin of the Loch Ness monster, really existed. A true believer, Kolchak's heartbeat accelerated, but as most often happened, disappointment quickly followed.

The email turned out to be another con. For just $500, the author promised exclusive rights to examine the evidence. As a show of good faith, the writer attached a grainy photo of a shadowy shape several hundred yards from the shore. Despite the effort the sender had put into photo-shopping Vermont's Green Mountains into the background, Kolchak immediately recognized it as the debunked "driftwood" photo of the Loch Ness monster. He deleted the email and added the sender's address to his junk mail filter.

Kolchak recognized the last email address. It was from one of his fellow paranormal enthusiasts, Sheriff's Deputy Fred Barnes in Piper Falls, NY. Fred had recently sent him an email about multiple ghost sightings at a Halloween party up there. While there were many eyewitnesses, with just a little research, Kolchak had learned that the hosts of the party were well known special effects enthusiasts. So, he didn't follow up with a trip to Piper Falls. If Fred felt slighted, he hadn't said anything about it. Fred wasn't the brightest bulb out there, but like Kolchak, he was a true believer.

Kolchak turned to his powder blue Budgerigar parakeet. "All right, Pandora, let's see what Freddy's got for us this time."

"Gotta believe, gotta believe," the parakeet replied.

Kolchak laughed. "You're right, Pandora, you can't find something if you don't believe it exists."

He opened the email. All it contained were three links to recent articles in the *Piper Falls Press*. Kolchak sighed again. "I think Freddy's still upset that I didn't show up in person to inspect that Halloween party."

"Gotta believe, gotta believe."

Kolchak looked up at Pandora and shook his head. "I guess I shouldn't have fallen asleep during that *X-files* marathon."

The bird stared back impassively.

Turning back to his computer, Kolchak clicked on the links and read through the articles. "Freddy thinks something from the world of Faerie has crossed into our world in Piper Falls. By the sounds of it, whatever it is has a rather nasty sense of humor, too. Pack your bags, Pandora. We're heading upstate."

"The truth is out there," replied the bird.

3

SUNDAY MORNING, THE DAY AFTER THE
INCIDENT AT SCHOEN PARK

PENNY AND DUNCAN SAT NEXT TO EACH OTHER ON THE LOVE
seat in Mr. Myrdin's living room.

Master Poe perched motionless on the mantle, looking more
like a statue than a living bird.

Mr. Myrdin walked in from the kitchen with a steaming
mug of his favorite Earl Grey tea, sat down across from them,
and said, "All right, why don't you tell us about last night's time
fold?"

After they finished, Mr. Myrdin nodded. "I'm glad no one
was seriously hurt and that your friends accepted Mr. Potter's
explanation of things. The last thing we need is anyone connecting
the two of you to these time folds."

"I agree, but how do you explain the behavior of the time strands? This was the seventh time fold I've closed, and I've never seen strands act like that before," Penny said.

"I would guess that the excess extra-dimensional energy from our defeat of the *Crom Dubh* interfered with the strands' weaving," Mr. Myrdin said.

"So instead of a new timeline, they formed a knot," Duncan said.

"Yes. Master Poe, what do you think?"

"I agree that higher levels of energy could interfere with the time strands' weaving. However, it has been several weeks since we defeated the *Crom Dubh*. While the energy levels remain higher than normal, the ripples are nowhere near powerful enough to explain the knot."

"What if something concentrated the ripples?" Mr. Myrdin asked.

Master Poe bobbed his beak up and down. "Yes, that's a possibility, but it would take a powerful talisman to do it."

"Could my amulet have done it?" Duncan asked.

Master Poe shook his beak from side to side. "No, your amulet only has three stones. It would take a talisman with at least five, and that would only work if it was wielded by someone who was naturally misaligned."

"Okay, but what about oak? Schoen Park has the oldest oak trees in town. Perhaps the trees' natural resistance to extra-dimensional energy created an amplifying effect," Mr. Myrdin said.

"So, you're saying the oaks acted like a magnifying glass," Duncan asked.

"I'd have said a telescope, but yes that's the general idea. What do you think, Master Poe?"

"Theoretically, it's possible. However, the oaks would have to be properly aligned with the singularity across all the dimensional planes. Given the power of this singularity, I suspect it reached into at least five, perhaps even six, dimensions. I'd have to take some measurements, but the odds against such an alignment are truly astronomical."

"Penny, you've been rather quiet," Mr. Myrdin said. "What do you think? After all, you are the only one of us who actually interacted with the strands."

Penny let out a sigh. "I'm sorry, but I think we're on the wrong track. Higher energy may have made the singularity more intense, but I don't think it created the knot."

"Oh, what makes you say that?" Mr. Myrdin asked.

"Well, the knot didn't form until after the braided red and yellow time strand arrived. It also acted oddly, almost like it was trying to create a knot rather than weave a new timeline. On top of that, why was one red and intertwined with another time strand?"

"Those are good questions, Penny. While they're outside my area of expertise, I think with your help, I might be able to get some answers."

"Okay, but how can I help you?"

"This will be similar to when we worked together to create Duncan's amulet, but this time we'll reach into the knowledge cloud of my dimension."

"What do you need me to do?"

"Recall the braided strand and concentrate on how it interacted with the other strands. Are you ready?"

Penny nodded.

"Now look into my eyes and keep the image of the braided strand in your mind. Recall everything you can." The temperature in Mr. Myrdin's living room dropped ten degrees. Lines of blue, yellow, and red power flashed between Penny and Master Poe's eyes. An instant later, the lines faded, but the chill remained in the air.

Duncan rubbed his arms with his hands. "What just happened, and why is it so cold?"

"With Penny's help, I accessed the knowledge compendium of the Time Harmonics Conservatory. As for the cold, when I opened the compendium, it sapped some of the energy from this dimension. I should have realized that and warned you."

"That's fine, but did you get any answers to our riddle?" Mr. Myrdin asked.

"There's a lot to digest. Give me a moment to sort things out." Master Poe flew down from the mantle, landed on the coffee table between the love seat and Mr. Myrdin's chair, and began pacing.

After almost a minute, he said, "Sorry, the math was a bit complex, but I think I can summarize. Yellow time strands represent specific events from the past. When a singularity forms within the dimensional fabric, it pulls strands from the past into the present. Those yellow strands work together to interweave their timeline within the fabric occupied by the present, which is represented by the blue time strands."

"Right, so that's why I remove the yellow strands from the blue fabric and send them back through the singularity to close a time fold. Why was last night so different?" Penny asked.

"I believe two uncommon things coincided to alter last night's fold. First, braided strands are quite rare. They represent two aspects of a single event that are bound together. Simply put, one cannot happen without the other. Because of that, it can be difficult for them to work effectively with the other strands from the past. Compounding things, the braided strand arrived after the original seven strands had already begun weaving their timeline. Something in their creation must have conflicted with the event represented by the braided strand."

"So the braided strand created the knot to stop them?" Duncan asked.

Master Poe bobbed his beak up and down.

"Okay, that explains the knot, but why was one of the braided strands red?" Penny asked.

"I couldn't find anything in the compendium about red time strands. It's clearly extra-dimensional in origin, but it's not an aspect of time."

"Could it be one of your higher-dimensional enemies using a time fold to enter this universe?" Mr. Myrdin asked.

"No, higher dimensional portals might allow time travel, but there's no way to use a time fold to create a higher-dimensional portal."

"Then what could it possibly be?" Duncan asked.

After a short pause, Penny said, "It's a *Bodach* from the past."

Mr. Myrdin stroked his chin and looked to Master Poe. "A time-hitching *Bodach*. What do you think?"

Master Poe ruffled the feathers at the tips of his wings. "Unfortunately, it's the only proposal on the table that fits the facts."

"What do you mean, unfortunately? Didn't we just solve the mystery?" Duncan asked.

"Yes, but now we have a new problem," Mr. Myrdin said.

"I never sent the braided strand back through the singularity," Penny said.

Duncan shook his head. "You mean . . ."

"We've got a new extra-dimensional visitor somewhere in Piper Falls," Penny said.

4

THE DIM AND DISTANT PAST

THE GROUND SHOOK VIOLENTLY. A VASE TOPPLED FROM ITS perch and crashed to the ground. Shards of clay scattered across the walkway tiles. Water meandered between the tiles and shards. Ash-covered blue petals rode the miniature river across the tiles.

Amunet ran through the debris. She trampled her precious lunar flower petals and crushed the shards of the vase beneath her feet.

The earth shook more violently. She fell to the ground. The only sound to penetrate the deafening roar of the exploding sky was the sharp snap of Amunet's elbow shattering against the stone tiles.

The earth ceased shaking. She rose from the walkway. Ignoring her pain and straining to be heard above the shrieking of the wind, she yelled, "Iosheka!" More tremors shook the earth. Clutching her shattered elbow, she stumbled across the courtyard. "Iosheka! Iosheka! Where are you?"

A violent tremor knocked Amunet from her feet.

A young and powerful hand grabbed Amunet's arm and steadied her against the shaking earth. "Mom, I'm here." The seventeen-year-old Iosheka helped her with one hand even as he carried a dark-stained oak case in the other.

With her good arm, Amunet hugged her son. Tears rolled down her cheeks.

Iosheka returned her hug, squeezing her tightly. The wooden box banged her elbow. She winced.

"Mom, where are you hurt?"

Amunet stepped back from her son. "I fell in the courtyard and hurt my elbow. I can't use my right arm."

Iosheka looked at his mother's arm. Her forearm extended at an awkward angle from her obviously broken elbow. Habitually, he bit his lower lip.

Amunet forced a smile. "It looks worse than it is. Once we're resettled, our medics will heal it, but until then, I'll need your help. I see you retrieved the Gaol; did you bring the Asclepia pods? Without them, the young Gaol won't be able to transform into their flying form."

Iosheka released his lower lip.

"Yes, mother. The case is stuffed with pods and leaves."

"What about the Sekhem? Surely, you didn't leave it in the lab?"

Iosheka reached into his tunic and withdrew the gem-encrusted silver scepter.

"I needed someplace to put the Gaol and their leaves. So, I used the Sekhem's case. It'll be safe in my tunic."

A thunderous explosion echoed through the sky, and the ground shook more violently. A cloud of dust engulfed them. When the tremor subsided and the dust settled, the lab entrance was gone, replaced by a pile of rubble.

"Your tunic pocket will have to do."

A gale-force wind laden with dust and debris ripped through the courtyard. Amunet clung to her son with all the strength her good arm could muster.

Iosheka sheltered his mother from the wind. Unable to reach around her while holding the Gaol, he gripped the case in both hands and squeezed his mother between his body and the oak box.

A piece of wind-driven glass embedded itself in Amunet's good hand. She gasped with pain. Her knees buckled. Only Iosheka's hold kept her from falling.

Just as quickly as it had risen, the wind passed. It became stiflingly hot, and soft gray ash fell from the sky, muffling all sound.

Amunet whispered into her son's ear. "We must hurry to the dock before the last ship sails."

The combination of the choking ashfall, tremors, and rising heat made for a hellish journey to the docks. Scores of buildings burned while dozens more were piles of rubble. Bodies of the dead and dying littered the capital city's once grand boulevards. The wounded cried out for help. With tears in their eyes, Iosheka and Amunet hurried through the devastation. They had to get the Sekhem to the last ship.

A strong tremor pulled Amunet from Iosheka's grasp and sent him crashing to the ground. He narrowly avoided falling into a gaping fissure that suddenly appeared in the earth. Regaining his senses, he felt the weight of the Sekhem in his tunic pocket. He scanned the area looking for his mother and the Gaol case. He saw the case wedged between two large rocks. It was scratched, but otherwise, it appeared to be intact. He saw no sign of his mother.

"Mother!" he screamed. No reply. "Mother, where are you?" Still no response. He persisted until he was nearly hoarse.

Then he remembered the fissure. It had opened next to him . . . right where his mother had been walking.

He looked toward the fissure and saw a dust-covered hand. He ran to the edge and peered over the side. His eyes met those of his mother.

"Mother," was all he could manage in response.

"I was lucky to grab the edge, but I can't hold on much longer."

Iosheka reached down with both hands and pulled his mother free. As her feet cleared the crevice, there was another powerful temblor, and the fissure closed.

Amunet hugged her son tightly. "You always had a good sense of timing." Breaking their embrace, she took a scrap of her dress and dabbed his lower lip.

Iosheka winced.

"Haven't I warned you about biting your lip?"

"Yes, Mother. We've got another half-mile to go. Do you think you can make it?"

"Yes, yes, I told you . . . other than my elbow, I'm fine."

He cocked his head slightly as he looked at her.

She picked up the Gaol case with her good arm and handed it to him. "After you went to all the trouble of rescuing them, it would be a shame to lose the Gaol now."

"Thank you."

"Good to see you still have your manners. Let's get moving."

The hardest part of their journey was witnessing the destruction of their civilization. Not a single building remained unscathed; even the great dome of the Ganondagan observatory, where Iosheka had dreamed of studying, was cracked.

They emerged from the desolation and found a crowd of fellow survivors lined up on the quay to board the last ship in the harbor.

"We're just in time," Amunet said with a reassuring smile.

The sight of the Toth's dual stacks emitting sparks into the air as the crew powered up her twin magnetos brightened Iosheka's mood. He returned his mother's smile.

"She's a beautiful ship."

"That she is," said a crewman, who stood on the quay helping the last of the refugees on board. "And Seskat's the finest captain a ship could have. With her at the helm, you've got nothing to worry about. She's brought us through worse storms than this little blow, that's for sure," the middle-aged man added without the slightest hint of exaggeration.

Just in front of Amunet stood a little girl clutching a stuffed rabbit close to her chest. Iosheka guessed that she was no more than seven. Through tears, she said to the crewman, "She can't see the stars or the sky. How will she know where to go?"

"What's your name?" the crewman asked.

"Everyone calls me Bes. What's yours?"

"Mine's Aker. Now as for getting lost, it's true that we might not see the stars for days, but Captain Seskat doesn't need the stars to steer the ship. The Toth has a special tool called a gyromagnet. No matter what the weather, we'll know where the polestar is. Even if we can't see the sun, the Captain will know our bearing. There's no way we can get lost."

He knelt and wiped away the young girl's tears.

Another temblor hit. The quay shook. The waiting passengers struggled to remain standing; many failed, and some fell off the dock. Iosheka fell and hit his head. The screams of those who'd fallen in the water jolted him back to reality.

He looked for his mother. She was nowhere on the quay. He ran to the edge of the dock and searched the water for her. The calls for help faded quickly as the victims were pulled out to sea by the receding harbor water.

One scream persisted. It was Bes. She'd fallen off the dock. Her dress was caught on one of the cross supports. It saved her life but left her dangling helplessly above the harbor.

Iosheka wanted nothing more than to find his mother, but he couldn't ignore the helpless little girl. Everyone else on the dock was rushing toward the Toth. He was her only chance for survival.

He lay down on the dock and reached over the edge. He grabbed her dress, but the girl was struggling too much. Her dress ripped. She screamed.

"Bes, my name's Iosheka. I'm going to pull you up onto the dock, but I need you to be still. Can you do that for me?"

"I'm scared."

"It's all right to be scared. I'm scared too, but if we help each other, we can chase our fear away. Can you help me with that?"

She nodded.

"Good. Now I'm going to grab your dress and pull you up here with me." With the girl remaining still, he easily pulled her onto the dock.

"Nice job!" said Aker, patting Iosheka on the back. "Now let's get moving; the Captain's taking the Toth out to sea before the water surges back into the harbor."

"Could you make sure Bes makes it onboard?"

"Of course, but what about you? I can't leave you here."

"I've got to find my mother."

"She's already on board. Fought us like a demon." Aker showed Iosheka several bruises on his well-muscled arms.

"Sorry about that."

"Nothing to worry about. But the only way I got her to stay on board was to promise that I'd come back and look for you."

"She's safe?"

"Yes, now come with me. I can't imagine what that woman will do to me if I return empty-handed."

Bes, Iosheka, and Aker fought against the powerful wind toward the Toth.

Just as they got there, Bes screamed hysterically. "Hapi! Hapi! I dropped Hapi. I need Hapi!"

Iosheka spotted the doll. It had blown down the dock and wedged itself next to the Gaol case which he thought he'd lost in the sea. He turned around.

Aker grabbed his shoulder. "Are you mad? The Toth's wheels are turning!"

"I can make it. It's not just her stuffed rabbit. I need to rescue the Gaol," Iosheka shouted.

"Do what you must, but the Captain won't wait for you."

Iosheka nodded, and the crewman released his grip on the boy.

Iosheka retrieved the stuffed rabbit and the Gaol case. The fierce wind and flying debris battered him as he ran toward the Toth. Above the din, he could hear Aker and other refugees cheering him on.

Less than fifty yards from the ship, an earsplitting crack knocked Iosheka from his feet. Together with the remnants of the destroyed pier, he collapsed into the cold embrace of the massive wave that engulfed the harbor.

From the Toth's wheelhouse, Captain Seskat shouted against the wind and the sound of the ship's magnetic powered engines.

"Aker, has everyone boarded?"

"There was one more, but the pier just collapsed."

She shot the crewman a questioning glance. He shook his head. She winced and turned back into the wheelhouse. "Helmsman, give me full power to the engines, and let's get the Toth to the safety of the open sea."

"Aye, Captain. Full power!" The helmsman drove both throttles forward.

Strong vibrations coursed through the deck as the engines drove the Toth's twin propellers faster and faster. The acceleration was so abrupt that passengers—and even some of the less seasoned among the crew—struggled to remain standing.

Amidst the chaos, Amunet broke free from the crewman holding her and ran to the rail, screaming, "Iosheka! Iosheka! No, you can't leave my son!" She ran to the wheelhouse and forced her way to the throttles.

Before she could disengage them, Aker grabbed her from behind and lifted her off the deck. She kicked the air wildly. Despite several painful connections with his shins, the first officer held her steadfast in his powerful grip.

"Put me down! Put me down! My son's back there! We can't just leave him behind!"

Aker altered her position so that her feet hit nothing but air. "That's enough. The pier's collapsed, and the sea is rushing out of the harbor. If we don't get out to deep water, we'll run aground, and the incoming wave will smash the Toth like she was made of paper. There's nothing more to be done."

Through her sobs and wails, Amunet continued to struggle, but it was clear that she wouldn't escape from the brawny officer. A minute later, the healer arrived. Before Amunet could react, he placed a thanojector on her arm. Amunet felt a small pinprick. She turned her head to scream at the healer, but the sedative quickly took effect, and she lost consciousness.

"That was fast," Aker said.

"Yes, I gave her a powerful dose. She'll be out for several hours."

"Good, now get her off of my bridge, and secure her in her quarters."

"Aye, Captain," Aker replied.

"And, Aker, be sure to assign a crewman to stay close by her for the next several days. After going through all the trouble to rescue her, I wouldn't want her jumping overboard."

5

LATE SUNDAY MORNING IN PIPER FALLS

WHILE SITTING ON HIS PORCH, SHERIFF'S DEPUTY FRED Barnes watched an old, beat-up, seventeen-foot U-Haul truck pull into his driveway. When the door opened, he recognized his friend.

"Kolchak!" Fred yelled from his chair. No one ever called him Darin. "I'm so glad you decided to come. What's with the truck? You plannin' on movin' in?"

"I'm happy to be here, Freddy. As for the truck, do you remember Mrs. Scully?"

"Your neighbor, the little, old red-haired lady."

"Yeah, that's her. Well, she got really sick back in the fall and passed away."

"Sorry to hear that."

"Yeah, she was a nice lady. Anyway, I guess she really appreciated me dropping by to fix her computer and internet connection. So, she included me in her will."

"And she left you this heap? Maybe she didn't like you as much as you think."

"She didn't leave me the truck. Do you remember that coffee can Mrs. Scully was always throwing loose change into?"

"Sure, but even this dilapidated, ol' thing must've cost more than a coffee can full of spare change."

"True, but when her lawyer gave me the can, he also gave me a note from Mrs. Scully."

Fred's eyes widened.

"What'd it say?"

"From one true believer to another, empty the can and solve all your problems."

"Empty the can . . . what the heck did that mean?"

"I didn't know either, but she was a nice lady. Besides, nothing good ever comes from ignoring the dead."

"Ain't that the truth."

"So, I dumped the coins onto the floor."

"Did you find any rare or valuable ones?"

"No, that's the first thing I thought of, too. I found $117.27 plus another $3.53 Canadian and seven Swiss Francs, but nothing rare or valuable.

"I started to put the coins back into the can when I noticed a series of numbers etched into the bottom of it. Do you know what those numbers were?"

"Let me guess, you played those numbers in the lottery and won," Fred answered with just a hint of sarcasm.

"No, they were the International Bank Account Numbers for a Swiss bank account with just over fifty thousand dollars in it."

"Fifty thousand dollars! Where'd she get that kind of money? And if she gave you $50K, why are you drivin' that heap?"

"I have no idea where she got the money. One of her relatives said she'd been saving loose change in cans for years. She must've put it all in the Swiss bank account and just left it alone. As Einstein supposedly said, 'Compound interest is the most powerful force in the universe,' so I guess it just built up. As for the truck, well, I needed more room for all the new equipment. It takes a lot of power to run all that high-tech gear."

"High-tech gear? All I see is a rundown U-Haul. Tires don't even look new." Fred idly kicked one of them.

"This is no ordinary U-Haul. Come around back, Freddy, and take a look." While Fred moved toward the back, Kolchak continued, "I bought this truck at an auto auction for only $500."

"Looks like you paid too much to me," Fred mumbled.

Ignoring his friend, Kolchak walked to the liftgate, flipped the latch open, and raised the sliding door.

Fred's mouth dropped open. Both walls of the truck were lined with LCD screens and sophisticated electronic equipment. Two swiveling chairs with harnesses were mounted on a track that ran down the middle of the trailer.

"Would you like a tour?"

"You bet I would." Fred climbed into the truck and sat down in one of the chairs.

"In front of you are the displays for the two 360-degree rotating digital cameras and three separate thermometers. Over here is the Geiger counter and a white noise generator."

"You've got thermographic and night vision cameras!"

"Yep," Kolchak smiled at his friend. Next, he pointed to a set of shelves and hooks. "We've also got a complete set of tactical equipment for use outside the truck."

"Why have you got both the K-II Electromagnetic Field meter and the original numerical kind?"

"The K-II's are more sensitive, but some of the older detection algorithms require the numerical input of the original meter."

"Oh," Fred nodded. "What's in them two large boxes?" He pointed to the compartment that hung over the cab.

"One has batteries. They're customized versions of the ones you'd find in a hybrid car."

"This thing's a hybrid?" Fred's eyes widened again.

"No, the engine's conventional gasoline combustion, but it does keep the batteries charged, and they power all of this equipment. I can run everything for more than twelve hours before I need to turn the engine on for a recharge. The other box contains an Ion generator."

"I take back what I said earlier, this truck is totally awesome!"

"I'm glad you like it."

"I give it two thumbs up!"

Fred turned and looked through the sliding window into the truck's cab. Clinging to the brass bars of a birdcage, a powder blue Budgerigar parakeet stared directly at him.

"Is that who I think it is?"

Kolchak nodded. "None of Mrs. Scully's relatives wanted her, so I agreed to take her."

"I guess every silver linin' comes with a cloud."

"Oh, Pandora's all right, as long as you don't let her watch too much TV."

Fred shook his head. "Enough about that annoyin' bird. Even with all of this stuff, you should've had some money left over to spring for a new paint job. You know, maybe black with a cool ghostly logo."

"I've got one more thing you need to see."

Fred hopped out and followed Kolchak around to the passenger side of the truck. A large mural of a flying saucer covered the trailer. Below the mural, a caption read, "Roswell, New Mexico. Out of this world."

SWIM PRACTICE LATER THAT MORNING

"YOU NEED TO PICK UP THE PACE, PRESTON!" COACH HARLOW YELLED from the pool deck.

Penny barely heard her. She touched the wall, and without looking at the clock, pushed off for the seventh of eight 100s in the set. It was slower than the previous six, and she missed the interval. She didn't even stop at the wall. Instead, she flipped straight into the final 100. She took a breath on her second stroke off the wall and saw Coach Harlow raising her hands and shaking her head as she followed her along the side of the pool. Penny abandoned her alternate side breathing and took the rest of her breaths toward the center of the pool.

When she finished, the other kids had already completed their warm downs and were heading toward the locker room.

Coach Harlow called out, "Penny, even at the end of practice you should be able to make hundreds on the 1:30! Just because you made States already doesn't mean you can loaf your way through practice."

"I'm sorry, Coach, I really was trying."

Coach Harlow tilted her head to one side. "Is something wrong? Are you sick or hurt?"

Penny was tempted to take one of the offered excuses, but she didn't want to lie to her coach. She shook her head and instead told a half-truth. "I guess I'm just tired. It's been a rough week at school, and I haven't been sleeping very well."

Coach Harlow pursed her lips and scratched the back of her neck with one hand. "All right, I want you to give me an easy 200 warm down, and I'll see you on Tuesday."

"Coach, what about tomorrow's practice?"

"I think you should take tomorrow off." Penny started to protest, but her coach raised her hand. "This is the first year you've come to the weekend practices. There is such a thing as working too hard. I don't want you running yourself down and getting sick before States. Okay?"

Penny nodded. "Okay, Coach."

By the time Penny got to her locker, everyone else was already dressed and gone. She rushed out the door and found Duncan leaning against the far wall waiting for her. Together, they began their walk home, neither saying a word.

After a few minutes, Duncan broke the silence. "What was up with you and Coach?"

"Oh, it's nothing."

"She called you Preston. She only calls swimmers by their last names when she *really* wants them to listen. Was she mad at you?"

"No, she just wanted to know why I was having trouble with the workout."

"Well, what did you tell her?"

"The truth of course."

Duncan cocked his head to one side and said, "Eh, which truth?"

"I told Coach Harlow that I haven't been able to sleep or think straight because I've been too worried about an extra-dimensional braided time strand that I encountered when I was closing a time fold."

Duncan narrowed his eyes. "You're kidding, right?"

Penny sighed. "Of course, at least about the time strand. I just said I was tired because school was keeping me up late. She told me to skip practice tomorrow."

"Okay, that makes sense. I mean, she did the same thing with a few swimmers last year. She doesn't want you to get sick before States."

Penny let out another sigh, then gently punched him in the shoulder.

Even though it didn't hurt, Duncan rubbed his arm. "Okay, I guess I deserved that one. So, you were kidding about telling Coach Harlow, but you *are* worried about the braided time strand, right?"

"How could I be so careless to lose a time strand?"

"Don't beat yourself up too much. I mean, you did close the fold, and nothing happened . . . well, nothing besides Mr. Potter getting a bit of a shock." Duncan laughed.

"I don't think it's anything to laugh about."

"Sorry, but Mr. Potter looked pretty silly with his hair all frizzed out and his smoldering glove."

"Yeah." Penny struggled not to laugh at the Einstein-like image of Mr. Potter. "But that's not what I'm talking about. What if there is a *Bodach* attached to that braided strand? Who knows what it might do, and it would all be my fault."

"I don't know much about time strands, but if we could beat the *Crom Dubh*, then I'm sure between us, Mr. Myrdin, and Master Poe, we could take care of a time-hopping *Bodach*."

At that moment, Simon appeared out of nowhere and rubbed against Penny's legs.

Duncan added, "And of course we also have Simon."

Yes, do not forget about me.

Penny reached down and scratched the young *Cait Sith* behind his ears.

Of course, I would never forget you, Simon. She turned back to Duncan. "You're probably right, but . . ."

"But what?"

"Something felt wrong when I helped Master Poe access the compendium's knowledge. Did you notice anything odd about it?"

Duncan pursed his lips, then shook his head. "I mean, that was quite a chill, but it always gets cold when you open rifts."

"That's just it. I don't think I opened a rift."

"Isn't that the kind of thing you'd remember?"

"Yeah, but all I can remember is concentrating on the braided strand."

"Do you think he and Mr. Myrdin are trying to hide something from us?"

"They've left things out before."

"Why would they do that now?"

"What if the time hopper isn't a powerful *Bodach* . . ." Penny just let it hang there.

"What else could it be?" Duncan asked.

"Another misaligned person."

6

SIX MONTHS AGO, AT THE HISCOCK ARCHEOLOGICAL SITE

"PROFESSOR RICHARDS! PROFESSOR RICHARDS! YOU GOTTA see what Meagan found!"

Dr. Richards carefully placed the ancient stone projectile point back among the flint knappings on the plywood topped sawhorses that served as his field desk and turned toward the entrance of the tent.

Not surprised, he saw a young undergraduate student panting with excitement.

"Professor Richards, you gotta come see what Meagan found!" she repeated.

"All right, calm yourself . . ." he squinted to read her name tag, ". . . Andrea. It's been there for thousands of years. I'm sure a few more minutes won't do any harm. Now, why don't you lead me to whatever it is that Meagan's found."

Andrea caught her breath and led him into the newest section of the dig. Another young woman wearing a baseball cap with a dark auburn ponytail hanging down her back stood by a fresh pile of dirt with a look of awe and confusion on her face.

"Okay, Meagan, what have you found?"

"I don't know. I'd just reached the 6,000 YA (years ago) level, and I found something that doesn't make any sense."

"Why don't you show me."

Slowly, she pointed to the ground next to the pile of fresh earth.

He bent down to take a closer look. Without turning from the object, he asked, "Are you sure you've followed timeline protocols?" His tone was a little harsher than he'd intended.

They both nodded vigorously, and from what he could see around the object, they were telling the truth. It wasn't the Mastodon tusk he'd been hoping for, and it would probably turn out to be some sort of site contamination.

If not, it might just end up being the most important discovery of his career.

------✦------

SUNDAY MORNING IN MR. MYRDIN'S HOUSE

MYRDIN LOOKED OUT THE WINDOW. SATISFIED THAT PENNY AND Duncan were safely down the street, he went to the kitchen, refreshed his mug of tea, and went back to the living room where Master Poe had returned to his perch on the mantle.

"All right, what was that all about?" Myrdin asked.

"Whatever do you mean?"

Myrdin rolled his eyes.

"I mean that little theatrical show you just put on. Time Harmonics Conservatory indeed. You and I both know you didn't just reach into the seventh dimension. Even with Penny's help, it would be much too dangerous. So why the story about accessing this fictional compendium of knowledge. What were you *really* doing?"

"I assure you that the Time Harmonics Conservatory exists, and its members maintain a compendium of knowledge which I did access. However, you are correct that I did not do so through the higher dimensions. I didn't need to because I have the entire compendium here with me."

"Then why the elaborate ruse?"

"Think of the compendium as a library that contains all my people's knowledge about time, but instead of being written in books or saved as ones and zeroes in computer files, the information is stored as pure thought."

"So, all you have to do is think of what you want to know, and it pops into your head?"

"In a manner of speaking, but the data is organized for seventh-dimensional thinking. Unfortunately, I only have access to the three spatial dimensions and time in this universe."

Myrdin stroked his chin. "So, finding the thoughts you want is like looking for the proverbial needle in a haystack while you're wearing a blindfold."

"Yes, if the needle is microscopic and the haystack is as large as a mountain."

"All right, I understand that the braided time strand is the needle, but if you didn't need access to the higher dimensions, how did Penny help you?"

"When Penny closed the time fold, she acted across multiple dimensions. When I asked her to concentrate on her memory of the event, she recreated those conditions."

"Ah, you whittled down the haystack then?"

"Actually, I magnified the needle, but you get the idea. Somehow the braided time strand had minimized its presence in her conscious mind. That's why she lost track of it. My link with her gave me access to her subconscious memories, and that allowed me to find what I needed."

"Why couldn't you have just said that instead of making up the story?"

"Human subconscious is a strange thing and I didn't know how the braided strand's manipulation worked. Frankly, I was afraid if I revealed my intentions, I would fail."

"Once you succeeded, why didn't you tell us?"

Master Poe ruffled the tips of his feathers. "What if I need to reach into her mind again?"

"On that pleasant thought, do you *really* think Penny's right about someone from the past using the time fold to jump forward into our timeframe?"

"We've done it many times ourselves, so why couldn't someone else?"

"Not to swell your head, but I doubt they have a Master from the seventh dimension to teach them how."

"No, I'm the only one in this universe."

Myrdin raised his eyebrows. "Are you sure? Your destruction of the *Crom Dubh* released a lot of energy. Maybe it damaged the dimensional fabric enough to let another entity into our universe?"

"I would *know* if someone else from my continuum entered this one, and no one has. However, one thing is clear. Our visitor must be someone with a great command of extra-dimensional energy."

"So, you agree with Penny that it's likely to be a powerful *Bodach*?"

Master Poe ruffled his tail feathers. "We've always assumed that the *Bodach* want to return to the time before my arrival when their own multi-dimensional portal was open, right?"

Myrdin nodded.

"Then why would one of them use a time fold to come to the future?" Master Poe continued.

"Good question. Maybe the *Bodach* was escaping from something, or it sensed all of the extra-dimensional energy released by the death of the *Crom Dubh* and came here to reenergize."

"Perhaps, but I fear we're overlooking another possibility," Master Poe said.

"I'm not sure I follow you. If the time hopper is not someone from your dimension, then it has to be a *Bodach*. What else could explain a connection to the higher dimensions?"

"Another misaligned person," Master Poe said.

Myrdin steepled his fingers in front of his face. After a few moments, he let out a long sigh. "Do you think this misaligned person accidentally fell through the time fold into our time? After all, we've never encountered an untrained misaligned person who could create and navigate a time fold on their own."

"True enough, but we've also never known one to fall through a time fold either. No, this was no accident. Whoever came through that fold knew what they were doing."

"If that's true, that person would have to be quite misaligned. Maybe as much as Arthur or even Penny."

"Perhaps even more so," Master Poe said.

"But how could we have missed someone as powerfully misaligned as that? And if such a person does exist, how have they survived without formal training? Not to mention, why would another misaligned person come to this time?"

"Good questions that I can't answer. What I do know is that if I hadn't linked to Penny's subconscious memories, we wouldn't have known the braided strand remained in our time at all."

Myrdin dropped his hands from his face. "So whoever it is, they don't want to attract any attention. That doesn't inspire confidence in their motives."

Master Poe shrugged his wings up and down. "No, it doesn't, but of course all of this is mere speculation. I have no doubt that Penny's right about someone or something using the fold to connect to our time. As to their nature and their motive, that remains a riddle worthy of Poirot or Holmes."

"Speaking of riddles, my former colleague Tom Holman from the Monroe Institute's Archeology department has asked me to help him solve one."

"Oh, what would that be?" asked the raven, cocking his head to the side.

"They found something strange at the Hiscock site up in Byron."

"Isn't that the archaeological site where they're always digging up bits and pieces of Mastodons?"

"That's the one."

"So now you're an expert on Mastodons?"

Myrdin shrugged. "All I know is that they came to the Monroe asking for code-breaking help and that Tom thought of me."

"I guess we've both got a mystery to solve," Master Poe said.

IN THE DIM AND DISTANT PAST

THE RAPID ACCELERATION OF THE TOTH'S MIGHTY MAGNETIC-
driven engines combined with the powerful undertow,
delivering a rough ride through the shallows of the capital's inner
harbor.

Using her intimate knowledge of the harbor and a near empathic
connection to her ship and crew, Captain Seskat guided the Toth to
the safety of the open sea.

"Reduce engines to two-thirds; secure all passengers, crew, and
cargo. Maintain present course until we breach the incoming surge."

"Aye, Captain, engines two-thirds," a crewman replied. He
pulled back on the throttles, reducing the engines' deep thrumming
to a barely audible hum.

Less than a minute later, the lookout cried, "Surge incoming from two-seven-zero at one half-mile!"

"Helmsman, come about to two-seven-zero."

"Aye, Captain steering to two-seven-zero." The helmsman turned the ship's wheel, and the Toth slowly turned to face the incoming wave.

"Surge incoming at one quarter-mile!" called the lookout.

"It's coming in mighty fast!" Aker said.

"The undertow's too strong. It's locked the rudder against the ship. We're not going to complete the turn!" the helmsman said.

"Brace for impact!" Aker yelled.

Seconds later, the powerful surge struck the Toth thirteen degrees to the port side of the bow. The sea crashed onto her deck, driving the Toth's bow down, while the surge lifted her stern into the air. For an instant, her screws turned freely through the air. Moments later, the surge passed. The stern dropped and met the sea with a deafening crash, knocking everyone off their feet.

Captain Seskat was the first to regain her footing. She stared back toward the distant harbor, but all she could see was an immense wall of water at least seventy feet high. It engulfed the entire waterfront. Several seconds later, a thunderous rumble reverberated through the ship.

After the echoes of their civilization's death cry passed, an eerie silence gripped the Toth's passengers and crew.

Captain Seskat was the first to speak with a simple, one-word command. "Status?"

With a quick look at his gauges, the chief engineer replied, "Engines online and ready."

"Helm's responding normally again," added the helmsman.

"One confirmed casualty," Aker said.

"Who?" Seskat asked.

"Kepri . . . he was on lookout duty."

After closing her eyes briefly, Seskat said, "Helmsman, come about to zero-three-zero and maintain two-thirds power."

"Aye, Captain. Ship coming about to zero-three-zero."

"Aker!"

"Aye, Captain?"

"After you run a complete damage report, stand down the crew and establish a normal duty roster. I want a full count of our passengers and a list of any special skills they might have."

"Aye, Captain. Where should we quarter everyone?"

"Double up the passengers in the staterooms. Place extras wherever you can find space but keep them out of the engine room and off my bridge. If necessary, stretch extra sleeping berths in the hold."

"Aye, Captain. What about rations?"

"Put everyone on spare rations."

"The crew won't like that, Captain."

"They won't like it if we run out of food either," she said, holding her first officer's eyes in her intense gaze.

Aker knew that look meant there was no room for debate. "Aye, Captain."

PRESENT DAY

"HI, TOM," MYRDIN SAID AS HE ENTERED ONE OF THE LABS IN THE archeology wing of the Monroe Institute.

"Myrdin, it's good to see you." The tall, dark-haired man with glasses vigorously shook Myrdin's hand. "I bet you didn't expect to be back so soon."

"No, I must say I didn't."

"How's retirement treating you?" Tom asked with a wink.

"Oh, I keep busy."

"I'll bet. Spending all day with a bunch of eighth-graders must be . . . tiring."

"Yes, it can be like herding cats, but occasionally you can get them to purr. Teaching has many rewards. Not a lot of pay but many rewards." Both men laughed. "Now just exactly why have you called me, Tom?"

"You're familiar with the Hiscock archeological site up in Byron?"

"A late Pleistocene and early Holocene dig where they've found a lot of mastodons and some paleo-American artifacts, arrowheads, spear points, things like that, right?"

"That's right."

"Okay, but I'm a physicist and language guy, not a mastodon or paleo-American expert. So why am I here?"

"Yeah, I always thought that was a strange combination. But anyway, it's not about those things, it's about . . . this." He pointed toward a polished wooden box on the table.

"May I see it?"

Tom nodded.

Myrdin picked up the box and turned it over in his hands. Besides some minor pitting and a single deep scratch, the nut-brown stained box was extremely smooth. Judging from the patterns in the wood grain, it appeared to be carved from a single piece of oak. The seams along the lid were so well matched that Myrdin could've sworn the box was solid. He couldn't imagine it was an authentic Stone Age artifact.

"You're not telling me this is from the Pleistocene, are you?"

Tom said nothing.

"Surely, there must be some mistake. The students are playing a prank on their professor. I hear the dig director's not the easygoing sort." Myrdin placed the box back on the table.

"You're right. Dr. Richards is a most fastidious field archeologist, but he assures us that this is no joke and that proper timeline protocols were strictly followed."

"Well, there must be some other explanation. Perhaps a farmer buried it there and forgot about it. That sort of thing happens all the time."

"We thought along those same lines. So, we had the box carbon dated."

"Well?"

"The box is a little over seven thousand years old."

"There must've been an error. Did you rerun your tests?"

"Yes, we radiocarbon dated the box using both the traditional method and the laser technique; they both agreed. The box is seven thousand years old, which implies it was a little over a thousand years old when it was buried."

"How can that be?"

"I don't know, but that's not the most amazing part. Open the box."

Myrdin did, and his jaw dropped.

"The butterfly scepter . . . at least that's what we're calling it . . . is pure silver. As pure as anything we can make with today's technology. The gems are all-natural stones with near-perfect crystalline structures. And before you ask, it's the same age as the box, give or take a few years."

Myrdin reached for the scepter and quickly pulled his hand away.

"It's all right, Myrdin, you can pick it up."

The scepter was about a foot long and shaped like a medieval mace with a small knob at one end and a larger head at the other. The head was set with six smaller gems surrounding a larger seventh one. Each of the circling gems was a different color—red, orange, yellow, green, blue, and purple—while the crowing gem was clear. The shaft was about the same thickness as a broom handle, and its entire length was engraved. The engravings included both pictures and what appeared to be some form of phonetic writing.

"Amazing, isn't it?"

"More than you can possibly imagine," Myrdin replied.

"Does that mean you recognize the writing?"

"No, but I have a few ideas. Has anyone else seen this?"

"Richards thought it might be some precursor to the Zapotec writing from Mesoamerica, so he showed it to Jean LeClerc before he brought it here."

"Zapotec wasn't used until thousands of years after this box was buried. Besides, these symbols are clearly phonetic, and it wasn't until the Mayans another thousand years later that phonetic writing evolved in the Americas." Myrdin shook his head. "I assume LeClerc told him as much."

"Yes, but Richards thought that the pictures might be part of the writing. He was really hoping to prove some connection to early Mesoamericans."

"Wants to rewrite history, does he?" said Myrdin, lifting one eyebrow.

"If by that you mean he's looking for his own wing at the university, then I agree with you. He's a very ambitious man."

"A man should never let his ambitions get in the way of the facts," Myrdin said, a bit more derisively than he intended. "The pictures show the lifecycle of a butterfly. The leaves look like milkweed, so I'd guess they're Monarch butterflies or their prehistoric relative."

"Yeah, we noticed that. That's why we call it the Butterfly Scepter."

"I suspect they're purely decorative."

"A curious choice, don't you think?"

"I don't know. The metamorphic lifecycle of the butterfly may not be miraculous to us, but I could see how it might inspire people's belief in spiritual renewal."

Tom smiled. "I didn't know you were a poet."

"Just because I'm a scientist, doesn't mean that I can't appreciate the beauty of things. Now, as for the script, it does bear some similarities to Minoan Linear A, but there are also some significant differences."

"Well, I'm glad we called you in. It sounds like you're the right man for the job."

"Don't be too hasty. Linear A may be older than Zapotec, but it's still several thousand years later than this artifact, and it's never been deciphered. Even cuneiform, the oldest known form of writing, came a thousand years after this was buried, let alone after it was made."

"I guess you've got a real challenge on your hands."

"Was there anything else in the box? Something that might give us a clue about its origins or purpose?"

"Oh, I almost forgot, there were several dried-out leaves and some fine dust in the box."

"Contamination?"

"No, the box was airtight, and the leaves dated to roughly the same timeframe where the box was found. The dust appears to be a mix of pulverized vitric shards, shattered phenocrysts, and lithic fragments."

"Sorry? For the non-archeologists in the room?"

"Oh right, it's volcanic ash, and judging from the fracturing of the crystals, it must've been at least as powerful as Krakatoa. We also found similar particles embedded in the outer surface of the box."

"Again, pardon my ignorance, but is there any evidence of such a massive volcanic event in North America six thousand years ago?"

Tom shook his head. "Nothing of this magnitude."

"Any other possibilities?"

"Well, the timing does correlate closely with the 5.9 kiloyear event that led to the creation of the Sahara."

"I thought that most climatologists attribute that to changes in Atlantic Ocean current patterns."

"True, but there's a minority who've always maintained that those changes were volcanic in origin, and they've got some ice core samples from Greenland to support their theory, but . . ."

"But what?"

"Well, the only volcanically active areas in the North Atlantic are in the Caribbean and Iceland. The Caribbean is too far west, and Iceland is too far north to affect the changes needed to support their theory. Some of the more adventurous of the group have proposed what is jokingly referred to as the Atlantis solution."

"You're kidding?"

"No, their basic hypothesis is that there was an eruption. It caused the desertification of North Africa, and the reason we can't find it is that the eruption was so violent that all traces of the volcano were swallowed by the ocean and destroyed."

Myrdin stroked his chin, "An intriguing theory. However, a mysterious wooden box with ancient volcanic ash found in upstate New York isn't the type of evidence that will stand up to peer review."

"No, you're right. It's probably just a coincidence—a very bizarre coincidence—but nothing more. Even if we could connect them, how did the box get to Byron? And we'd still have to find the volcano or its remains."

"Perhaps the leaves will give us a clue," Myrdin suggested.

"Oh yes, Dr. Richards sent them to a botanist for analysis. The results just came in yesterday." Tom searched through an overstuffed inbox and pulled out a sealed manila envelope. "I haven't had a chance to look at them yet."

"Mind if I take a look?"

"No, of course not." Tom handed him the envelope.

Myrdin broke the seal and took out the papers. He finished reading them and handed the papers back to Tom.

"Why are you smiling?"

"I just skimmed the analysis, but it appears the leaves were left in the box on purpose."

"What makes you say that?"

"They came from a milkweed plant. And they also found something else."

"Oh, what was that?"

"Butterfly scales."

ACROSS TOWN

A CHILL RAN DOWN HIS SPINE, AND THE HAIR ON HIS NECK STOOD up. The little man in red stared up at the sky. Something was searching for him. Something from his past; something that meant him harm. Fear gripped his alien heart. How had it followed him here? How had it known about his new home?

He fought back his rising fear by talking to himself. "Don't ya go and panic now, Farsyl," he said, using the name he'd adopted from one of his long-dead summoners. His real name being unpronounceable in this realm. "All ya have to do is find a nice safe place to hide from the nasty, dark fiend."

He looked frantically from side to side, searching for a place to disappear. He needed something red, something natural. When he reached the end of town, he found what he was looking for—a dense thicket of holly bushes. Their leaves were green, but the boughs were filled with red berries. There were more than enough to meet his need. He dove into the thicket, momentarily shifting out of phase with the local dimension to protect himself from the sharp thorns.

In that brief instant, a deep chill washed over him, and he knew the fiend had detected his use of extra-dimensional energy. The dark shape began spiraling down over his hiding place.

"Curse this body's weakness," he gritted his teeth and stroked his beard. "Well, Farsyl, there's nothing for it now."

He made several signs with his fingers and muttered a few words in an ancient tongue, opening a tiny rift in the dimensional fabric. Sweat poured down his face as he fought against the bounds of his summons to keep the pinprick hole open.

Ultimately victorious, he reached down into his inner core and touched his true being. Carefully, he drew forth a tiny fraction of his inner essence. Deftly, he wrapped the diaphanous essence around the misshapen form he was forced to wear in this dimension. He wove the delicate overlapping wisps of his extra-dimensional energy to form an opaque cloak that even the dark fiend could not pierce.

The dark one circled the thicket several more times before flapping its wings and flying away.

Exhausted from his effort, the little red man slipped into what passed for sleep.

AS HE FLEW OVER PIPER FALLS, MASTER POE DETECTED NUMEROUS cross-dimensional anomalies. Two of the strongest were Penny and the *Cait Sith*, Simon, but he also sensed several other sources. Two were the powerful talismans of Myrdin's ring and Duncan's amulet. Two others were weak *Bodach* scampering about, but their energy levels were so low, that he was certain they weren't the time hopper. He also sensed a very strong stationary irregularity coming from the Monroe. Its lack of movement and strength suggested a lab experiment. The Monroe's particle physics experiments occasionally sent spikes of energy through the higher dimensions and gave him false readings. He made a mental note to ask Myrdin to verify his hunch.

Initially, the last one appeared to be nothing more than another weakened *Bodach* slinking through town. To be sure, Master Poe altered his search pattern and circled above it. As he did, a sudden eruption of higher-dimensional energy spiked through the first five dimensions. For the blink of an eye, the intense flash of energy blinded Master Poe's senses. He couldn't feel the wind in his feathers, hear the cars on the street, or see anything but a faint red glow.

An instant later, his senses returned to normal. Everything was exactly as it had been. Everything except the *Bodach* he'd been following. It was gone without a trace. Master Poe circled the area a few times, and when he didn't detect any new energy emissions, he decided to return to Myrdin's house.

IN THE DIM AND DISTANT PAST

ONCE SHE CLEARED THE SHALLOW WATERS OF THE HARBOR approach, the deep water of the open ocean protected the Toth from the power of the waves. Having swept through the capital city, the waves returned to the ocean filled with the debris of their fallen civilization. Most of it was unrecognizable wreckage, but some items were identifiable. Pieces of furniture, storage trunks, and numerous articles of clothing littered the sea. One passenger began crying uncontrollably when she spotted the sign that hung over her family's apothecary shop. Mercifully, other than one early wave filled with dozens of chickens, there were few bodies.

Even within her quarters, Amunet was not spared the anguish of the debris-filled waves. The flotsam banged against the copper-sheeted hull of the Toth, sending a cacophony of sound resonating through the ship. The nearly endless clanging and clanking provided a constant reminder of her civilization's downfall and the loss of her son. She teetered on the brink of irrationality and would've happily succumbed if not for the presence of her tiny roommate, Bes.

During the first few days, Bes latched on to Amunet, and Amunet clung back. For different reasons, each had adopted the other.

"Amunet, are we going to live on the Toth forever?" Bes asked.

"No, Bes, Captain Seskat is taking us to a new home."

"How does she know where to go?"

"She has instruments and maps to help her find her way."

"I learned in class that the closest lands are either covered in ice or filled with unfriendly savages. How can we build our new home in such a place?"

"I've heard those same stories, but the captain has sailed far and wide. She says there is a land to the east where a great river flows into the sea. The waters are full of fish and the land near the river is rich and fertile."

"Will any others be coming with us?" Bes asked.

"According to Captain Seskat, directions and orders were prepared for every captain in the capital city. I don't know how many survived, but I'm sure some did."

Bes hugged Amunet. "We're pretty lucky to be on the Toth, aren't we?"

"Yes, we are indeed."

BACK IN THE CAPITAL CITY

IOSHEKA GAGGED AND COUGHED UNCONTROLLABLY. WATER DRIBBLED out of his mouth and over his chin. He opened his eyes, hoping to see his mother's face.

"Well, hello. I'm glad you woke up. I thought I was going to have to carry you to the platform," said an unfamiliar female voice.

As his vision cleared, he saw that the voice emanated from a woman with sun-blonde hair, light brown eyes that sparkled mischievously, and a smile that reached from ear to ear. He guessed she was his age or perhaps a little older.

"Platform? What platform? Where am I? How did I get here?" He struggled to sit up.

"Full of questions, aren't you?" She dropped her smile. "Fair enough; I'll go first. You are on the mooring platform at the capital city aerodyne station. Near as I can tell, you were caught in the great wave and washed up here. I came down to release the Onatha's mooring lines, and I stumbled across you lying here. I saw you were still alive and came over to resuscitate you. It was just dumb luck, really."

"Who are you, and what is the Onatha?"

"My name is Ataensic, and the Onatha is my aerodyne. Well, it's not *mine*, but I need it, and the real owners aren't likely to complain about me borrowing it now, are they?"

"Thank you for saving me, Ataensic. My name is Iosheka."

"Nice to meet you, Iosheka." She flashed her smile again. "Now as I was saying, I'm going to use the Onatha to get us out of here before the whole place sinks to the bottom of the sea."

"You know how to fly it?"

"Well, not exactly, but I did date a member of the ground crew."

"That's your qualification? You dated a guy on the ground crew?"

"Only for a few weeks, mind you, but he was a chatty fellow, especially about himself and his job. Lift coefficients, wind speed, propulsion, thrust, and all kinds of other terms. I think he thought it would impress me or something. All I wanted to do was hitch a ride in the Onatha. Never did happen." She sighed.

"You mean you've never even been *in* the Onatha?"

"Oh, I've been *in* it many times. It's just that his idea of soaring the heavens and mine were a bit different. You know what I mean?"

"So, what happened?" Iosheka half-guessed the answer.

"Well, I slapped him, of course." She grinned.

"I gather that was the end of the flying?"

"Yeah, but he'd already shown me all of the controls and explained how everything worked."

"But you never really flew the Onatha?"

"No, but I guess that's going to change. I mean, given that the alternative is a permanent home on the ocean floor, I think it's worth the risk."

The ground shook, and fresh ash fell from the sky. Iosheka looked into Ataensic's eyes and saw that despite her bravado, she was scared, too. He recognized that she needed him as much as he needed her, and her smile was almost as irresistible as she thought it was. "When you put it that way, it's hard to argue. What do I need to do?"

"I knew you'd come around. Now, help me with these mooring lines, except for the one attached to the gondola. We'll cut that once we're ready for liftoff."

He checked his tunic pocket and felt the Sekhem and immediately thought of the Gaol. "Before we start, did I have anything with me when you found me?"

"Yes, as a matter of fact, you did." She handed him the wooden box that contained the Gaol and tossed him Bes's stuffed rabbit. "I'm not one to judge, but aren't you a little old for stuffed toys and bug collections?"

"It's a long story."

"You can tell me when we reach our new home. Now help me with the lines." She scrambled to one of the mooring points.

The ashfall and tremors intensified as Iosheka and Ataensic cleared the last of the mooring lines and climbed into the Onatha's gondola. The gondola consisted of two compartments. The larger of the two sat above the other and had berths for six passengers. It was filled with wooden crates and jars of supplies.

"Secure your things and join me on the bridge," Ataensic said.

Iosheka did as she asked and stepped down the small ladder onto the bridge. It was much smaller than the passenger compartment. The two seats were set in tandem. Ataensic sat in the front seat flanked by the throttles and several dials, which Iosheka guessed were for monitoring the engines.

"I'm going to power up the magneto drive to help us clear out of here as fast as possible. The ash shouldn't hurt the aerodyne's skin, but I don't want to be anywhere near here when the heavier stuff starts falling. Once we begin to move forward, you go to the passenger compartment and cut the last mooring line."

"Understood," he replied with a crisp nod.

Ataensic grabbed the throttles and engaged the magneto drive. As the gentle hum of the drives kicked in, she turned to Iosheka. "Now."

He went up to the passenger compartment, found the line, and cut it. Immediately, the Onatha sprung forward, nearly knocking Iosheka to the floor. He regained his balance and carefully worked his way down the ladder into the bridge room.

"Sorry about that, I gave her a little too much throttle, but I'm getting the hang of it now."

Iosheka nodded. The glass surrounding the bridge room afforded him a panoramic view of the devastated city. He was mesmerized by the scope of the destruction. Virtually nothing recognizable remained. He found the cracked dome of the Ganondagan observatory. As he watched, there was another tremor, and the dome of the observatory collapsed into a heap of rubble and dust.

"Hold on tight, I'm going to open the engines up to full speed. It's going to get a little rough."

Iosheka gripped the sides of his chair tightly and let the tears roll down his cheeks unabated.

9

PRESENT DAY, IN PIPER FALLS

SOBEK TUCKED IN THE BOTTOM OF HIS HEAVY FLANNEL SHIRT and pulled the leather belt tight, fastening the clasp in the last hole. Other than the corduroy trousers being a tad too generous in the waist—apparently food was plentiful in his new timeframe—he was quite pleased with his *borrowed* clothes.

He especially liked the zipper. Once he figured out how it worked, it was much more efficient than the buttons and hooks he was used to. He hadn't found any shoes to borrow, so he kept his old ones. Open gaps may have been the height of style for late seventeenth-century footwear, but he was happy to have his unfashionable closed latchet shoes in his new timeframe's cold winter.

He also thanked his good luck to have landed in a location where they spoke English. Admittedly, it was different than the English he knew, but it was fairly close, and he was a very skilled linguist. He'd lost count of the number of languages he'd learned, and in quite a few cases, forgotten. After eavesdropping on the local conversations, he felt pretty comfortable. He could imitate their accents well enough, although contractions still gave him some trouble. He even managed to pick up a few of their idiosyncrasies. He knew that sneakers were a type of shoe, a sucker was a hard candy, and that pop was a beverage.

Before discarding his old clothes, he reached into a pocket and took out the coins he'd stolen from Master Giles. He held them in his hand. Four guineas had been a princely sum in the seventeenth century. He'd known that a time tunnel was coming, but he hadn't known precisely when to expect it.

He'd made enough hops forward in time to know that it was best to bring money, preferably gold. So, he'd stolen five guineas and a few shillings.

To cover his theft, he'd carefully placed the shillings and one of the guineas among his colleague Oliver's things. Once the coins were found and Sobek's sworn testimony was taken, Oliver was quickly convicted. To avoid prison and an all but certain death sentence, Oliver agreed to indenture himself to one of the colonial sugar companies in the Caribbean; an only slightly slower path to death.

Some of the proceeds from his indenture went to repay Master Giles, and the remainder went to the judge and the local magistrates who used their contacts to arrange the indenture.

While more than three centuries of real time had passed and Oliver was long since dead, it had all happened only a few weeks ago for Sobek. He didn't like the dishonesty, but he was Amun-Ra. His most sacred duty was to protect the people and their culture. Nothing else mattered, certainly not the innocence of an uncouth outsider. The leaders of his order had failed, and the people's civilization had perished. Only he was left. Only he could right their wrongs.

Enough reminiscing, he thought. He needed to get some local currency. Satisfied that he could blend in with the locals, he stepped out of the alleyway and onto Elm Street. It was a small town, but it appeared to be prosperous and much cleaner than its seventeenth-century equivalent; due in no small part to its lack of horses in the streets.

Breathing deeply, he was greatly relieved to finally be in a timeframe that didn't depend on animals for transportation. Through the centuries, he'd come to loathe horses. The belching combustion vehicles of this timeframe lacked the elegance of the magneto trams of the capital city, but at least his nostrils weren't under constant assault from the smell of those beasts. And the paved roads were a nice touch. Not as aesthetically pleasing as the stone of the people's capital city, but much better than the amalgam of mud, refuse, and animal waste that dominated his most recent stop.

The teller at the Empire State Bank wouldn't take his guineas. Instead, she referred him to Caleb's Collectibles, which was conveniently just down the street.

Sobek walked around the corner and into the shop.

"Hello, what can I do for you?" said a short, thin, balding man whose eyes matched in color just like everyone else's he'd seen. In the man's case, they were light brown.

"Are you Caleb?" Sobek asked.

"Yes, I'm Caleb Cowling. Is there something I can get for you?" Without waiting for a response, Caleb reached under the counter and pulled out a watch and chain. "I just got a wonderful pocket watch from 1901."

He handed the watch to Sobek who held it dangling in the air by its chain.

"Fine works. Still keeps accurate time. See the engraving on the back. 'Pan American Exhibition 1901,' that's the one in Buffalo. You know, the one where President McKinley was shot."

"It is very nice, but I am not here to buy anything."

"Oh, I see, I see. That's a shame. So, you've got something to sell then?"

Sobek nodded. "Four gold coins."

"Well, you've come to the right place. I'm an appraiser." Caleb pointed to a framed document hanging on the wall behind him. "Certified by the American Numismatic Association. Why don't you show me what you've got?"

Sobek reached into his pocket, pulled out the coins, and handed them to Caleb.

"I thought you said you had four coins. There're only three here."

Sobek put his hand in his pocket and searched for the fourth coin. He didn't find it, but he did find a big hole.

It was a wonder he hadn't lost more than *one* of the coins. He muttered a curse in a language so old that even he couldn't remember its exact meaning.

"I'm sorry, what did you say?" Caleb asked.

"My apologies. I seem to have only brought three with me. I must have misplaced the fourth."

"Well, if it's anything like these, please bring it in. These are very old, very old indeed." Caleb lifted his glasses onto his head, took a lens from his pocket, and examined the coins more closely. "Oh my, oh my, William & Mary gold guineas from 1692, and they're in very fine condition! I've never seen their like before, at least not in Piper Falls." Caleb took the lens from his eye and looked up to Sobek. "If you don't mind my asking, where did you get them?"

"A friend of the family was in the trade and left them to me." Sobek smiled showing his overly large, pointy teeth.

Caleb winced.

Sobek quickly hid his teeth. "I need some local currency and would like to sell them."

"Local currency, well yes, yes, that's what I offer," answered Caleb with a grin. "Hmm, that must've been some friend; these are very valuable. When would you like to sell them?"

"Now, I need the currency as soon as possible."

"I could get more for them if you would give me a week, or even a few days, to find a buyer. Coins like this don't come up that often. It would be a shame not to get multiple bids for them."

"No, I am afraid I cannot wait that long."

"I won't be able to find a buyer here in Piper Falls."

"Does that mean you are not interested in buying them?"

"No, no, of course I'm interested. It just means that I'll have to make some calls to New York to find a buyer."

"Calls?" asked Sobek with a look of confusion.

"You know, phone calls?" Caleb raised his right hand to his face with his pinkie at his mouth and his thumb at his ear. "I've got some contacts through the Numismatic Association down in the city, and I'm sure they'll know someone who'd be interested in buying these. Although, as I said, I won't be able to give you full value for them."

Sobek frowned.

A chill ran down Caleb's spine.

He shook it off.

"I mean, I have to cover my costs. My contacts will need to make a profit too, and the buyers of coins like these . . . well, unless there's a bidding war, they won't overpay."

"I understand. What can you give me?"

"Bear with me a minute." Caleb pulled a thick book off a bookshelf and began rapidly flipping through the pages and punching numbers into a calculator. "Let's see, Elephant and Castle, 1692, very fine condition, twenty-four hundred pounds each, $1.54 to the pound, less commission, taxes, and insurance." He tore the printout off the calculator, lifted his glasses, and held it close to his eyes. "I can give you $6,500."

Sobek stared back at Caleb without saying a word.

Misinterpreting Sobek's stare, Caleb said quickly, "I can see you're disappointed. I know they're worth a lot more than that. I'll have to cut a few corners and bargain harder with my city contacts, but I can add another $500 to make it an even $7,000. That's the best I can offer."

"Can I have the currency right now?"

"My, my, you are in a hurry, aren't you? I don't have that kind of cash here in the store, but I can write you a money order that you can take to the bank, and they'll give you the cash."

"Like a letter of credit?"

"Not exactly, I see you're a bit new at this. Tell you what, I'll close the shop and walk over to the bank and get the cash for you."

"How long will that take?"

"Oh, I'll need to tidy up a few things here before I go. How about you come back in an hour or so, would that work for you?"

"Yes, that would be acceptable." He smiled, once again revealing overly long and pointy teeth.

Better prepared this time, Caleb didn't wince, but he couldn't avoid thinking of crocodiles.

A GENTLE TAPPING SOUND ROUSED MYRDIN FROM HIS DEEP CONcentration. He took a sip from his mug of Earl Grey before setting it down and walking over to the window.

Master Poe was sitting on the windowsill staring at him with a look of mild annoyance. Myrdin opened the window, and the large black raven flew into the room.

"What took you so long?" asked Master Poe as he flew to the mantle. He shook his wings in an unmistakable shivering gesture. "It's cold out there!"

"Sorry, I guess I got caught up in my research."

Looking from one stack of books to another, Master Poe bobbed his head up and down. "I didn't know you had so many books on Mastodons," he said with a slight cackle that passed for laughter.

"I don't. I wasn't researching Mastodons."

"No, I don't suppose you were. But I'm curious what research requires Demosthenes' translation of Khotep's *Definitive Demon Defenses*, Van Hussen's classic *Introduction to Hyper-dimensional Fractal Solutions*, and Julia Child's *Mastering the Art of French Cooking*. Are you trying to bore them to death, cook them a fine meal, or is there a connection I'm missing?" Master Poe cackled again.

Myrdin ignored his friend's jibe and picked up a piece of paper from his desk. He walked over to the mantle and held the picture up for Master Poe to see.

"The *Teyrnwialen o Saith*," Master Poe said with a bob of his beak.

"Correct. Give the bird a cracker," Myrdin said with a little more bite than he'd intended.

Master Poe ignored his friend's sharp tone. "All right, so why are you showing me the mythical talisman, and what does it have to do with all of these books?"

"I'll answer the second question first. I was looking for this picture. I knew I had placed it between the pages of a book for safekeeping, but I couldn't remember which one. So, I started randomly searching through them." Myrdin waved his hand around the room, which was full of books randomly strewn about.

"It's not easy getting old, is it?"

Myrdin shot the bird a furtive glance, then nodded. "No, it's not."

"Let me guess, it was in the cookbook."

"Yes, one of my colleagues at the Monroe gave it to me. Thought it would do me some good to eat properly cooked food." Myrdin made a derisive snort. "I never did try it. I stuffed the picture in there so that I wouldn't lose it. I never really thought I'd need it again. Anyway, even after I got the right book, there are over seven hundred pages in it. I found it just before you arrived."

"That explains the books, but how about my first question?"

Myrdin placed the picture on a table and steepled his fingers at his chin. "The talisman is not a myth."

"You can't be serious!" Master Poe squawked.

"Quite serious."

"Are you sure?"

"That's what they found out in Byron. I held it in my hands this afternoon. I suspected it was something significant and powerful, but I wasn't sure what it was until I found the picture."

"And now you're positive?"

Myrdin nodded.

"Tell me everything."

When he'd finished, Master Poe said, "That explains one of the unidentified energy sources I found in my search."

"What unidentified sources? I think you need to fill me in on your flight."

When Master Poe finished, Myrdin took in a deep breath and let it out slowly. "This changes everything."

10

PRESENT DAY, IN PIPER FALLS

After Monday's swim practice, Duncan met Penny at the school library.

"So, did the day off from practice help you clear your head?"

Penny gathered her books and stuffed them into her backpack. "Not really. Instead of being unfocused at practice, I was distracted while doing my homework."

"What were you working on?"

"Geometry proofs for Mrs. Berardino's class."

Duncan raised his eyebrows. "What could possibly distract you from that?"

Penny hefted her pack, then glared at him.

"All right, I'm sorry. I assume you're still having trouble with . . . you know."

Penny nodded.

"I think I might have an idea to help with that."

"Why don't you tell me on our way home."

Once they were clear from the school, Duncan looked around to make sure no one was nearby. "Maybe we should ask Deputy Barnes."

Penny looked at Duncan and raised the brow above her brown eye. "I don't think it's the kind of mystery he can solve."

"No, maybe he can't, but his friend with the U-Haul might be able to help."

"Friend? U-Haul? Uh, what are you talking about?"

"His friend's name is Kolchak."

"Is that his first or last name?"

"I don't know, but Deputy Barnes calls him Kolchak, and he was fine with me calling him that, too. Anyway, he's got this old U-Haul that's loaded with all kinds of really cool electrical gadgets in the back. Looks like something out of *Star Trek*."

"He's not one of those Trekkies, is he? You know, with the pointy ears and funny clothes."

"No, I didn't mean exactly like *Star Trek*. He's a paranormal investigator." Seeing a blank look on Penny's face, Duncan added, "You know, he uses the latest technology to track down ghost stories, find werewolves, the loch ness monster, stuff like that."

"You mean like a real version of *Ghosthunters* or the *X-files*?"

"Exactly."

"Okay, but I don't see how that helps us. I mean seriously, we probably know more than he does."

"Maybe, but we don't know about the braided strand," Duncan said with a smug look on his face.

"Does *he*?" she asked.

Duncan shrugged.

"I didn't think so."

"Well, what do you think we should do?"

"I think we should go back to the park."

"Trying to jog your memory?"

"Yeah, something like that."

"Okay, but if we don't find anything there, we'll try Deputy Barnes's friend?"

"Agreed."

Fifteen minutes later, they reached the entrance to the park. "What do you expect to find here?" Duncan asked.

"I don't really know."

"You're not expecting to find the braided strand hiding in the bushes or behind one of the oak trees, are you?"

"No, of course not, but this is the last place I saw the strand." Duncan nodded.

"And the last place you saw something is usually the best place to start looking for it when it's lost."

"Precisely."

"Okay, but if we're not looking for the strand itself, what exactly are we looking for?"

"Something that looks out of place."

"It's one of those 'you'll know it when you see it' types of things?" Duncan rolled his eyes.

Penny frowned. "First, I think we should look for something extra-dimensional."

"You think the braided strand may have left some kind of trace that we can follow?"

"Yeah, something like that. You look along that side of the path, and I'll take this one."

"No problem." Duncan moved off the main path and into the snow-covered grass.

Penny watched Duncan disappear into the bushes before venturing off the path in the opposite direction. Even in winter, many people walked in the park, and the snow on the main track was well packed, but few people ventured *off* the path. Although there hadn't been a major snowfall since they'd closed the time fold, the snow was still deep enough to make walking through it difficult. Penny was glad she'd lost the argument with her mother about wearing her boots to school.

Penny extended her extra-dimensional senses and spent several minutes searching for some extra-dimensional disturbance, but all she sensed was Duncan's amulet and the familiar outline of Simon.

What are you looking for? her *Cait Sith* protector asked.

I'm looking for some clue about the braided time strand. Do you think you can help?

I do not know anything about a braided time strand, but there are some unusual footprints over here.

Over where?

They are in a small clearing between these holly bushes.

I see the bushes, but I don't see the clearing.

The bushes have grown intertwined in a tight circle, but there is a narrow pathway between them.

Penny circled the bushes. *I can't find the pathway. Can you lead me through?*

Of course, I am Cait Sith, replied Simon, suddenly appearing at her feet.

Penny followed Simon through more twists and turns than she thought could possibly fit in the park, much less within the small stand of holly bushes. At one point, the path was so overgrown with prickly holly branches that she had to crawl through on her stomach, but eventually, she reached the small clearing Simon had mentioned.

Inside the clearing, she found the unusual set of footprints Simon had told her about. Whoever made them had very long feet, almost twice as long as hers. The heels were narrow, while the toe area widened before closing in an elongated point.

I see a dim reddish glow coming from the footprints. What is it? Penny asked.

I am not sure, but it looks like the traces I found when I was looking for the black bird.

You think these were left by an extra-dimensional?

Yes, but not by the black bird. His traces were a mix of red, yellow, and blue. I can only see red here.

When Penny bent down to look more closely at the print, she heard Duncan yell, "Penny, I think I may have found something!"

Not wanting to leave the clearing, she yelled back, "Me too!"

"Where are you? Your voice sounds like you're far away."

"It's hard to explain. Simon's on his way to get you. Just follow him."

After a few minutes and several loud curses, Duncan found his way into the clearing. "How did you ever find this place?" he asked, brushing leaves and snow from his coat. "It's like one of those garden mazes, although, I'd swear there's no way it should all fit here."

"I didn't find it, Simon did. And you're right, it's too big to be here in our dimension."

Duncan raised his eyebrows. "What exactly do you mean?"

"I think we're in some kind of pocket of extra-dimensional space. I can see a faint glow of extra-dimensional energy all around the edges of the clearing."

Duncan touched the Celtic triskele amulet he wore around his neck that allowed him to perceive the higher dimensions. After a few moments of concentrating, he too saw the sheen of extra-dimensional energy. "Cool!"

"That's not all." Penny pointed to the ground. "Look at these footprints."

Again, Duncan furrowed his brow. "Uh, they look like elf-prints to me."

"A rather *large* elf," Penny said.

"Maybe it was Santa Claus," Duncan chuckled.

"Maybe, but I wouldn't bet on it. Do you notice anything odd about them?"

Duncan stared at the prints for a few moments. "Yeah, they've got the same reddish glow that surrounds this whole clearing. You think that's connected to the disappearing braided strand, don't you?"

Penny nodded. "If not, it would be one strange coincidence."

"Okay, but what does it mean?" he asked, scratching his head.

"I'm not sure, but if I had to guess, I'd say that these footprints belong to our visitor from the past." After a brief pause, she added, "Now, what were *you* so excited about?"

Duncan's eyes lit up. He reached his hand into his pocket and pulled out a gold coin that was about an inch in diameter and handed it to Penny.

One side featured the silhouetted heads of a man and a woman with a small elephant and castle below them. The other side had a crown over a shield with lions and several other symbols that Penny couldn't make out. There was writing around the edges of both sides. Penny recognized the words as Latin, but she didn't know their meaning. The date on the coin was 1692.

She rolled the coin in her fingers before handing it back to Duncan. "Where did you find this?"

Taking the coin and placing it safely back in his pocket, Duncan answered, "Under a tree just a little bit off the main path."

"Was it buried in the snow or anything like that?"

"No, it was just sitting there like someone had dropped it yesterday."

"I wonder."

"You wonder what?"

"We'll have to go to Caleb's to be sure."

"To be sure of what?"

"We need to find out if this coin is genuine. If it is, we just may know what time period our hitchhiking guest came from."

IN THE DIM AND DISTANT PAST

TWO DAYS AFTER THEY LEFT THE AERODYNE STATION, IOSHEKA woke with a shiver. He let out a deep breath, and a cloud of mist formed in front of his face. Besides the lack of heat, he no longer heard or felt the gentle humming of the Onatha's magneto drive. His heartbeat quickened as he raced from the passenger compartment down the stairs and into the bridge room. "What's happened to the engines? Have they failed? Why's it so cold?" he asked Ataensic between his panting breaths.

"Well, good morning to you too," she replied, unleashing her smile.

"Uh, good morning, Ataensic," he stammered.

"Now, as for the engines, I turned them off."

"You did what?"

"I didn't turn them *completely* off, I just shut down the propulsion system and turned the heat down a bit."

An involuntary shiver shook Iosheka. "Why did you do that? Are you insane?"

She pointed to one of the many dials in front of the pilot's seat. "To answer your first question, we used a lot of energy getting away from the capital, and we've been fighting a strong wind out of the east. As for the second, well, I've always thought sanity was a bit overrated."

With some effort, Iosheka broke eye contact with Ataensic and looked at the dial she pointed to. It was labeled 'Energy.' He noticed that the indicator needle was just above the red zone, about three-quarters down from the top.

"Doesn't this thing have rechargers?"

"Of course, the Onatha's one of the latest aerodyne models. The entire skin of the buoyancy balloon is covered with sunlight collectors."

Iosheka looked outside. There wasn't a cloud in sight. Turning back to Ataensic, he said, "I don't see any clouds."

She nodded.

"So, what's the problem?"

"I don't know. Maybe the collectors were damaged when we left the station, or they're covered with ash. It's even possible that they're working just fine, but all of the ash in the atmosphere is blocking the light we need to charge the cells. How should I know? I only dated the guy for a few weeks. All I can tell you is that we've been steadily losing energy since we left, and if we continued to run the engines as we were, we'd run out in a matter of hours."

"So, your solution was to turn them off?"

Ataensic pursed her lips.

"I'm not real happy about it either. First, I turned all non-essential systems off."

"Non-essential?"

"Yes, we no longer have lights in the passenger compartment, there's no power in the galley, and the bathroom might be a bit dicey."

"What do you mean by a bit dicey?"

"I turned the waste incinerator off."

Iosheka scrunched his nose in disgust.

"With just the two of us, it shouldn't be too bad for at least a week or so. If we're still in the air at that point, we'll have bigger problems."

"What could be worse than drifting through the sky in a cold, dark box accompanied by the smell of raw sewage?"

"Well, even cutting all of those corners, we're still losing energy."

"Oh, it's a lot slower than before, but it's still dropping."

"I'm not sure I understand the problem. We're not going to fall out of the sky, are we?"

"Don't be daft! The buoyancy balloon doesn't need any power to keep us aloft. As long as it doesn't spring a leak, we'll be fine. It's getting *down* that'll be the problem."

"What do you mean?"

"Well, you see, we don't need the power to fly, but we do need it to make a safe landing." She pointed to the indicator again. "The red zone indicates the minimum energy levels for a safe landing."

Iosheka bit his lip.

"The red zone is for a fully loaded ship and includes a decent safety margin. With only two of us, we can probably make it down safely with about half of that."

"How long until we reach that level?"

"At the current rate, we've got four, maybe five, days."

"So, we just drift about aimlessly with the wind for four days and hope we find land?"

"I wouldn't have put it so bleakly, but that's about the gist of it."

"Which way are we drifting?"

"A little north of due west," she replied.

"The Toth and the other survivors are going east."

"I know, but there's nothing to be done for it. If I restart the engines and turn east, we'll run out of energy in less than a day, then we'll be adrift and unable to safely land."

Iosheka realized that Ataensic was telling him the truth, but that didn't make her words any less bitter. He thought of his mother, and tears rolled down his cheeks.

11

IN THE DIM AND DISTANT PAST, ABOARD THE TOTH

A S THE FLAGSHIP OF THE MARITIME SERVICE, THE TOTH WAS the finest vessel in the fleet. Built for exploration and trade, her crew accommodations were adequate, if not luxurious. Her designers had never envisioned her as a refugee ship. Survivors and supplies were crammed into every available nook and cranny. Half-rations, frayed emotions, and the cramped quarters were a volatile mixture.

To diffuse the tensions, Captain Seskat created the Leaders Council. In addition to the Captain, the council included the Toth's First Officer, Aker, and the ship's Chief Engineer, Herys. The passengers were represented by the highest-ranking members from each of their professional guilds: Jehut for the healers; Neper for the merchants and tradesmen; and Amunet from the scientists and educators. The seventh member was Sobek, the senior Amun-Ra among the survivors.

Like all the Amun-Ra, Sobek had two eyes of different colors, and he possessed the gift of second sight. Using those abilities, the Amun-Ra served as protectors of the people's traditions and customs. The conservative nature of their mission made them suspicious of scientists, and most scientists reciprocated in kind.

Amunet had enjoyed better relations with the Amun-Ra, which is why she'd been trusted with the Sekhem. She'd never met Sobek but knew him by reputation as a hard-liner who'd opposed her use of the Sekhem. No doubt he'd supported her persecutors among the Order. The recent loss of the Sekhem did not bode well for their relationship, so she entered the council meeting with trepidation.

Captain Seskat began the meeting. "Early tomorrow, we'll reach our destination."

"You mean our new home?" Jehut asked.

"Not exactly. We've been on course for a great river delta, and tomorrow we'll reach it. The point of this meeting is to decide how to proceed."

"I'm not sure I understand," Neper spoke up. "Shouldn't we rendezvous with the other survivors and get to work building our new home?"

"It's not quite that simple. As you know, all ships in the harbor received orders to evacuate the capital with as many survivors as they could carry." Everyone nodded. "What you probably *didn't* know is that not everyone was ordered to the same location."

"Many of the members of our medical team have family on other ships. They're expecting to see them when we arrive. Now you're telling us that their hope was misplaced." Jehut said.

"We did our best to keep families together, but there just wasn't enough time to keep *everyone* together," the Captain said.

"Let me guess, you were just following orders," Neper said with a hint of indignation.

Sobek spoke first. "You're correct, my merchant friend. The good Captain *was* following orders, and those orders came from the Amun-Ra. With so few of us likely to survive, the Amun-Ra counseled the minister and the admiralty against sending everyone to the same location."

"Surely, we'd have a better chance to survive if we stayed together," Neper said.

"I agree," Jehut said.

Amunet shook her head. "Just as a plant scatters its seeds in the wind, going to different locations improves the chance that some of our people will survive. One group might fail, but others will likely continue."

Seskat nodded in agreement. "Also, it's been a long time since our last visit to some of the locations. We couldn't guarantee which ones were safe."

"All right, so the Amun-Ra and the government agreed to diversify. When you put it that way, it makes sense. Any merchant worth his salt knows that many small customers are better than a single large one. Besides, what's done is done. I doubt the Captain called us here to tell us about things we cannot change. Right, Captain?" Neper asked.

"Yes, in addition to dispersing the fleet, the admiralty also agreed to a communication protocol for survivors and locals at each site."

"Locals?" Jehut asked.

"The good Captain means the uncouth," Sobek said. His lip turned up in a snarl at the last word.

Captain Seskat glared at the senior Amun-Ra and paused before she spoke. "The disaster hit us so quickly that we didn't have time to adequately prepare. Aker?" she pointed to her first officer.

"Yes, Captain?"

"On half rations, how many more weeks of food do we have?"

"Eight."

"Do we have tidal tables for the river, maps of the interior, an understanding of the local plants and animals, or knowledge about local weather patterns?"

"No, on all counts, Captain."

"Eh, pardon me for asking the obvious, but without that information, how do we figure to survive?" Neper asked.

"Our situation is not ideal, but according to the survey logs from the last visit here, the natives are both friendly and very knowledgeable about the local conditions," Seskat said.

"But they're uncivilized," Jehut said.

"Perhaps, but we need their knowledge to survive. If we alienate them, we won't have a chance."

Both Jehut and Neper stared down at the table and shook their heads.

The Captain turned to her Chief Engineer. "Herys, you were aboard the Pef, the last ship we sent to the delta, right?"

"Aye, Captain. It was thirteen years ago, but I doubt much has changed."

"What's your appraisal of the natives?"

"They have very limited scientific knowledge—"

"So, no magneto technology?" interrupted Neper.

"I'm afraid not. They possess only rudimentary metallurgy skills," answered Herys.

"Uncouth!" Sobek hissed through clenched teeth.

Herys shook his head. "They may lack many things we take for granted, but their understanding of their environment and how to survive in it is second to none."

"Could we survive without mingling with the uncouth?" Sobek asked the engineer.

"It would be much more difficult."

"I understand, but we could do it?"

"Yes, the privations would be great, but we could survive on our own."

"Ah, so our choice is between preserving our culture at the cost of some discomfort and debasing ourselves by mingling with the uncouth. In effect, to make life a little easier on ourselves, all we must do is surrender some of our values. If that is all that is at stake, we could all agree that it was a reasonable compromise." Sobek paused, inviting the others to express their opinions.

Aker and Neper were nodding their agreement.

Sobek continued. "Ah, but my esteemed colleagues, it is not that simple. Values and culture are the levees holding back the floods of ignorance and barbarity. Dikes do not burst instantaneously. No, they corrode slowly over time. What starts as a single drip begets more drips. The drips coalesce into a dribble, then a trickle. The trickle grows into a stream, which spurts and surges, tearing away the mortar and stones of the dike. Eventually, the dike is no more—washed away by the floodwaters of our baseborn instincts. Without the dike, there is no culture, and without culture, there is no real life. There is only uncouth barbarity."

Sobek folded his arms, sat back in his chair, and smiled, revealing his sharp crocodilian teeth.

Amunet looked around the room. Sobek's argument had hit home with several of her fellow council members. Neper, Aker, and even Jehut were still nodding their heads. Was she the only one who recognized Sobek's speech for what it was? Couldn't they see that he was counting on their emotions and prejudices to consolidate power for the Amun-Ra? Controlled by the nervous, backward-looking, paranoid philosophies of the hardline Amun-Ra, the people could not survive. Amunet looked past Sobek's smile and gazed deeply into his blue and brown eyes; all she saw was lust . . . an arrogant lust for power.

If she remained silent, Sobek would win. The despair of all they'd been through washed over her: the destruction of their civilization; the privations of the journey; and most painfully, the loss of her son. Despair was easy and seductive. She almost succumbed, but she didn't. She remembered young Bes drying her tears, the warmth of Bes's hand in hers, and the joy of her smile. She'd stared into the abyss and recognized it for what it was. She knew that only *she* could prevent her people from slipping into the seductive chasm offered by Sobek.

"Any other comments before we vote?" Captain Seskat asked.

Amunet raised her hand. "Yes, I'd like to say something."

Captain Seskat gestured for her to proceed.

"Jehut, as the chief healer on the Toth, what's the condition of the crew and passengers?"

"We've all lost a little weight, but for the most part, given what we've been through, everyone's in pretty good shape."

"A tribute to your team's hard work."

Jehut smiled and nodded at the unlooked-for compliment.

"However, weeks of half rations and being cramped aboard the Toth have taken their toll, especially among the old and the young. Correct?"

"Yes," agreed the healer.

"Is it safe to assume that eight more weeks of half rations would only make things worse?"

Jehut nodded. "Yes, that's reasonable."

She turned next to the Chief Engineer. "Herys, you said that we could survive without turning to the natives, but that the privations would be great. What exactly did you mean by great?"

"Once we exhaust our rations, we could supplement our diet with fish and some wild grains, but there will be some lean times until the next planting season."

"By lean, you mean *less* than even half rations?"

"Aye," Herys replied reluctantly.

"When you previously visited this area, did you interact with the locals?"

"Yes."

Amunet ignored the audible hiss that escaped from Sobek. "How would you describe them? Were they friendly?"

"Aye, once they got over their fear."

"Fear?"

"Aye, see every time we approached them, they'd scatter into the reeds. We tried to follow them, but they knew the area better than we did."

"So, if they ran away and you couldn't catch them, how did you interact with them?"

"We cleared an area and left them gifts. Things like beads, combs, and even a few metal blades. They quickly understood and left us food and clothing in return. Eventually, we built up trust and traded in person."

"Was there ever a confrontation or violence?"

"No, an occasional misunderstanding, but nothing you wouldn't see in a spirited negotiation in one of our markets."

"Are you confident they would help us again?"

"Yes, unless we make trouble, I can't imagine a problem."

"Jehut, if we didn't get more food and had to live under the conditions Herys described, who among us would be hit hardest?"

"The young and the elderly."

"They would be the first to succumb to malnutrition and illness. And given their already weakened states, many would die. Would you agree, Jehut?"

"Yes."

"So if I might reframe the question put to us by our colleague from the Amun-Ra, we can either choose cultural purity at the expense of the most vulnerable in our society or we can be true to our values and protect our children and elderly by working with the natives, who've readily helped our people in the past."

Amunet paused to let her words sink in before closing her argument. "I agree that culture is important, but culture without a people is nothing but ruin. Ruin is what we left behind. We're here to build a *new* civilization."

Sobek dropped his smile and pursed his lips so tightly that the color left them.

No one else moved to speak, so Captain Seskat passed out red and blue shards of pottery. "This is a secret ballot. If you agree to work with the natives, drop a blue shard in the vase; if you disagree, drop a red one."

Herys was the first to vote conspicuously dropping a blue shard in the vase. The others followed protocol more tightly so that Amunet didn't know if she'd swayed any of the vacillating members until Captain Seskat emptied the vase. The final tally was five blue and two red shards.

PRESENT DAY, IN PIPER FALLS

"That's strange, it looks like Caleb's is closed," Duncan said.

As they approached the shop, they noticed that while the sign was flipped to closed, a light in the back room of the shop was on.

"Maybe Mr. Cowling just forgot to flip the sign?" Penny said.

Duncan tugged on the door which refused to budge. "I don't think so. It's locked. I guess we'll have to come back tomorrow."

"Maybe he's in the back room."

Duncan knocked on the glass door, but there was no sign of Mr. Cowling.

"Something's not right here. I don't think we should wait," Penny said.

Duncan shrugged. "Well, what else can we do? The door's locked, and no one's answering."

With an effort that had become almost second nature, Penny opened a small trans-dimensional rift, reached through it to the other side of the glass door, and unlocked it.

Duncan shook his head. "Do you think that was a good idea? What if someone saw you stick your hand through the door?"

"Unless they can see into the higher dimensions, all they'll see is me pushing my hand against the door. Besides, I think Mr. Cowling might be in some sort of trouble, and we should do what we can to help him. Now, if you'd please try the door again."

Duncan rolled his eyes and did as she asked. The door opened, and they stepped into Caleb's Collectibles to the sound of the door's bells clanging against the glass.

"Mr. Cowling? Mr. Cowling, are you here?" Penny called out.

No one answered.

"I told you this wasn't a good idea." Duncan looked around the shop, which was crowded with an odd assortment of items. One wall was lined with musical instruments including everything from ukuleles and guitars to trombones and flutes. Wild animals, including fish, foxes, and even a bear, stared out from the opposite wall. The aisles in between contained everything from used power tools to fine china. Toward the back of the store, but still within view of the front door, was the cash register. It sat on a waist-high glass counter that contained several shelves filled with jewelry, coins, and other fine valuables. To the right of the cash register, a small brass chain ran between the counter and the wall. A sign on the wall read, "Employees Only."

Penny walked to the back of the shop and unhooked the chain's latch.

Duncan placed his hand on her shoulder and pointed to the sign. "What are you doing? We can't go back there."

Penny clipped the chain's latch on the open side. "What if Mr. Cowling is in the back and something has happened to him?" Without waiting for an answer, she stepped through the counter and into the back.

Duncan followed her.

The room was littered with piles of books, boxes, and assorted oddities. There were commemorative plates, bowls, and cups for just about every event imaginable. One of the strangest sat on a small table next to a box. It was a porcelain tea set honoring Nixon's visit to China. The white teapot was emblazoned with a full-color image of Nixon shaking hands with Mao Zedong; the date was February 21, 1972.

Penny picked up one of the cups and looked at it more closely. It featured the American and Chinese flags in an X-pattern with the same date across the bottom.

As she was returning the cup to its tray, the back door opened, and Mr. Cowling stepped into the room. "Penny, don't tell me you've broken into my store to steal that tea set."

Penny shook her head vigorously. "No, no, Mr. Cowling. We saw the closed sign and the light on in the backroom and, well, we were worried something might have happened to you."

"We?" Mr. Cowling asked.

As if on cue, Duncan stepped out from behind a shelf.

"Ah, I see, this was a two-man job, was it?" He smiled at them.

"Hi, Mr. Cowling."

"Hello, Duncan. Nice to see you."

"I'm sorry we ignored the closed sign, but we thought something might be wrong; you're not usually closed at this time of day."

"Yes, yes, so Penny was telling me. I guess I must be getting forgetful in my old age. I was sure I locked the door when I left for the bank. Well, no matter. Now that you can see I'm fine, what brought you here in the first place? Have you got a closet Nixon or Mao fan in the family?" He pointed to the tea set.

Penny took her hand away from the tea set. "Oh, no, no."

"Good. You see, I've lined up a buyer in Ithaca for that tea set."

Duncan scrunched his nose. "Really?"

"Yes, yes, I know what you're thinking. Who in their right mind would pay good money for something like that? Well, the world is full of strange people . . . and a good thing, too, or I'd be out of business." He chuckled. "Anyway, in this particular case, my client's mother met the president during his tour of China, and she'd like to give her the set as a memento of the occasion. I was just wrapping it up for shipment. Now that we've settled that, why don't we step out front and discuss what really brought you to my shop."

Following his lead, they walked out of the back room and into the front of the store. Instead of stopping behind the counter, Mr. Cowling walked to the front door and turned the sign around to indicate the store was open. "So, are you here to buy or sell?" he asked.

"We're not quite sure," Penny said.

"You do know that's what I do, right?"

They both nodded.

"All right, all right, let me guess, you've found something and you're not sure what it's worth, and you want me to help you appraise it."

"Exactly!" Penny and Duncan said in unison.

"Well, why don't you show me what you've got?"

Duncan reached into his pocket, pulled out the gold coin, and handed it to Mr. Cowling.

"Well, well, isn't Mr. Sobek a very lucky man?" Mr. Cowling said.

"I'm sorry, who?" Penny asked.

"Yeah, we don't know anyone named Mr. Sobek," Duncan added.

"No, no, I don't suppose you do. I didn't know him until he came in here about an hour ago. He was in a real hurry to sell four coins just like these."

"What's that got to do with this coin?" Duncan asked.

"Well, as I said, he wanted to sell four coins, but he only had three with him."

"You think this coin belongs to him?" Penny asked.

"It seems likely. There aren't a lot of three-hundred-year-old gold coins floating around Piper Falls. Anyway, those coins are very valuable, and he insisted on cash. I don't normally keep that much cash in the store."

"So that's why you were out?" Penny asked.

Mr. Cowling nodded.

"How much cash are we talking about?" Duncan asked.

"Seven thousand dollars for the three coins."

Duncan whistled.

"And he needed the money right away?" Penny asked.

"Most of my clients want their money quickly, especially if they're selling something valuable. Usually they're in some kind of financial pickle. I mean it's not every day that you decide to sell a prized possession or family heirloom."

"So, do you think Mr. Sobek was in financial trouble?"

"I couldn't say for sure, but I told him if he needed the money today, I wouldn't be able to give him their full value because I'd have to arrange the sale through my contacts in New York City."

"And he was okay with that?" Penny asked.

"As he put it, he wanted local currency as quickly as possible."

"Can you describe Mr. Sobek to us or tell us where we can reach him to return his coin?" Penny asked.

"Yeah, and did you notice anything peculiar about him?" added Duncan, earning another quick look from Penny.

"Anything peculiar? Why would I . . . actually, now that you mention it, I did notice something strange about him." Mr. Cowling paused when they heard the bells clang against the door.

"Ah, there's Mr. Sobek now," Mr. Cowling said, clearly happy to be saved from explaining himself.

Penny and Duncan turned to the entrance as a dark-haired man wearing faded corduroy pants and a flannel shirt stepped into Caleb's Collectibles.

"Ah, Mr. Sobek, I see that you are a prompt man."

"Can the same be said about *you*?" Sobek asked without a smile. "Do you have my local currency?"

"Of course, of course, but first I'd like to introduce you to two of my friends." He pointed toward Duncan. "This is Mr. Duncan O'Brien."

Duncan waved his hand and gave a weak smile.

Sobek nodded.

"And this is Miss Penny Preston."

When Penny looked up, she was startled to see one blue and one brown eye staring back at her.

Sobek raised his eyebrows and held Penny in his gaze for an uncomfortable moment before smiling and nodding to her.

Penny winced at the sight of his sharpened teeth.

He turned away from her, back toward Mr. Cowling. "I don't mean to be rude, Caleb, but do you have my local currency?"

"Of course, but before we get to that, when you came in earlier, you mentioned four coins."

"Yes, I did, but as I said, I lost one of them," he replied.

"I know, I know, but that's why I introduced you to Duncan and Penny." Seeing Sobek's confusion, he added, "They found your coin and brought it to me. Isn't that wonderful?"

Sobek turned toward Penny and Duncan. "That is an uncanny bit of good fortune. If I might ask, where did you find my coin?"

"At Schoen Park in the snow," Duncan replied.

"How did you know to bring it here?"

"We didn't know what it was but figured Mr. Cowling could tell us. It was just luck that he knew it belonged to you."

"You are to be commended for your honesty." Sobek smiled once again revealing his oddly pointed teeth. After another lingering stare at Penny, he turned toward Mr. Cowling. "Can you purchase the fourth coin?"

"Yes, yes. Fortunately, I got extra money from the bank, so I can pay you for all four coins."

"The same price for the fourth coin?"

"Of course," Mr. Cowling replied.

After completing the exchange, Sobek turned again to Penny and Duncan. "As you might have guessed, I am a stranger in your country. In my culture, it is customary to reward the virtuous. Would you accept a token gift for your honesty?"

Duncan began to reach out his hand, but Penny spoke first. "No need, Mr. Sobek. Here in Piper Falls, we believe virtue is its own reward."

Sobek met Penny's gaze and again held it for an uncomfortable few seconds. "Well, if you change your mind, I'm staying at the local inn." With that, he turned and left.

13

"WHY'D YOU TURN DOWN THE REWARD?" DUNCAN ASKED Penny. "Did you see the amount of money Mr. Cowling gave him? I bet he would have given me at least fifty dollars without missing a penny."

"Something about him bothered me. Maybe it was the way he stared at me or his grin. Did you see his pointed teeth? They gave me the creeps." Penny shivered. "I just wanted to get away from him."

"You've never seen someone else with eyes like yours, have you?" When Penny glared at him, he quickly added, "I mean, I'm used to seeing your eyes, but the first time you meet someone, they usually stare at you, right?"

Immediately, he knew he'd only made it worse. He wanted to say something else, but with one foot firmly in his mouth, all he managed was a feeble, "I'm sorry. I wasn't thinking."

Penny's cheeks reddened. "It's okay. I know what you meant, but that's not it. Yeah, I was surprised at seeing his eyes and his teeth, but there was something else about him that bothered me. I can't quite put my finger on it."

"Do you think he's our time hitchhiker?"

"Do you have a better explanation for the coins?"

"Maybe he found them while he was walking through the park. I mean, *I* found one."

"True enough, but that's an awful strange coincidence, don't you think? And if he did find them, why'd he make up the story about them? Not to judge a book by its cover, but if you were Mr. Cowling, would you believe a stranger claiming he found valuable three-hundred-year-old coins in Schoen Park?"

"Okay, I agree that the coins had to have come through the time fold. And Mr. Sobek's lying about how he came by them. He's almost certainly from the past himself, but besides giving you the creeps, I don't think he's the real threat."

"Why do you say that?"

"Did you see his feet?"

"No," she replied.

"Well, I did, and other than his shoes not matching his clothes, they were normal-sized."

Penny stopped for a moment . . . then nodded in agreement. "So, there's no way he left those footprints we found in the holly thicket."

"Not only that, but I also bet if we went back to where I found the coin, we'd find prints that match his shoes."

"So, you think Mr. Sobek was caught on the wrong side of the time fold when I closed it."

"It fits the facts."

"He still creeps me out."

"Well, if you'd been plucked out of your time frame and dropped three hundred years into the future, you'd probably freak out a few people, too. I mean, customs change a lot in three hundred years. Just think how different things were in Piper Falls. Heck, there wasn't even a Piper Falls three hundred years ago. Now, why don't we head over to Costello's for some ice cream."

14

PENNY WALKED UP THE STEPS TO THE FRONT DOOR AT THE Hughes's house and rang the doorbell. It was her first babysitting job, and she was a little nervous.

A man wearing a coat and tie opened the door. Penny recognized Mr. Hughes, who worked with her parents at the Monroe. "Hi Penny, you're a little early."

"Sorry."

"Oh, no worries. Tammy will be right down. She's still getting ready. Why don't you come in and have a seat?" Mr. Hughes motioned Penny through the foyer and into the living room.

Penny sat down, and Mr. Hughes disappeared up the stairs. She looked around the room and noticed that everything was neat and orderly. There was a large bin of Mega Bloks, another with a wooden railroad set, and a third with rings, cups, and soft squishy balls.

Mrs. Hughes came down the stairs and into the living room. "Hello, Penny."

Penny stood up and held out her hand as they taught her in class. "Hi, Mrs. Hughes."

Mrs. Hughes shook her hand and smiled. "Is this your first babysitting job?"

"Yes, but I completed the town's babysitting class. I brought my certificate if you'd like to see it." Penny reached into her pocket.

Mrs. Hughes waved her hand. "Oh, that won't be necessary. Sam's getting the kids into their jammies. They go to bed at eight o'clock. They're used to a bedtime story. There are plenty of books to choose from in Michael's room."

Penny nodded. "Okay."

"Please make sure that they use the bathroom before you put them to bed. Michael will say he doesn't need to go, but if he doesn't, he'll have to go in the middle of the night. And he doesn't always wake up in time. Don't let him talk his way out of it."

Penny nodded again. "No problem, Mrs. Hughes. Anything else I should know?"

"Oh yes, Elizabeth's just learning to use the potty."

"Don't worry, I helped with my young cousins, and we also covered that in class."

"Well, you've got to watch her and make sure she sits down."

Penny raised the eyebrow above her brown eye.

"She's stubborn and doesn't want to use the potty. Sam told her if she wanted to be a big girl, she needed to use the potty like her older brother, Michael." Mrs. Hughes paused to see if Penny understood. When it was clear Penny hadn't, she continued, "She saw her brother using the bathroom standing up and thought her father meant that *she* should stand up, too."

From somewhere upstairs, Penny heard, "Lizzie a big girl, she use potty like Michael!"

To keep from laughing, Penny scrunched her nose.

Misunderstanding Penny's reaction, Mrs. Hughes said, "Yes, it was a bit of a mess, but she only did it once. If you remind her to sit down, everything should be fine."

Mr. Hughes came down the stairs carrying Elizabeth, who was already dressed in blue pajamas with rabbits and butterflies on them. He was followed by Michael, dressed in light blue pajamas with rocket ships, moons, and stars.

"I said I was sorry about that, dear." His look of sincerity could've been borrowed from Penny's dad. Penny thought it must be one of those survival skills all husbands developed, at least if they wanted to stay married.

"I know, dear, I just wanted to make sure it didn't happen to Penny." She took Elizabeth from her husband and kissed him on the cheek.

"Here are our cell phone numbers, and the doctor's number is on the fridge. We're going to dinner first, then a movie. It's an early one and should end around nine o'clock, so we'll be home no later than nine thirty."

"Okay, I'm sure everything will be fine. My house is just across the street, and my parents usually stay up until eleven or so," replied Penny with what she hoped was a confident smile.

"Yes, I'm sure." Mrs. Hughes turned toward the children. "Michael and Elizabeth, make sure you're on your best behavior for Penny. Okay?"

Both dutifully nodded their heads.

And with that, Mr. and Mrs. Hughes went out the garage door.

Penny and the children played trains until bedtime. Other than a minor argument over who got the blue engine and who got the red, everything went well. Just as his mother predicted, Michael griped about using the bathroom, but when he saw that Penny wasn't going to back down, he reluctantly went.

Lizzie was an altogether different problem.

"Lizzie, it's your turn to use the potty," Penny said as she set the cushioned insert into the toilet seat.

"I don't wanna sit down. I wanna stand."

"Lizzie, big girls sit down on the potty."

"No, no, no," Lizzie screamed. Then she grabbed the insert out of the toilet and threw it on the floor.

"Lizzie, what are you doing? If you don't use the cushion, you'll fall into the potty."

"No, I won't. Wanna stand like Michael!" Lizzie insisted. Then she pulled down her pajama bottoms and underwear, stepped out of both, and walked to the edge of the toilet bowl.

Penny's mind raced through her training, but she couldn't recall anything about girls standing up to use the bathroom. She briefly considered creating a rift to close the lid extra-dimensionally but quickly dismissed it. Just seconds away from a catastrophe, inspiration hit. "Lizzie, if you sit on the potty, I'll tell you a funny bedtime story."

"What kinda story?"

"How about 'The Princess, the Beanstalk, and the Frog'?"

"I never heard of that before. Is it a real story?"

"You bet it is, but you only get to hear it if you sit on the potty. Will you do that for me?"

"Will you tell it to us in my room, instead of Michael's?"

"Sure. Now, will you sit on the potty?"

Lizzie nodded.

Penny placed the cushion back on the toilet, and Lizzie took care of business.

A few minutes later, Penny sat cross-legged on the floor of Lizzie's room with the children in front of her.

"The title of this story is 'The Princess, the Beanstalk, and the Frog,'" she began.

"That doesn't sound like a real story," interrupted Michael.

"Oh, it's a real story," she assured him.

"What's it *about*?"

"There once was an unhappy princess who lived in the kingdom of Beans," Penny said.

"Why was she unhappy?" Lizzie asked.

"Because in the kingdom of Beans, every meal included beans, and the princess hated beans."

"What kinda beans?" Lizzie asked.

"She hated all kinds of beans: red beans, kidney beans, green beans, navy beans, and lima beans. You name the bean, and she hated it."

"Even baked beans?" Michael asked.

"Yup, she couldn't bear to eat a single kind of bean, but every night, her dinner included beans, and every night, she refused to eat them and sent them back to the royal chef. This angered her father, the King, who'd decreed that all subjects in his kingdom must eat their beans, but the princess refused to obey him."

"What did he do?" Michael asked.

"He commanded the princess to eat her beans or he'd throw her out of the castle."

"He's a big meanie," Lizzie said with a frown.

"Did she eat her beans?" Michael asked.

"No, but she didn't send them back to the chef either. Instead, she scraped them off her plate and hid them under her bed.

"That night, there was a blue moon—a rare and strange time of magical moonbeams. The beams shined through her window, onto her mirror, and were reflected under her bed, where they found her hidden beans," said Penny as ominously as she could.

"What happened to the beans?" Lizzie asked.

"Nourished by the blue moonbeams, the beans sprouted into a massive beanstalk that carried the princess's bed out of her window and up into the sky while she slept. When she woke, she found herself high in the clouds outside a small house with an open door."

"A small house? I thought there was a giant's castle at the top of the beanstalk," Michael said.

"Not in this story, Michael. So, the princess walked across the clouds and went into the small house. What do you think she found there?"

"I dunno. What?" Lizzie asked. Michael just shrugged.

"The house was so small that she had to crawl through the front door. Inside, there was only one room. The only thing in the room was a bathtub."

"A *bathtub*?" Michael said.

"Yes, a bathtub, and sitting on a lily pad in the middle of the tub was a Frog." Penny said with a creaky and croaky voice, "I'm a prince trapped in this house by an evil warlock. If you kiss me, you'll set me free, and we can rule my lush and bountiful kingdom together."

Switching her voice to play the princess, she said, "Will I have to eat beans in your kingdom?"

Croaking again, she said, "No, as my princess, you will never eat beans again."

"The princess bent down and kissed the frog. The moment her lips touched him, there was a bright flash and a puff of smoke. The house in the clouds vanished, and she found herself sitting next to the frog on a lily pad in a lush swamp. She was no longer a beautiful, young princess. She was a frog. She and the frog prince lived happily ever after eating flies and swimming in his swampy kingdom, and she never ate beans again."

Lizzie and Michael smiled and laughed with delight as Penny tucked them into bed.

Just after nine o'clock, there was a knock at the front door. Penny's first thought was that Mr. and Mrs. Hughes were back early, but why weren't they at the garage door, and why would they knock?

With some trepidation, she walked to the front door. She turned on the house light and stared out the peephole. She was surprised to see Duncan standing on the stoop. She opened the door but didn't let him in.

"What are you doing here? I'm not supposed to have any visitors when I'm babysitting."

"Sorry, but there's been another unexplained event."

"Where?"

"At Ms. Johnson's house."

"Which one?" There were two Ms. Johnsons in Piper Falls. One was a middle-aged woman who owned a bakery, and the other was a retired widow who owned lots of cats.

"The one with all of the cats."

"You think it's our hitch-hiking friend?" she asked.

"Yeah, it's too weird to be anything else. You gotta come and see it."

"As much as I'd love to, I can't right now."

"Oh yeah, right. When are the Hughes getting home?"

"Any minute now, why don't you wait for me across the street on our front porch? As soon as I'm done here, we can head over to Ms. Johnson's."

"Sounds like a plan."

15

A S SOON AS HE ARRIVED ON THE SCENE, DEPUTY BARNES PULLED out his cell phone and called his friend Kolchak.

Minutes later, Kolchak pulled up with Pandora in his specially equipped U-Haul. He stepped out of the cab and stared wide-eyed at the strange panorama in Ms. Johnson's front yard. Hanging anywhere from eight to ten feet off the ground were thirteen cats, each suspended by a single line secured to a branch. Cats hung from every large tree in the yard . . . except, he noted, for the lone oak.

Adding volume to the milieu were the surreal sounds of thirteen cats meowing and screeching as they struggled to free themselves from their undignified suspension. Kolchak didn't consider himself a cat person, but even *he* felt sympathy for the dangling felines.

Taking his eyes from the strange scene, Kolchak quickly found Fred consoling an elderly woman. He approached them.

"How much longer do my poor kitties have to endure this inhumane torture?" the woman asked through a flurry of sobs and tears.

"Just a few more minutes, Ms. Johnson. We're still gatherin' evidence. We need to take pictures of the crime scene, look for footprints, that kinda stuff," replied the deputy.

"Oh, please hurry." The distraught woman turned and walked back to her porch.

"We'll get 'em down as soon as we can." The deputy turned to his friend. "Hey, Kolchak, did you ever see such a thing?"

"No. I've seen many strange things, but never anything quite like this. Tell me, Fred, when did this happen?"

"We're not really sure."

"Well, Fred, why don't you tell me what you've got?"

Fred flipped through his notebook. "At about 7:00 p.m., a short, disheveled man, dressed in red knocked on Ms. Johnson's door. He complained about the cold and asked her if he could come in to warm up. She said no. He mumbled somethin' that she didn't understand, but by his tone, she assumed he said something unfriendly, if not downright insultin'. She closed the door on him.

"Just before 9:00 p.m., she heard her cats meowin'. She opened her door to let them in, but none came. She stepped outside and saw this." He motioned to the spectacle in the front yard.

Kolchak glanced at his watch. "So, it could've happened two hours ago?"

"Yeah, I suppose so," Fred replied.

"I'd better use the K-IIs. They won't give me the numerical reading for my computer algorithm, but they're more sensitive to older electromagnetic disturbances. Can you give me a few minutes to scan the area before you free the cats?"

"I think so, but you'd better hurry. Ms. Johnson's pretty upset."

Before Kolchak went to the back of the truck to get the K-II, he decided to check on Pandora. "How are you doing, Pandora?"

"I tawt I taw a puddy tat," replied the bird. After a short pause, she added, "I did! I did!"

Kolchak chuckled. "I think we might need to cut down on your TV watching, Pandora."

THE HUGHES GOT HOME A LITTLE BEFORE NINE THIRTY. IT WAS JUST over three blocks from the Prestons' house to Ms. Johnson's. Running most of the way, Penny and Duncan arrived just as Kolchak completed his electromagnetic sweep of the area. They sidled up against one of the trees and eavesdropped on his conversation with Deputy Barnes.

"There's definitely been some sort of electromagnetic disturbance in the area. Are there any buried power lines in town?" Kolchak asked.

"No, there was talk about buryin' the cables a few years back, after the big ice storm, but it was too expensive."

"Same with the phone lines?"

"Yep, other than sewer and water, the only thing that's buried is the cable TV line. Could that've caused your readings?"

"No, the cable access box is on the other side of the house, and the readings were in a different frequency band than cable uses. Besides, the K-II has a filter function that suppresses false reading from the cable TV line. Just to be sure, we should check with the utility companies."

"If it wasn't one of them things, then what's causin' your readings?"

"Well, my best guess is that the K-II is picking up the residual energy signature of a paranormal event."

"You mean ghosts? Ghosts right here in Piper Falls?" Fred asked.

"Maybe, but I don't think so." Motioning his friend over, Kolchak continued. "Look at these readings. They're weak here on the ground but stronger as we get near the cats."

"Well, I'll be . . . supernatural cats!"

Kolchak pursed his lips. "No, Fred. Look. See how the energy's in the red band near the rope but fades as I move the monitor further away?"

Fred nodded.

"Also, look at the rope. Does that look like the kind of rope you'd buy at the local hardware store? You should take some of it in for analysis. I'll bet it's 100 percent natural hemp. You don't see much of that these days. Almost everything's got at least some synthetic fibers in it. Not only that, but did you notice what the cats are hanging from?"

"Uh, trees."

"Yes, but did you notice what *kinds* of trees?"

"Well, let me see . . . there's a maple, two lindens, a honey locust, and an oak." Fred paused for a moment. Then he snapped his fingers. "No cats are hangin' from the oak!"

"That's right. Every tree with branches big enough to support a cat has one, except for the oak."

"What's it all mean?"

"I'm not sure, but quite a few paranormal entities have aversions to modern substances. And certain types of wood interfere with their powers." Kolchak stroked his chin with his left hand. "If I had to guess, I'd say we've got ourselves one of the faerie folk, and the K-II's detecting where it touched the rope."

"You mean an elf?"

"Yeah, but by the looks of things, a rather ill-tempered elf."

Ms. Johnson yelled from her porch, "Deputy, you said just a few more minutes and you'd get my poor kitties down!"

Fred glanced over at Kolchak who nodded. "I've got all I can get."

"Okay, Ms. Johnson, we've got the evidence we need. I'll start gettin' the cats down."

"Now you be careful with them, 'specially Sofie. She's got a bad foot from the time Mr. Greenbaum accidentally parked on her."

"He parked a car on your cat?" Kolchak asked.

"No, a truck, but it wasn't his fault. See, since my James passed on," she paused briefly to look skyward, "Mr. Greenbaum's been helping me with the little things around the house. You know, leaky faucets, running toilets, squeaky doors, that kind of thing." Her face lit up with a girlish smile.

Kolchak nodded.

"Anyway, he was coming over to fix my chimney flue last fall. It wouldn't close properly, and there was a terrible draft. Nothing worse than an open flue; might as well heat the whole town. That's what my James used to say."

"True enough, but what's that got to do with your cat?" Kolchak said.

"Oh, I'm getting to that. You see, Sofie's a sweetie, but she's stubborn as a mule. She thinks the world revolves are her. It was sunny that day, and she was lying in the drive when Mr. Greenbaum drove up, and he didn't see her. Anyway, she refused to move.

Poor Mr. Greenbaum nearly had a heart attack when he heard her screech."

"Which one is she? I'll get her down first," Deputy Barnes said.

"She's the white Persian over there." She pointed to the largest of the hanging cats.

"She is a big one, isn't she?" Kolchak said, shaking his head.

"Well, after the accident she did become a little less active. You know, because of her foot."

"Understandable." Kolchak turned to Fred. "You might want to be careful with that knot. Unless I'm mistaken, it's a barrel sling. It's strong and easy to tie, but it's also easy to undo. That's a good thing when you're unloading cargo from a ship's hold to a dock, but I'm not so sure about suspended cats. It might be safer to cut the line instead of trying to untie the knot."

Concentrating too much on the knot, Fred didn't hear his friend. Talking to himself, he said, "I think if I pull this one, this'll go through there and the knot'll come undone." He pulled on one end of the line and the sling supporting Sofie rapidly unraveled.

Predictably, Sofie fell.

Like all falling cats, she twisted her body to orient her feet toward the ground. Unfortunately for Deputy Barnes, he was between her and the ground. Legs outstretched and claws deployed, she landed squarely on the deputy's chest.

"Aiyee!" he screamed.

"Good catch, Deputy!" Ms. Johnson rushed over and took Sofie from him. Holding the cat tightly in her arms and rocking from side to side, she purred. "Oh, mommy's so happy to have you down from that terrible rope."

After surrendering the cat, Fred examined his uniform shirt. It was filled with pinprick holes from Sofie's claws, but luckily it didn't tear, and there wasn't any blood. He rubbed his chest. "I think I'll cut the rest of the lines first and untie the cats on the ground." Fred turned to his friend. "Now what were you sayin'?"

"Oh, nothing important."

"IT'S GETTING COLD. WHY DON'T WE GO TO MY HOUSE FOR SOME hot chocolate?" Duncan suggested after Kolchak put away his gear and drove off. "My brothers and sisters are all out tonight, and my parents are playing bridge with the Watsons. We can talk there."

Penny was more worried about someone overhearing their conversation than the cold, but the thought of a cup of hot chocolate was too tempting to pass up, especially O'Brien hot chocolate. "As long as you make it with real milk and chocolate," she replied with as straight a face as she could manage.

Duncan raised an eyebrow and stared at her. "Is there any other way to make hot chocolate?"

Simon followed unobtrusively behind them as they walked to his house. They went straight to the kitchen. Duncan got out a pot, the milk, a chunk of chocolate, and a cheese grater.

While he was grating the chocolate over the pot, Penny said, "You weren't kidding about Deputy Barnes' friend having a lot of high-tech gear. Outside of my parents' lab at the Monroe, I've never seen so much high-tech stuff in one place. I couldn't even name half of it."

"Yeah, it's way cool." He poured the milk into the pot and began stirring. "You know, I think I'm going to need some more chocolate. Would you mind getting it for me? There should be some more in the pantry."

Penny was pretty sure he had enough chocolate and that Duncan just wanted to get her out of the kitchen while he added the secret ingredient that made O'Brien hot chocolate so good. Mrs. O'Brien had told her two years ago that it was vanilla, but she'd sworn Penny to secrecy. "Sure, I'll be right back."

"What do you think of Kolchak's ideas about the cats?" Duncan called to her while he sneakily added two teaspoons of vanilla extract to the milk. "Do you really think it was some malicious elf?"

Before Penny could answer, Duncan's grandmother stepped into the pantry. "Hello, dearie, he's stirring in the vanilla, isn't he?" she whispered.

Initially startled, Penny quickly recovered and whispered back, "Hi, Mrs. Cadogan. I think you're right, but I'm not supposed to know."

Mrs. Cadogan put her index finger to her lips. "Not to worry, dearie, I won't tell."

As they walked back to the kitchen together, Duncan said, "Did you hear me, Penny? What do you think about Kolchak's theory that a malicious elf's behind the recent mischief?"

"Sounds like a Red Leprechaun to me," replied Mrs. Cadogan, walking into the kitchen ahead of Penny.

Duncan turned from his pot of hot chocolate. "Oh, uh, hi Grandma. I didn't know you were still up."

"Is that any way to greet your grandma? Now come over here and give me a hug and a kiss."

While Duncan was hugging his grandma, he raised both eyebrows at Penny. She just shrugged. Duncan's grandmother was the one person outside their inner circle who had an inkling of what was really happening in Piper Falls. She'd lived in rural Wales as a child and seemed especially in tune with the old myths. "Here's the chocolate you asked for," Penny added.

"Uh, thanks."

"Aren't you going to put it in the pot?"

"Uh, uh, no, on second thought, it looks like I had enough, but thanks for getting it."

Mrs. Cadogan faced Penny and winked.

Penny smiled in return. "What were you saying about a Red Leprechaun?"

"I said, these pranks sound like the types of things we used to blame on the Red Leprechaun, or as my mum would say, the *Coch Coblyn*."

Duncan looked up from the hot chocolate. "I thought leprechauns wore green and hid pots of gold."

"Oh, I suppose some of them do, but not the *Coch Coblyn*. They're a far more ornery and irritable lot."

"And you think there's one here in Piper Falls?" Penny asked.

"Oh, I don't know, dearie. It's probably just a bunch of mischievous kids. But if you're going to blame the fairy folk for strange happenings, you should at least blame the right ones. Most elves are generally good-natured. You know, like the elves who helped the shoemaker."

Penny and Duncan nodded.

"But none of them take kindly to being blamed for something they didn't do. And there's no sense in bringing the lot of 'em down on your head."

Duncan stopped stirring the hot chocolate and stared quickly at Penny. She met his gaze and shrugged ever so slightly.

Despite their best covert efforts, Mrs. Cadogan's smile broadened. Penny and Duncan both blushed.

"Now, Duncan, make sure you keep stirring that pot, or the milk'll burn. Nothing tastes worse than hot chocolate with burned milk."

"Yes, Grandma." Duncan began stirring the pot again.

"Good, you two enjoy your hot chocolate; I'm going back up to bed." As she turned the corner, she looked back into the kitchen and caught Penny's eye and winked at her. Penny brightened several shades of red. She was grateful that Duncan was facing the stove and had missed the exchange.

Duncan turned off the burner. "Hot chocolate's ready." He poured a mug for each of them.

"What do you think about what your grandmother said?"

Duncan shook his head. "I've never heard of a Red Leprechaun or *Coch Coblyn*, but she was right about Simon, and she knew about the *Bodach*."

"Yeah, and these pranks started right after we closed the rift."

"You think it's a coincidence?" Duncan asked.

Penny gawked at him, but didn't say anything,

"Okay, okay, I know, there are no such things as coincidences. What do you think we should do?"

"I think it's time we had another meeting with Mr. Myrdin and Master Poe. First thing tomorrow morning."

"Okay, I'll come by your house at seven thirty."

"I know I said first thing, but isn't that a little early?"

Duncan grinned. "Well, maybe for visiting, but not for breakfast."

Penny playfully punched him in the arm.

Duncan rubbed his arm. "I'll take that as a yes for breakfast."

AFTER THE CHILDREN HE'D MET AT CALEB'S AND THE REST OF THE onlookers were safely out of sight, Sobek stepped out of the shadows and onto the street. In a habit he'd picked up through the long lonely years of his quest, he began softly talking to himself.

"A most peculiar evening, yes indeed. The hanging cats were clearly the work of our time-traveling companion. If one of the townsfolk would just invite the Red Man into their home, the pranks would probably stop." He shook his head. "Of course, that never happens. No doubt the residents of this fine town will experience more of the Red Man's mischief. The real question is, why did he come here?"

Sobek stroked his chin and thought through the events and conversations of the evening. "Perhaps he was interested in the tools the constable and his friend—Kolchak I believe—were using to examine the scene."

After a moment's contemplation, he shook his head dismissively. "No, their uncouth toys are certainly interesting, but we did not sense any higher plane activity from them, did we? That's what draws the Red Man. It must be something else. Maybe he came for the girl."

"Perhaps," he answered himself. "She clearly possesses the Amun-Ra's gift of second sight. We had our doubts when we encountered her earlier. However, her presence here under the watchful eyes of her *Cait Sith* protector confirms her gift. The *Cait Sith* never serve the ungifted. Maybe the Red Man chose to suspend the cats as a warning to *her*. His sense of humor always tends toward the absurd."

Even as the thought escaped his lips, he recognized the flaw in his logic and shook his head. "No, no, that cannot be it. Even if she was gifted enough to draw the Red Man, her *Cait Sith* would prevent him from detecting her. She still may be involved, but something else must have drawn the Red Man here."

He stroked his chin again. In all his transits with the Red Man, there had always been something that had prompted his jumps. His last stop had been triggered by the disturbances caused by the hysterics of several gifted girls. Unconsciously, he shook his head. The Amun-Ra would have recognized the girls' talents and brought them into the Order for training before it was too late. Unfortunately for the girls, their uncouth society lacked the guidance of the Amun-Ra. He shuddered, thinking of the barbarity of the proceedings. Witch cakes, spectral evidence, touch tests, and all the other foolishness resulting in the persecution of hundreds and the execution of nineteen. No, he was certainly happy to be out of Salem, but he still needed to learn why the Red Man was in Piper Falls.

16

IN THE DIM AND DISTANT PAST

A TAENSIC'S REVELATION ABOUT THEIR DIRE SITUATION SENT Iosheka into a state of despair. He greeted her attempts at conversation with little more than token responses. When even her most charming smile failed to penetrate his dour mood, she, too, became dejected and gloomy.

For the next three days, the Onatha drifted on the wind in near silence. The only sounds were the barely audible hum of its idling magneto drive and the perfunctory acknowledgments of its two passengers as they relieved each other from watch duties.

That all changed on the fourth morning during Iosheka's turn at the watch. After hours of staring down at the seemingly endless rippling blue of the ocean, everything suddenly disappeared. No matter where he looked, Iosheka saw nothing but an impenetrable field of white. His heart raced with excitement. He'd never been more thrilled to see nothing in his entire life.

Instantly shaking his gloomy malaise, he raced up the ladder into the passenger compartment, strode to Ataensic's bunk, and shook her awake.

She opened her eyes and stared back at him groggily. "It can't be my turn already."

"It's not."

"Then why did you wake me?"

"The ocean disappeared." Iosheka smiled broadly.

"What do you mean the ocean disappeared? And why are you grinning at me like that?"

Unable to hold it back any longer, Iosheka said, "We're in a fog bank."

"Are you sure?"

Iosheka nodded. "One minute I was staring at the ocean, and the next minute, everything disappeared in dense whiteness."

"We're in a fog bank," she repeated. Then she leapt out of her bunk, and before Iosheka knew what was happening, she hugged him harder than he imagined possible.

He hugged her back, and the two of them jumped up and down screaming, "We're in a fog bank! We're in a fog bank!"

Before he was ready for it to end, Ataensic broke her embrace and held him at arm's length. She stared into his eyes . . . then she kissed him.

He kissed her back. The moment seemed to stretch into days.

Then she backed away and unleashed her beaming smile. "Come on, let's get down to the bridge and see our new home!" Without waiting for his response, she stepped past him and raced down the ladder.

Unconsciously, he bit his lip and stood in the cold darkened passenger cabin without moving. For the first time since the destruction of his world, he felt happy.

From the bridge, Ataensic yelled, "Do you want to help me power up the engines, or would you rather drift back out to sea?"

Her voice snapped him out of his reverie, and he followed her down into the bridge room.

Without looking back at him, she said, "We've already drifted quite a few miles inland from the coast. The fog's thinning out, and it looks like we're over some heavily forested hills. We need to find a good place to land."

"What should I be looking for?"

"Someplace that's flat and preferably without too many trees."

Iosheka scanned their new-found home from one end of the horizon to the other. All he saw were rolling hills. What wasn't shrouded in fog was covered with the densest forest he'd ever seen. "Good luck with that," he said with a little more sarcasm than he intended.

"Yeah, I'd rather not take her down in this type of terrain if I don't have to."

"How much time do we have?"

"We conserved more power than I expected, and there's no headwind, so we'll probably run out of light before we run out of power. The only thing worse than landing in a dense forest during the day is trying to do it at night."

"Makes sense."

"All right, while we're looking for the right site . . . and now that you're speaking to me," she paused to deliver an impish grin, "I think it's time for you to explain what's so important about that box, the butterflies, and whatever it is you're keeping in your tunic."

Iosheka took a deep breath and pulled the Sekhem out of his tunic and handed it to Ataensic.

"Is this what I think it is?" she asked with more reverence in her voice than Iosheka thought possible.

"Yes, you're holding the Sekhem."

"Where did you get it? Why do you have it? You didn't steal it during the eruption, did you?"

"Full of questions, aren't you? Fair enough, I did promise to tell you the story," he replied with a wry smile.

Ataensic's eyes flashed in response, and Iosheka knew that she also recognized the role reversal from their initial meeting.

"I'll answer the last question first. I did not steal the Sekhem, although some of the Amun-Ra would probably disagree. I rescued it from the lab." He paused and looked at Ataensic, who raised one eyebrow questioningly.

"My mother is, or I guess I should say *was*, one of the senior members of the Science Academy, and she'd been granted permission to use the Sekhem."

"I take it that didn't go over well with the Amun-Ra."

"Actually, the leadership supported her work, but some members of the Order were quite against the idea. To them, using the Sekhem's power for anything as mundane as research bordered on blasphemy. I'm afraid that after a thousand years, they've imbued their role as cultural guardians with almost mythic infallibility."

Ataensic nodded her agreement.

"I never really cared much for the Amun-Ra. They always struck me as living in the past, you know. Don't get me wrong, I appreciate all our ancestors did to create our civilization, but there is such a thing as progress. I mean, without progress, we'd have never discovered the magneto drive. And without the magneto drive, we never would've been able to build this aerodyne. Then where would we be?"

"Yes, well, they were particularly unhappy with my mother's research."

"Let me guess, that's where the butterflies enter into it."

"Yes. The population of the Gaol had been dwindling for several decades. My mother thought that the increased use of the magneto drive was interfering with their migration. She and her team were using the Sekhem to enhance the Gaol's migration capabilities."

"So, what was the big deal? Shouldn't the Amun-Ra have been happy? I mean, your mother's work would save the Gaol, right?"

"True, but the cultural significance of the Gaol is especially sacrosanct for the Amun-Ra. Its metamorphosis from the uncouth caterpillar to the beautiful butterfly is more than just an allegory to them. It's the spiritual essence of our culture. They view any threat to the Gaol as a direct threat to our civilization."

"What were we supposed to do, eliminate the magneto drive?"

Iosheka raised his eyebrows and smiled.

"You can't be serious! They *actually* wanted to abandon the magneto?"

"Only the most extreme members, but yes, that was their preferred option."

"What a bunch of ideological nutters! They'd have never gotten away with that."

"I wouldn't be so sure. The Council rarely defies the will of the Amun-Ra, but fortunately, we didn't have to find out. A majority of the Order agreed with you and approved the Science Academy's request to use the Sekhem to save the Gaol. But the extremists didn't accept defeat graciously."

"Oh, what did the whackos do? Threaten the end of the world?"

"That's exactly what they did."

"You don't think they had anything to do with the eruption, do you?" she asked, her eyes wide.

"No, of course not." He paused for a moment before adding, "But it may be hard to convince the survivors that it was only a coincidence. And my mother's survival without the Sekhem won't help her cause."

Ataensic touched Iosheka's shoulder. "I'm sorry, but there was no way for us to follow her."

In a barely audible whisper, he replied, "I know. You did what you had to do."

"I gather the butterflies you're carrying have been modified somehow?"

"Yes, the interference from the drives permeates the energy spectrum in this plane. So, my mother's team used the Sekhem to enhance the Gaol's antennae to detect energies outside our plane."

"She gave the butterflies second sight, like the Amun-Ra?"

"It's a bit more complicated than that . . . but yes."

"I bet that went over *well* with the Order."

"Unfortunately, many of her allies abandoned her. And without their support, her enemies controlled the Order."

"I don't suppose they invited her in for tea and cakes, did they?"

"No, they didn't." Iosheka paused for a moment and swallowed hard. "They called for a Desecration Inquest."

"A Desecration Inquest! You're kidding, right?"

Iosheka shook his head.

"That's ridiculous. Even an unrepentant non-traditionalist like me knows that a Desecration Inquest is reserved for the most heinous crimes against the people. There hasn't even been one for like a hundred years."

"It's been 211 years since the last Desecration Inquest, and that was an utter disaster, but that didn't stop the Amun-Ra. They not only succeeded in calling the Desecration Inquest on my mother and her team, but they also insisted on destroying the Gaol she'd modified."

"Obviously that didn't happen."

"No, my mother and I decided to free the Gaol before they could be destroyed. That's what we were doing . . ." Iosheka's voice trailed off.

"When the eruption began?"

Iosheka nodded.

17

PRESENT DAY, IN PIPER FALLS

M<small>R. PRESTON PLACED A PLATE FULL OF PANCAKES ON THE</small> kitchen table. "I think it's great that you two want to get an early start on your schoolwork, especially on a Saturday."

Duncan wasted no time moving half the stack of overly large pancakes onto his plate, shoving aside several strips of bacon and the remains of his scrambled eggs in the process.

"Would you like a *second* plate?" Mr. Preston asked.

"No thank you, Mr. Preston. I'm all right," Duncan answered, oblivious to his host's tone.

He was too busy carefully slathering butter onto each pancake, after which he poured half the maple syrup onto the mammoth stack.

Penny was always amazed, not only at the amount of food Duncan ate but at the rate at which it disappeared from his plate. If she didn't know better, she'd have sworn his *stomach* had extra dimensions.

Fortunately, this wasn't Duncan's first breakfast at the Preston's and her father made a double batch of pancakes, although to be fair to Duncan's appetite, it almost wasn't enough. When he reached his fork for the final two pancakes, Penny surreptitiously kicked him under the table. "Dad, you haven't had any pancakes yet. Would you like the last two?"

Her father turned from the sink. "Sure, thanks, Penny." As he sat down, he glanced at Duncan's nearly spotless plate. "I guess we'll have to go with a *triple* batch next time." He smiled. "So how are things going in Social Studies? I mean, it's not every day that your teacher turns out to be part of an international antiquities smuggling ring. At least not here in Piper Falls. So, who's your new teacher?"

At the mention of Ms. Morgan, Penny and Duncan exchanged a quick look . . . one that didn't go unnoticed by Mr. Preston. Fortunately for them, he misread the exchange.

"Come on, the new teacher can't be that bad."

Penny seized the opportunity. "Her name's Ms. Parsons, and she's not bad at all."

"As in Mr. Parsons, the gym teacher?" Mr. Preston asked.

"Uh yeah, his daughter," replied Penny while Duncan widened his eyes and nodded.

"Mr. Parsons has a bit of reputation as a hard case, doesn't he?"

"You could say that," Duncan answered.

"I guess that could be intimidating," Mr. Preston said.

"Oh, I'm sure that's it for some, but Duncan's problem is more with our project."

Mr. Preston looked at Duncan. "After your stint in a dress as Hammurabi, I'd have thought you were open to just about anything."

Duncan's face flushed.

Mr. Preston smiled. "So, what's the project?"

"The Metropolitan Museum Director of Antiquities is expanding the Egyptian Exhibit, and she's looking for ideas from expert Egyptologists on what to put in the new section," Penny replied.

"Let me guess, the students are the experts, and your teacher is the museum director, right?"

Penny nodded.

"While everyone's projects will be graded on their own merits, the project selected as the new museum piece will earn ten extra credit points."

"That sounds like it'll be fun. What's your area of expertise?"

Penny said nothing, but Duncan rolled his eyes.

"That bad?" Mr. Preston asked.

Penny shook her head. "No, it's not that bad."

"Not that bad? Eddie and Steve get mummification, the Anderson twins get the Pyramids, and what do we get? We get Hatshepsut!"

Personally, Penny was happy they hadn't gotten mummification; the whole process of removing the brain through the nose and storing the other organs in clay jars didn't motivate her, at least not in a positive way.

"Oh, come on, at least Ms. Parsons didn't assign us clothing and personal hygiene."

"Sure, but Hatshepsut's still lame."

"Oh, I don't know if I'd agree. I may not be an Egyptologist, but I think you'll be surprised by what you learn about Hatshepsut," Mr. Preston said.

AFTER A VERY COLD AND BLUSTERY WALK, THEY ARRIVED AT MR. Myrdin's house just before 9:00 a.m. As they walked up to the door, Duncan looked around.

"Where's Simon?"

"I don't know. I told him we were planning to go to Mr. Myrdin's this morning."

"Strange, he's always around; even when you don't see him, he's usually there."

"He is *Cait Sith*," Penny said with a little laugh.

"Huh?"

"Sorry, a bit of an inside joke."

Duncan shrugged. "Uh, okay, maybe this time we'll get to knock on Mr. Myrdin's door."

He reached his hand up to do just that when the door suddenly opened.

"Good morning, Miss Preston and Mr. O'Brien. We've been expecting you."

"What do you mean *we*?" Penny asked.

As if in answer to her question, Simon stepped out from behind the open door.

Nice to see you, he greeted Penny through their mental link.

What are you doing here? she asked in return.

Why, waiting for you, of course.

"So how did you know we were at the door this time?" Duncan asked Mr. Myrdin. "Let me guess, Simon told you," he pointed at the *Cait Sith*.

"In a manner of speaking, I guess you could say he did."

"Don't tell me he talks to you, too?" Duncan asked.

"If by talking to him, you mean hearing his thoughts . . . no, I can't do that. Only the person bonded to the *Cait Sith* can do that." Mr. Myrdin nodded toward Penny.

"Then *how* did you know we were at the door?"

"Call it a shrewd guess."

Duncan raised an eyebrow.

"A few minutes ago, I went to the kitchen to refresh my tea. When I came back, I found Simon lounging on the hearth."

"How'd he get in?" asked Duncan.

"I assume he teleported here, and I figured that meant you were coming. So, I sat down to enjoy my tea. When he got up and walked to the door, I followed him and opened it to find you standing on my doorstep."

Why did you do that? Why didn't you just walk with us? Penny asked Simon.

I knew you were coming to visit the gray-haired man and the black bird. I decided to meet you here. It was just a short hop. I knew you would be safe on your walk here. Besides, it was cold outside.

Penny reached down and rubbed him behind his ears. Simon began to purr.

"Well, come in from the cold. There's no point in paying to heat the whole town," Mr. Myrdin closed the door behind them. "Would either of you like to warm up with a spot of tea?" They both shook their heads. He motioned them toward his living room. "Please make yourselves comfortable while I refresh my mug." He disappeared into the kitchen.

After glancing around the book-filled room, Penny and Duncan looked self-consciously at each other and settled into the only free spaces left . . . on the love seat with the purring *Cait Sith* wedged between them. A cackle of laughter alerted them to Master Poe's presence.

"Good morning, Master Poe," Penny said.

"Good morning, Penny. And to you, too, Duncan."

Duncan nodded toward the large bird.

Mr. Myrdin returned from the kitchen and sat in his favorite overstuffed chair across from Penny and Duncan. "To what do we owe this visit? I don't imagine you've come here this early for a social call."

"No, we didn't," Penny said.

Mr. Myrdin smiled. "Well, then why don't you tell us what brought you here on this cold morning."

Penny and Duncan took turns describing their search for the braided strand, finding the coin, their encounter with Sobek, and the hanging cats at Ms. Johnson's.

When they were finished, Mr. Myrdin sat silently across from them with his fingers steepled in front of his face.

Master Poe broke the silence first. "Is that everything?"

Penny and Duncan exchanged glances but didn't say anything until Mr. Myrdin dropped his hands from his face. "All right, out with it?"

After a few more moments of silence, Penny said, "Well, Mrs. Cadogan—"

"My grandmother," interrupted Duncan.

"Yes, an amazing woman, I still want to meet her. Maybe you should arrange something. Perhaps an afternoon tea."

"What my old friend means to say is, what about her?" Master Poe interrupted.

"Well, she overheard us talking about Kolchak's theory that mischievous elves were to blame for Ms. Johnson's cats, and she disagreed."

"Yeah, she said it didn't sound like something elves would do," Duncan added.

"Is that all?" Master Poe asked, cocking his head to one side.

"No, she said it sounded like the work of a Red Leprechaun. What did she say its Welsh name was, Duncan?" Penny asked.

Before Duncan could answer, Mr. Myrdin said, "*Coch Coblyn.*"

"Yeah, that's it," Duncan said. "How'd you know?"

"We've dealt with the *Coch Coblyn* before," Master Poe said.

Mr. Myrdin stared at the floor and twisted his ring. "If by 'dealt with' you mean watched idly as hundreds died and seventy thousand of the old city's residents lost their homes, then yes, we've 'dealt with' the *Coch Coblyn.*"

"Don't be so hard on yourself, old friend. It wasn't your fault or even the baker's. Neither of you could have done anything to prevent the fire. The blame lies solely with the *Coch Coblyn.*"

Mr. Myrdin shot the raven a hard look. "If that idiot of a Lord Mayor, Sir Bloodworth, had been worth anything and done his job . . ." Mr. Myrdin stared vacantly at the fireplace. "She was my only love. We only had that one week together." His glare softened as tears welled up in his eyes.

An uneasy hush settled over the room. After several long moments of awkward quiet, Master Poe broke the silence. "I know this life has been hard on you, but at least you had that week with Abigail. Tis better to have loved and lost than never to have loved at all."

Mr. Myrdin dabbed his eyes, and anger flashed briefly across his face. "A great quote, and true enough, but you know how much I despise Tennyson."

Master Poe bobbed his beak up and down. "Indeed."

"As if I would let Morgana beguile me into giving her the knowledge to imprison me in an oak tree."

"Of course, you wouldn't," Master Poe agreed.

"Everyone knows that oak wood is impervious to extra-dimensional energy. It's in all the books." Mr. Myrdin turned to Penny and Duncan, who dutifully nodded. "An Alder would at least make sense, but oak? What a preposterous idea!"

When no one said anything in response, he continued. "Using Art and Gwen's love and their loss as an allegory for the shortfall of Victorian virtues was bad enough. But blaming that loss on Gwen, even metaphorically . . . what a bunch of nonsensical twaddle! His bungling of the facts to cater to the baser instincts of his audience preserved women's inequality for another generation!"

"Undeniably," Master Poe agreed.

"And they made that man the poet laureate?" Mr. Myrdin shook his head. "It's truly a shame that Samuel Rogers' old age prompted him to turn down the post!"

"Perhaps, but *Tears, Idle Tears* and *Ulysses* were masterpieces worthy of recognition. And who would argue that Tennyson didn't make good use of his post with *The Charge of the Light Brigade*," Master Poe said.

Before Mr. Myrdin could respond, Penny said, "I'm sorry, but what does this discussion have to do with the *Coch Coblyn*?"

"Yeah, it reminds me of that time I got stuck listening to Mrs. Waldron and Mr. Taylor arguing about Dickinson and Wordsworth," Duncan added.

Mr. Myrdin's smile returned. "Thanks, old friend. My apologies for getting lost in past grief."

"You've nothing to apologize for. Abigail was a wonderful woman and her loss a tragedy. But the blame for her death and the destruction of old London belongs to the *Coch Coblyn*, not you. Perhaps, you should fill in the blanks for our younger guests."

Master Poe pointed his beak toward Penny and Duncan.

"Yes, yes, of course. It was late in the summer of 1666. Master Poe and I had just materialized in London. I was posing as a down-on-his-luck Master Carpenter—"

"*You're* a Master Carpenter?" interrupted Duncan.

"Strictly speaking, no, I never got past the journeyman level. It's hard to serve a full seven year apprenticeship when you're constantly hopping forward in time. Nonetheless, while I'll never be confused for Norm Abram, I picked up enough knowledge to convince Thomas Farynor to give me free lodging in return for building a set of cooling racks in his Pudding Lane bakery."

"Wait a minute, wasn't 1666 the year of the great fire in London? And didn't it start in a bakery?" Penny asked.

"Yes, on both counts," Mr. Myrdin answered.

"Is that what brought you there? Were you trying to stop the fire?" Duncan asked.

"In a way, yes, but not exactly."

Duncan frowned. "What kind of answer is that?"

"A truthful one," Mr. Myrdin replied. "Master Poe detected a large multi-dimensional disturbance in 1666 London, and that's what brought us there."

"Let me guess, it was the *Coch Coblyn*," Penny said.

"Yes, we'd run into him before, in Amsterdam, shortly before a fire destroyed three-quarters of that city in 1452."

"I don't get it . . . what's the connection between two fires hundreds of years ago and Ms. Johnson's cats dangling from trees, or Ms. Jenkins' underwear being displayed for all the neighbors to see?" Duncan asked.

"Are you familiar with the quest for the Holy Grail?"

Duncan nodded.

"Sure, it was the ultimate test for the knights of King Arthur's roundtable. Many sought the grail, but their own imperfections betrayed them. Finally, after many harrowing tests, the purest knight, Sir Galahad succeeded."

"That is the most popular interpretation of the tale. While it is derived from the truth, it's mostly the imaginings of Chrétien de Troyes' epic twelfth-century poem *Perceval, le Conte du Graal*, which means *The Story of the Grail*," Mr. Myrdin said.

"So, it's kind of like the rest of the Arthurian legend . . . a little bit of truth with a lot of poetic license?" Penny asked.

"In a way, but the story of an all-powerful artifact is older than Arthur. It was old when my Master taught it to me. In the Druid version, the artifact is a talisman in the form of a scepter known as the *Teyrnwialen o Saith*, which is Welsh for 'Scepter of Seven,' because it contains seven multi-dimensional stones. All apprentices were required to memorize the story and repeat it verbatim before beginning their formal training."

"Do you still know it?" Duncan asked.

"Yes, my Master followed the training regime diligently, but it's a very long tale. The short version is that Adda, the first owner of the *Teyrnwialen o Saith*, used its power to harness the spirits of nature—"

Duncan interrupted. "You mean the *Bodach*, right?"

"Yes, of course I mean the *Bodach*. Please refrain from interrupting. Now, at first, everything went well and Adda and his people prospered. All the cows had twins, the harvests were plentiful, the hives produced the sweetest honey, and so on, but it didn't last."

"What happened?" Penny asked.

"Adda's wife, Carys, became mysteriously ill and died."

"Why didn't he save her?" Duncan asked.

"He was away when she became sick and didn't arrive until after she died. His grief was so great that he tried to use the power of the *Teyrnwialen o Saith* to bring her back from the dead."

"I gather that didn't go well," Penny said.

"No, it didn't. Compelled by the *Teyrnwialen o Saith*, some of the spirits attempted to carry out his command, while others opposed them. Their battles ravaged the land and destroyed the people's paradise."

"Did that really happen or is it just a myth?" Duncan asked.

"Most of my fellow apprentices and Druids believed it just an illustrative story to remind us that there were lines we shouldn't cross."

"Most, but not all," Penny said.

"Perceptive as always. My Master believed there was more truth to the tale than his peers. Perhaps that's why he was one of the last druids to survive. I don't know, but I do know that the *Teyrnwialen o Saith* exists. I even held it in my hands."

"How is that possible?" Penny asked.

Mr. Myrdin shrugged. "I don't know, but this summer, some undergraduate students found a strange oak box at the Hiscock archeological dig. The *Teyrnwialen o Saith* was inside the box. Here's a picture." He handed them the same picture he'd shown Master Poe.

"Okay, but I still don't see the connection between the underwear, the cats, and the talisman," Duncan said.

"Well, until you mentioned the *Coch Coblyn* just a few minutes ago, I wouldn't have thought there was any connection either. But if Mrs. Cadogan is right, and I suspect she is, then I doubt it's a coincidence that the *Coch Coblyn* just happens to show up right after the most powerful talisman ever created is found."

"What exactly is the *Coch Coblyn*? Is it some kind of *Bodach*?" Duncan asked.

"Literally, the name translates to *red leprechaun*, which is a good description, as far as it goes. But as for the *Coch Coblyn's* true nature, well, that's open to some debate. While we didn't meet the *Coch Coblyn* until the fifteenth century, I've been able to trace tales of him back to Roman Britain. According to the myths, the *Coch Coblyn* was a powerful faerie summoned by Celtic druids at the request of Boudica to help her overthrow the hated Romans."

"Why's he called a red leprechaun?" asked Duncan. "Aren't leprechauns those short tricksters who wear green and hide their pots of gold at the end of rainbows?" When Mr. Myrdin nodded, Duncan continued. "I don't get how a small practical joker could help defeat the Romans? I mean, what's he going to do . . . tickle them to death?"

Mr. Myrdin shook his head.

"His name is a bit of a misnomer. You see, the *Coch Coblyn* is not a true Leprechaun; he merely resembles one. He's short, bearded, and has overly large feet, much like a true Leprechaun. But that's where the similarity ends. While true Leprechauns are a friendly, albeit slightly mischievous, weaker type of *Bodach*, the *Coch Coblyn* is an altogether different character. He wears red because it is the color of blood and battle and the *Coch Coblyn* was summoned to help the Celts fight."

"But the Celts lost, didn't they?" Penny asked.

"Yes, but initially they were quite successful. With the *Coch Coblyn's* help, Boudica led the Celts to victory over the Romans in three great battles. Goaded on by the *Coch Coblyn* and their desire for revenge on the Romans, the Celts not only defeated the Roman army, they devastated the towns that later became Colchester,

London, and St. Albans. They slew everyone they found in the cities and burned them to the ground."

"Even children?" Penny asked.

"Women, children, young and old, it made no difference. They were infused with the bloodlust of the *Coch Coblyn*. People retold the tale of the slaughter for years. Even three centuries later, when I was born, my Master Druid told the story of Boudica's battles as a warning against cooperating too closely with powerful *Bodach*."

"I can see why," Duncan said.

"Yes, unfortunately, Boudica didn't have the benefit of that lesson. Too late, she realized the evil of her bargain with the *Coch Coblyn*. Revolted at watching her daughters participate in the wanton slaughter, she attempted to revoke her covenant with him."

"Attempted?" Duncan asked.

"Yes, pacts with extra-dimensional beings are never easy to escape. In return for her life, the *Coch Coblyn* agreed to free her people from his bloodlust. She died thinking she'd saved her people."

"The *Coch Coblyn* didn't keep his end of the deal?" Duncan asked.

"On the contrary, he kept it to the letter. In the next battle, he remained neutral. Valiant as the Celts were, without his help, they were no match for the reinforced and well-trained Romans. They were slaughtered, and their lands were absorbed into the empire."

"What happened to the *Coch Coblyn*?" Penny asked.

"When his summoning Druids were killed by the Romans, he became trapped in our dimension. Like his *Bodach* cousins, he wants to return home, but can't. In our dimension, he appears as a small, misshapen man with overly large feet. He always dresses in red. He follows his *own* interpretation of Celtic law and customs, punishing violators with pranks and tricks. The tricks start small, but always escalate."

"He's the connection to those two fires, isn't he?" Duncan asked.

"Yes, and quite a few others. While it's a small consolation to Boudica and her followers, the first was the Great Fire of Rome in 64. After wandering through the empire, he made his way to Rome, where it didn't take long for the local customs to run afoul of his adopted Celtic ways. The fire burned ten of Rome's fourteen districts and contributed to Emperor Nero's downfall."

"I guess he never bought into the old 'When in Rome, do as the Romans do' saying," cracked Duncan.

"No, and judging from the pranks we know of here, I don't think he's taken too kindly to the ways of twenty-first-century Americans either," Master Poe added.

"Why bother with pranks? And why hasn't he faded like the other *Bodach*?" Duncan asked.

"In answer to your first question, I think the pranks are meant as a warning rather than a punishment."

"A warning to who?" Duncan asked.

"To fellow travelers, that the home in question is not a friendly place. Now, as for your second question, Master Poe and I have been pondering that for centuries."

"And?" Penny asked.

"We haven't made much progress. The death of his summoners should have severed his connection to the higher dimensions, and without that connection, his energy should've dissipated. But it didn't and near as we can tell, he's as strong as he was when he was trapped here," Master Poe said.

"Maybe he's been feeding on the other *Bodach*," Duncan offered.

"We thought of that, but if that were the case, then I'd see fluctuations in his energy levels, which I've never detected," Master Poe said.

"I think I get it," interjected Penny. "I mean, I could be wrong, but it might make sense." She paused, waiting for their full attention.

"Yes, go on," encouraged Mr. Myrdin.

"He was brought here through the power of the Druids to defend the Celts. Well, maybe as long he stays within the bounds of his original summoning, he can avoid fading."

"What do you mean?" Duncan asked. "The Celts have been gone a long time."

"As a nation, but not as a culture. Think of all the traditions we follow that have roots in Celtic customs. Like Halloween and its costumes, Groundhog Day, and mistletoe."

"Okay, but do you honestly think the *Coch Coblyn* is interpreting Ms. Johnson and Ms. Jenkins as threats to Celtic tradition?" Duncan asked.

Mr. Myrdin sighed. "Oddly, it makes good sense."

"Huh?" said Duncan.

"The Celts were active traders, but their lands were sparsely populated. Travel was slow, and larger towns with inns were often days apart. With frequent bickering and fighting between rival clan leaders, travel was a risky proposition, so common Celts looked out for each other. Homesteaders were expected to offer safe board to travelers, even if it was no more than a spot of hay in an animal shelter. When Ms. Johnson and Ms. Jenkins turned him away, the *Coch Coblyn* could have interpreted their actions as violating Celtic tradition."

"A most interesting debate, but somewhat irrelevant. Something has protected the *Coch Coblyn* from fading, and Penny's hypothesis seems to fit the facts. That said, the real issue before us is why is he here and what are we going to do about it?" Master Poe said.

"As usual, you're right, old friend."

"Earlier, you said he's here because of the *Teyrnwialen o Saith*," Penny said.

"Yes, he can sense dimensional disturbances, and the discovery of the *Teyrnwialen o Saith* certainly counts as a dimensional disturbance," Mr. Myrdin said.

"If he can jump through time, why did he bother with all of those intermediate jumps? Why not just come straight here?" Penny added. "Or even to the time before the *Teyrnwialen o Saith* was lost?"

"Good questions, while we don't have perfect answers, we can make some good guesses. First, in this dimension, the *Coch Coblyn's* ability to time travel is limited to skipping forward. So, presumably, the *Teyrnwialen o Saith* was lost before he was summoned. Second, if he's like Master Poe—"

Master Poe interrupted with a loud squawk. "Sorry, old friend. No offense meant." Master Poe ruffled his feathers but said nothing else.

"Second," Mr. Myrdin continued, "jumping forward is not a precise science. It's hard to land exactly *when* you intend to land. Finally, the *Teyrnwialen o Saith* wasn't just lost, I believe it was hidden."

Penny raised the brow above her blue eye. "Hidden?"

Mr. Myrdin nodded.

Penny pursed her lips for a moment before answering. "It was in an oak box."

"Very good, Miss Preston, very good."

"How'd you figure that out?" Duncan asked.

"I figured if you want to hide something as powerful as the Scepter, you'd have to hide it in oak."

"Okay, so the *Coch Coblyn* came here because of the *Teyrnwialen o Saith*, but what's he going to do with it?" Duncan asked.

"With *Teyrnwialen o Saith*, he would be able to reconnect with his higher-dimensional home," answered Master Poe.

"Well, that doesn't sound so bad. I mean if he's a menace here, then why not let him use the scepter to leave?"

"I'm afraid it's not that simple," said Mr. Myrdin.

"He could use the *Teyrnwialen o Saith's* power to break the bonds of the Druids' summoning incantation. Couldn't he?" Penny said.

"Exactly," said Master Poe. "Freed from the summoning restrictions and with direct access to higher dimensional energy—"

"He'd become unstoppable," finished Penny.

T HE PUNGENT AROMA OF GARLIC WAFTED FROM THE BLUEBIRD'S kitchen and up the stairs . . . and found Sobek's nostrils. The scent invoked a memory from the dim and distant past when he and the rest of the Toth's survivors abandoned their culture to assimilate into the Egyptian village of Buto Maadi . . .

A FEW HOURS AFTER SUNRISE AND IT WAS ALREADY UNBEARABLY hot and humid. Sobek wiped the mixture of dust and sweat from his brow with his sleeve. He cursed and wondered how Buto Maadi could be both humid and dusty at the same time.

The uncouth residents were all busy with their daily tasks. The men had departed before sunrise to work the fishing nets from their crude reed boats. The older boys were out tending flocks of sheep and goats. Women and younger children sat in front of the entrances to their half-buried clay hovels, grinding grain between stones. Others baked the flour into a coarse bread or stirred cauldrons containing onions, garlic cloves, and salted fish. Sobek had never cared for onions, and after months in Buto Maadi, he'd developed a strong aversion to garlic.

No one paid attention to Sobek, which was exactly what he wanted. He loathed the residents and everything else in his new home. There was only one member of the uncouth clan who interested him: Heka, the spirit-seer and magical protector for the village. While her second sight was weak, with the proper training she would have made a serviceable Amun-Ra acolyte. Unfortunately, she had the misfortune of being born among the uncouth where her minor talents were wasted auguring futures and creating useless charms.

Her hovel, at the edge of the village, consisted of a single room with a bare dirt floor several feet below street level. Half-burying the huts kept them cooler in the heat of the day and warmer on the chilly nights, but it also made them dark and dreary.

Sobek stooped to fit under the low eave and entered Heka's hut. After his eyes adjusted to the dim light, he saw a young woman sitting with her back turned to him.

Heka was speaking quietly to the woman.

Sobek cleared his throat. "Ahem."

"I'll be with you in a minute, Sobek," replied Heka without bothering to make eye contact. She took the young woman's hands in hers and sang the words of a mantra three times before releasing them.

The girl—for to Sobek's eyes she was little more than that—silently dropped her hands into her lap.

Heka reached into a bag and pulled out a small ceramic statue depicting a woman with a frog's head. Sobek recognized it as a faience or good luck charm which the locals relied on as wards against evil spirits. He made no attempt to hide his derisive snort.

Heka ignored him. "This is Heqet, the spirit of fertility. Keep her with you at all times, and you will have healthy children." She placed the faience into the girl's hands.

Heka rose slowly and motioned for the girl to do the same. When they were both standing, Heka started toward the door. Before she took her second step, the girl wrapped her arms around the spirit-seer.

Heka held the girl's embrace for a few moments and whispered something in her ear that Sobek didn't hear.

The girl released Heka and hurried out the door.

"What few skills you have, you *waste*. If you used your second sight properly, you would know that the girl's already pregnant; very early, but the signs are there for anyone with the gift to see."

Heka met his gaze but said nothing.

"You did her no favors telling her that faience will guarantee her healthy children," he added with a mocking crocodilian smile.

"I know the statue holds no real power, but she's lost one child already and fears she will never have another. The statute will give her an outlet for those fears and allow her to enjoy the lives of her four children."

Sobek dropped his smile and cocked an eyebrow.

"Yes, I *know* she will have four healthy children. The three boys will become respectable villagers, and her daughter will become a great spirit-seer. I also know why you are here."

A part of him—his typically dominant, more confident self—was prepared for her response. But if she was telling the truth, then she *knew* what he intended. The other weaker part of him—the part containing his doubts and fears—rose up and asserted itself. Perspiration beaded on his forehead. He fought the urge to wipe it away. The beads on his brow coalesced and a rivulet of sweat dribbled down his face. In the folds of his robe, he tightened his grip on the crude cudgel he carried and prepared to strike.

Seemingly oblivious to his internal struggles, Heka continued. "You are here to ask me to auger your future, correct?"

Her question quelled his rising panic. He released his grip on the cudgel. He smiled confidently and looked down on the diminutive spirit-seer. "Yes, of course. Tell me what you see."

"As you wish, but I will need silence to accurately read your future. Speak only when spoken to. Do you understand?"

Sobek nodded. She motioned for him to sit on a small woven mat directly in front of her.

Heka closed her eyes, reached into a bag, and pulled out a ceramic figurine. Smaller than the faience she had given to the girl, this one depicted a short misshapen man. Everything from its long-pointed shoes to its comical hat was a shade of red. Its eyes were set with red gemstones that sparkled. Heka held the statue over her heart and extended her left arm; her hand up, palm toward him with her thumb, index, and middle fingers raised. She began to sing.

Sobek couldn't understand her words, but he recognized the pattern as a mantra. A reddish glow emanated from the statue in her right hand. The Amun-Ra forbid divining and auguring, but he understood that she was using the faience to enhance her power. She was calling for assistance from the upper planes, or what the locals referred to as the spirit world.

When she'd repeated the verse five times, she stopped singing.

A chill enveloped the room, goosebumps rose on Sobek's arms, and a shiver ran down his spine. The faience's reddish glow faded, and its gemstone eyes flickered to blue and yellow.

The faience was the power amplifier he'd come to steal. He shot his hand toward the spirit-seer, agonizing pain raced up his arm. He pulled his hand back, then slowly extended it across the gap. Two feet from the spirit-seer the hair on his knuckles stood on end, and the tips of his fingers tingled. The air around the spirit-seer shimmered with power. Using the faience, she had surrounded herself with a protective shield.

Silently cursing, he rubbed his hands over his arms as the air in the hut became even colder. He needed all his mental control to keep his teeth from chattering. His breath formed visible clouds of mist that crackled as the moisture turned to ice. A few feet away on the other side of the energy field, the diminutive spirit-seer sat comfortably cross-legged on the floor. Nothing about her visage gave any indication that she was the least bit cold; if anything, her red cheeks gave the impression that she was overheating.

Studying her through the shimmering field, Sobek noticed that her eyes were closed, and beads of sweat ran down her flushed cheeks. Maintaining the shield was pushing her beyond her meager limits.

He reached into the higher planes, but before he completed the connection, a blinding flash of blue and yellow light filled the room. The intense light burned through his closed eyelids. He raised his hands to cover his eyes, but the light seared through his flesh. His hands became translucent. The bones of his fingers glowed back at him.

Just as suddenly as it had appeared, the blinding light faded. Cautiously, he lowered his hands. The first image he discerned was the shadowy figure of the spirit-seer sitting cross-legged in front of him. Her eyes stared back at him; two fiery jewels, one a piercing blue, and the other a fiery yellow.

As if struggling against an unseen force, Heka's mouth moved, but her soft lilting voice was replaced by a stentorian snarl. Sobek recognized it as the otherworldly speech of a being from a higher plane.

"You are Sobek, of the Amun-Ra?"

Sobek nodded.

"Good, it's always best to properly discern one's enemies before dispensing with unpleasant business."

"Enemy?" asked Sobek. His voice sounded positively mouse-like in comparison to the words echoing from the spirit-seer.

"Hmm, it would be civil of me to give you an explanation. As much as I detest the extra-dimensionally aware beings of this plane, this spirit-seer followed the summoning procedure precisely. Additionally, her protections were properly constructed and, much to my chagrin, proof against my admittedly limited capabilities in this plane. By the terms of her summons, I am bound to her will until sunset or until she issues me three commands; whichever comes first. While I have some latitude to interpret her directives, I must carry them out to the best of my abilities. Her first command is to defend her from all harm. If you persist in attacking her, I will not hesitate to eradicate you from every plane of existence. Do I make myself clear?"

Sobek's fear asserted itself; all he could muster was a nod.

"Good. Just because neither one of us is happy with our current situation does not mean that we should abandon professionalism. That brings us to her second command which for some strange reason, she chose to spend on you."

The spirit-seer's eyes flashed more intensely for a fraction of a second, and a deeper chill raced through Sobek's body. Everything in the room went dark. Sobek lost himself in a miasma of nothing, drifting and falling through eons and moments, with no sense of causality or direction. All he could see was the piercing light of the spirit-seer's unnaturally blue and yellow eyes. He concentrated on those lights, fearful that if he lost sight of them, he would spin into the void of nothingness. He fought desperately to keep his mind, his consciousness, his very essence, from dissipating into the abyss.

Just when he thought he could no longer endure the strain, he snapped back into his normal reality, and the entity spoke. "Sobek of the Amun-Ra, I have read your heart's greatest desire. You did well to survive the reading; not many from your plane could have endured the perils of disambiguation. However, you must know that the task you set for yourself is well-nigh impossible."

"Impossible?"

"I said, well-nigh impossible, which means that there is a path with a greater than zero probability of success."

"How much greater than zero?"

"Let's just say that it's lower than the probability of a monkey banging out the complete works of Shakespeare on a typewriter but higher than the chances of the Cubs winning another World Series."

"Who is Shakespeare? What is a typewriter? And what is a World Series?"

"Eh, minor details, nothing for you to worry about. My point is that to win your heart's deepest desire, you must tread an arduous path, but not one without hope. With enough power and the proper tool, you could return to the past and reset the timeline to avert the destruction of your people. Unfortunately, you cannot hope to succeed by yourself."

"Are you offering to help?" Sobek asked.

"No, no, no," replied the entity in what to Sobek's ears almost sounded like laughter. "Don't get me wrong, I almost certainly wouldn't even if I could, but I can't. You see, while in this plane, I can only do what I've been commanded to do."

"So, I am *doomed* to failure and a meager existence among the uncouth?"

"Perhaps not, perhaps not."

Annoyed with the entity's vacillations, Sobek snapped, "You just said you could not help me, but even if it were possible, you would not."

"No, what I said was that I almost certainly wouldn't help you."

"I fail to see the significance of the distinction."

"Ah, until the spirit-seer gave me her third command, there was none, but now . . ."

"What has she commanded you to do?" asked Sobek.

"How shall I put this delicately?"

"Just give it to me straight."

"She's ordered me to eliminate you as a threat to her people."

Sobek sighed. "At least I won't have to endure a lifetime with Amunet and Seskat's crew trying to teach science and culture to these uncouth savages."

"I think you're being a bit too hasty with your judgment again, my Amun-Ra friend."

"How so? Do you plan to renege on your promise to the spirit-seer?"

"Of course not, but she did not command me to kill you. No, she commanded me to eliminate you as a threat to her people. I believe I can do that and help you along on your path as well."

"But why would you help me?"

"Don't mistake my assistance as generosity. I'm doing it for purely selfish reasons. While there's a small chance that you might succeed in your desire, there's a greater chance that your efforts will destroy this plane and free me to return home. If I simply eradicate you, that won't happen; but if I help you and you fail . . . well, you see how that might, how do you say it, make my day."

"Just what do you intend to do?"

"You need help from outside your world. I wasn't sure who I should burden with your presence. Then I remembered the faience the spirit-seer used to summon me."

"You're going to give me her faience?" Sobek's smile revealed his crocodilian teeth.

"Absolutely not. If I gave it to you, you might figure out how to command me with it, and that's unacceptable."

Sobek's stomach rose in his throat as the entity dashed his hopes.

Somehow, he mustered the courage to ask, "So what are you going to do?"

"This faience draws its power from a particular entity in my home realm."

"One of your kinsmen?"

"I suppose you could call him a distant relation, say a third cousin twice removed on my mother's side, if I had a mother, which of course I don't. In any event, he's tied to this statue, which is most inconvenient for him."

"You plan to free him?"

"No, that's beyond my abilities in this place. Besides, he might think I was doing him a favor, and I wouldn't want to give him the *wrong* impression. I'm going to bind the two of you together and cast you into the future. That will keep you from threatening her people. And who knows . . . at some point, he may help you achieve your desire."

"How far into the future?"

"That depends on how long it takes for someone to summon my erstwhile relative. The concept of linear time is strange to us, but it could be years, centuries, or eons."

Sobek swallowed hard.

"Oh, don't worry; it will seem no more than an instant for you. Completely painless, too," added the entity.

"How do I know I can trust you?"

"Oh, you can't, but since your alternative is eradication, I assume you'll cooperate."

"You make a most compelling argument."

"Why, thank you. I appreciate it when my partners recognize the facts and accept their fate without all that needless begging, pleading, and crying. Your professionalism is so refreshing. One other thing. The entity I'm binding you with is a rather ornery fellow. But remember, you cannot reset the timeline without him. To succeed, you will need to find the Sekhem."

19

PRESENT DAY, AT THE MONROE INSTITUTE

TONY PAGIA LOOKED AT THE NUMBERS FOR THE THIRD TIME. They still didn't add up. He threw his pencil onto his desk in disgust.

"Hey, Tony, what's got you so disgruntled?" asked a lilting voice from the hallway.

Tony looked up to see the concerned face of Sharon Wallis from public relations peering around his door.

"Oh hi, Sharon, come on in." He motioned her through the door with his hand. She sat down in the chair on the other side of his desk. "It's this presentation for the Monroe Institute's board meeting."

"Aren't they usually just a formality?" she asked.

"Usually, but not this time."

"Oh, why is that?"

"Well, with all of the budget problems down in Washington, there's a lot of talk about cutting funding for 'non-essential' research."

"They're not talking about our cryptography or basic science research, are they?"

"No, no, anything remotely scientific is safe, even the crazy stuff. I saw a program to study the impact of methane emissions from dairy cows to improve the taste of milk get approved."

"The government's funding a study on cow gas?" she asked.

"Yup, it's amazing how many favors Vermont's Senator Blutarski can call in. I'm pretty sure if our archeology group had some digs in Vermont, we could've gotten some of those $700,000, but unfortunately . . ." his voice trailed off without finishing the thought.

"How bad is it?"

"Even with my most creative accounting, we're talking about no funding for half the archeology department. What we really need is someone to step in and fund the group or we're going to have to let some people go."

"The Monroe's never laid off anyone before."

"True, but I guess there's a first time for everything."

"How long before the board meeting?"

"It's the day after tomorrow," Tony replied.

"So, if we could find a donor before then, the board would spare the department?"

"Sure, but where are you going to find that kind of money in two days?"

"Hey, I'm in PR, I'll find a way, trust me." She flashed him her biggest smile.

SHARON WALLIS PEEKED OUT FROM THE WINGS OF THE PIPER FALLS
Library auditorium; there were more than a dozen newspaper
and radio reporters as well as a camera crew from the Discovery
Channel sitting among a large crowd of interested locals, which
included Mayor Thompkins and several prominent businesspeople.
She'd had to call in most of the emergency favors she'd been saving
to get them all here, but they weren't her most important guests.

That distinction belonged to the Jesse Cornplanter, Sachem
of the Heron clan from the Tonawanda Band of the Seneca Tribe.
Their home was just twenty-three miles west of the Hiscock site.
The discovery of such a game-changing artifact linked to the
earliest arrival of their ancestors had struck a chord with the tribe.
In a matter of hours, Sachem Cornplanter had contacted the other
members of the Iroquois Confederacy and raised pledges of almost
a million dollars to support additional archeological research. She
hoped it was enough.

Turning away from the stage, she found Tom Holman nervously
rifling through his note cards. She tapped him on the shoulder. He
just about jumped out of his skin.

His carefully arranged note cards fell from his hands and scattered
across the stage floor. Without thinking, they simultaneously bent
down to pick up the cards, and their faces came within inches of
each other.

They paused, staring into each other's eyes for a long moment.
Sharon smiled.

"Tom, I'm so sorry. Here, let me help you."

Without breaking eye contact, they both reached to the floor
to pick up the scattered cards. Their hands touched and lingered

in a gentle caress. Sharon looked briefly down at their intertwined hands before returning her gaze to Tom's face.

His cheeks flushed, and he smiled awkwardly back at her.

"Ahem, can I help you two?" said Rick Testerman, who was coordinating the press event for Sharon. "Where would you like me to wheel the, uh, artifact? The Discovery Channel people want to make sure they can get a good shot for their exclusive. We've got 60 seconds before we go live."

Sharon and Tom quickly pulled their hands apart, gathered the rest of the cards, and stood up. "Just put it next to the podium," Tom said, his face still flush. "I'll make my opening remarks. Then I'll open the case."

"Sounds like a plan. We'll put it to your right, and I'll have Janet put a spotlight on it just as you reveal the box." Rick hurried off to find Janet.

Tom stared after Rick. "I wish Myrdin was here with me. He's the linguist who can best explain the significance of the markings."

Sharon replied, "Don't worry, Tom, the artifact and its age are the wow factor here; you don't need to go into those details. There will be time enough for Myrdin's expertise later. We've already received the funding from the tribes of New York; this conference is just for show. You're going to be great." Without thinking about it, she kissed him on the cheek.

"Ten seconds!" said a member of the production crew.

Tom checked his cards one last time and stepped up to the podium. Besides the press and local dignitaries, the audience included dozens of local residents, most of whom Tom knew. He swallowed hard and looked toward the eaves and at Sharon.

She raised her hand and waved with her fingers rippling one at a time, punctuating it with a full smile.

Even if he flopped, it would still be his best day in a long, long time. His confidence renewed, Tom smiled back at Sharon, turned toward the audience, and launched his presentation.

"Good afternoon. While searching for Mastodons at the Hiscock archeological dig in Byron, New York last summer, two undergraduate students, under the guidance of Doctor Marshall Richards from the State University in Buffalo . . ." Tom paused briefly and nodded to the professor seated in the front row, who waved and nodded at the acknowledgment, "stumbled upon something far more interesting." Pausing again, Tom slowly scanned the room and forced himself to silently count to five before saying, "In a layer of earth dating to six thousand years ago, they found this." With a flourish, he pulled the black cloth that was covering the stand to his right, revealing the oaken box containing the Butterfly Scepter. He'd wanted to skip the theatrics, but Rick and Sharon had insisted it was necessary.

Someone from the audience shouted, "A block of wood?" Mumbles quickly spread through the auditorium.

"It's not just *any* block of wood. This artifact is over seven thousand years old."

Another member of the audience yelled, "Okay, an *old* block of wood."

Laughter rippled through the crowd. Tom recognized several of his neighbors fighting to control themselves. He waited a few moments before raising his hands and motioning for the crowd to settle down. "This old block of wood is actually a precisely carved box. Even today, with all our fine machine tools, we'd be hard-pressed to replicate the tightness of its seams. Yet, somehow seven thousand years ago, the people living in upstate New York created this box.

"But that's not the most amazing part," he paused as Sharon had suggested.

It took less than five seconds for one of the reporters to lose patience and ask, "What's inside the box?"

Making sure he held the box squarely in the spotlight, Tom carefully slid the lid open to reveal the gem-topped silver scepter. "Ahs" and "Ohs" filled the auditorium, and Tom was nearly blinded by the flashes from the photographers' cameras. "We're calling this the Butterfly Scepter. Like the box, it, too, is seven thousand years old."

"What's it made of?" asked one of the reporters.

"Silver, as pure as anything we could make today."

A writer for a science magazine guffawed. "That's impossible. I bet those undergrads got careless with their procedures. It wouldn't be the *first* time," the writer said. Several others nodded their heads, and a few mumbled in agreement.

"Now see here!" Professor Richards stood up from his seat. "No one works at my site without a full understanding of how to follow protocols. I can assure you that this box and its contents were found in soil from six thousand years ago."

Tom spoke up. "The dates were independently verified using both traditional and laser carbon dating techniques. Copies of the results are included in your exit data packets."

"How can that be possible? It's got to be a hoax or error of some kind. The Native Americans of that time were Stone Age hunter-gatherers with no knowledge of metallurgy. You can't be suggesting that we believe they created the artifact," one writer said.

Before Tom could reply, Sachem Cornplanter stood up. "It would appear that my ancestors knew a great deal more than your experts thought."

The writer bristled at the Sachem's words. Tom feared the growing tension would ruin the event.

Fortunately, the correspondent from the Discovery Channel spoke up. "Why do you call it the Butterfly Scepter?"

"The scepter is covered with engravings depicting the life-cycle of the Monarch butterfly, and inside the box, we found the desiccated remains of milkweed leaves, the Monarch's favorite food."

"That's amazing. I can't quite make it out from here, but there appear to be other markings on the scepter. What can you tell us about them?"

"You're right, there are carvings interspersed among the butterfly images . . . we believe them to be some form of writing."

"Are you sure? Based on the age of the artifact, that would pre-date the earliest known writing by more than a thousand years."

"Of course, we can't be 100 percent certain, but our linguistics expert believes them to be a form of phonetic writing with similarities to Minoan Linear A."

"Are you saying this artifact is Minoan, or are you suggesting some sort of parallel development, or a common forbearer to both?" another reporter asked.

"Honestly, we're as mystified as you guys. All we know is when these artifacts were made, they were buried a thousand years later, and that the writing bears a resemblance to Minoan Linear A. Anything beyond that . . ." Tom spread his hands, ". . . well, that's just pure conjecture."

TINGLING WAVES OF ENERGY COURSED THROUGH SOBEK'S BODY, racing up his limbs and through his torso in ever-increasing intensity until they met and released their power in his mind. The explosion of extra-dimensional energy forced him out of his garlic-induced memory and back to the present. He shot up from his hotel room's overstuffed chair and stood ramrod straight.

He lifted his head slightly and sniffed the air. Happily, he detected no hint of garlic. Without moving the rest of his body, he closed his eyes and slowly turned his head from one side to the other. After completing the circuit, he opened his eyes wide and smiled, the crocodilian points of his teeth sliding over his stretched lips. After countless hops through time and innumerable false starts and failed hopes, finally, his time had come. Finally, he'd found the Sekhem. Now he needed to retrieve it.

20

As Tom fielded the last question from the press, Deputy Sheriff Barnes, who'd watched the presentation from the back of the auditorium, turned to his friend Kolchak.

"C'mon, he's goin' to invite everyone up to take a look, and I need to be down there."

"Do you really think there's going to be any trouble?"

"No, of course not, but we don't want people getting the idea that the Sheriff's department isn't prepared."

Kolchak slapped Fred's shoulder with his hand. "Besides, that scepter *is* pretty cool."

"Yeah, let's get down there and take a look." The two men swam against the current of the departing attendees to reach the stage where Sachem Cornplanter, Dr. Richards, and Sharon surrounded Tom.

"Can you believe the nerve of that guy? I mean, I may not have won a Nobel Prize or anything, but I do have a reputation for running a well-controlled dig," Dr. Richards vented.

"Yes, everyone knows that," Tom agreed.

"Well, I'm glad we put him in his place. Oh, and Sachem Cornplanter, thank you so much for organizing the additional funding. We'll be able to open another dig at the site next year."

"It was my pleasure, Professor. With few exceptions, our people have been divided and downtrodden for many years. This gives us an opportunity to come together."

"Excuse me, Sachem Cornplanter, would you mind posing for a photo with the Butterfly Scepter? It would make a great PR piece for the Monroe," Sharon said.

"Oh please, be my guest." The Sachem reached out toward the oak box, but before he touched the scepter, he paused. "I do this in thanks to the seven who have gone before and for the benefit of the seven who have not yet risen."

"What does he mean the seven who have gone before and those who have not yet risen?" Sharon asked.

"He's thanking his ancestors for their good stewardship and asking that what he does now will serve the generations to come," Professor Richards said.

Sachem Cornplanter turned toward the professor. "You know the Great Binding Law?"

"Not in detail, but I know that the Iroquois Constitution greatly influenced many of our founding fathers, including Benjamin Franklin and Thomas Jefferson. Even today, its concept of seven generation sustainability is one of the pillars for some in the environmental movement."

Sachem Cornplanter smiled. "I'm glad to see that I have invested the tribe's money with good people."

"We feel the same way, Sachem. Would you like to pose for the camera with the scepter?" Tom asked.

"Yes, of course." The Sachem carefully extended his hand into the oak box and wrapped his fingers around the Butterfly Scepter. He smiled at everyone before removing it. As the scepter left the box, the Sachem's eyes opened wide and froze. He stood silently still, his unblinking eyes, staring into nothing while his face wore a beatific smile.

Tom, Sharon, and Professor Richards exchanged furtive glances. Deputy Barnes broke the silence. "Is he okay? What happened?"

"He appears to be in some sort of trance." Everyone turned away from the frozen Sachem, toward the source of the voice . . . Darin Kolchak. He raised a finger to his lips in the universal sign for quiet. Dropping his finger, everyone huddled closer to him, and he continued softly, his voice barely above a whisper. "It bears some resemblance to a traditional Shaman's trance."

"You've seen one?" whispered Tom.

"No, but I have read first-hand accounts of them written by participants in the ceremonies."

"What should we do?" Sharon asked.

"The last thing we want to do is jolt him out of it. If he is in a Shaman's trance, his subconscious mind has risen into balance with his waking mind. If we wake him suddenly, we would destroy that delicate balance," Kolchak said.

"Assuming you're correct, I'm not sure I understand why that would be a bad thing," the professor said.

"Shamanists believe in a universe that consists of multiple planes of existence. The earth and everything we can sense with our conscious mind exist in one of those planes while the spirits of nature and those of our ancestors occupy others."

"Sounds a little bit like the concept of the multiverse from string theory," Tom said.

"Maybe science is finally catching up with mysticism," Kolchak said without a hint of sarcasm. "In any event, the Shamanists also believe that it's possible to make connections between the various planes."

"How would they do that, and why would they want to?" Sharon asked.

"Why do it? Well, for the same reason members of other religions pray to their gods and saints . . . to seek assistance from the spirits or guidance from their ancestors. As for the how, they believe that each of us has the ability to contact the other planes, but for our protection, the connection is blocked by our conscious mind. By entering a trance and raising the level of their subconscious mind, the Shamans remove that block and communicate with the other planes."

"But how'd he get into a trance? I didn't hear any chantin' or prayin'."

"Chanting and meditation are the most common ways to enter a trance, but there are others," Kolchak replied.

"Wait, what was it he said just before he reached for the scepter?" Sharon asked.

"He thanked the seven who've gone before and the seven who've yet to rise," said Deputy Barnes.

"That's it." Kolchak snapped his fingers.

"That's *what*?" asked the professor.

"The combination of the words from the Great Binding Law, his emotional state, and touching the scepter together induced his trance."

"Makes sense, I guess," Deputy Barnes said.

The professor glared at the deputy and shook his head.

"So, if we disturb his trance, shouldn't his subconscious fade into the background, leaving his conscious mind in charge?" Tom asked.

"Maybe, but some of the trance stories I've read suggest that breaking the trance suddenly allows the elements from the subconscious to cross permanently into the conscious mind."

"That's ridiculous. By its very nature, the subconscious is subservient to the conscious," the professor said.

"True, but would you agree that while in a trance, the boundary between the two states of mind blurs, and isn't that the entire basis for hypnotherapy?" Kolchak asked.

Professor Richards nodded. "Yes, there's ample scientific evidence to support that hypothesis."

"A Shamanistic trance, even a mild one, creates a stronger connection between the two levels of consciousness. All of us carry demons." Kolchak paused and looked at the people circled around him. Everyone nodded. "We hide those demons, personality quirks, and alter egos in our subconscious where they can harmlessly dissipate in our dreams and nightmares. Imagine if that release valve is realigned into our *conscious* mind instead of our subconscious one."

"You're sayin' that if we wake the Sachem from his trance, we may release his inner demons?" Deputy Barnes asked.

"Or perhaps something worse, Freddy," Kolchak said.

"What could be worse than that?" Sharon asked.

"Something from the other planes?" Tom suggested.

"Exactly," Kolchak said.

"Oh, this is nonsense," Professor Richards said. "It's cargo cult science of the worst kind. It's pure speculation without a shred of substantial evidence. I'll grant you that something strange is happening to Sachem Cornplanter. I'll even accept the possibility of some sort of hypnotic-like trance, but I draw the line at interfering entities from other planes. It's a bunch of hokum; that's what it is, hokum. I mean, look at him, does the Sachem look like he's possessed to you?"

While they were speaking, everyone had stopped paying attention to the Sachem. At the professor's reminder, they returned their attention to him. He stood exactly as he had been before, unblinking eyes staring off into nothing.

Deputy Barnes waved his hand in front of the Sachem's face with no results.

"What should we do?" Tom asked.

"I'm not sure, but—"

Kolchak never finished his sentence. The stones on the scepter began to flash on and off. First the red, then the yellow, followed by the blue. When they stopped flashing, the orange, green, and purple stones lit up in a similar alternating pattern.

"What's it mean?" Sharon asked.

"Did you detect any power source when you examined the scepter?" Kolchak asked Tom.

"No. All of our tests showed that other than the gems, it's solid silver."

"Do you think it's, uh, one of the spirits trying to communicate with us?" Deputy Barnes asked.

"Well, if it is, it's not using Morse code," Sharon said, earning her quizzical looks from Tom and the professor. "What? My father was an amateur radio enthusiast. He taught me Morse code."

"You're right, it's not Morse, but there are some differences in the two flashing patterns," the professor said.

"Really? They look pretty much the same to me," the deputy said.

The professor pointed to the scepter. "The primary colored gems take a little more than three seconds to flash through their sequence which repeats five times before the other gems begin flashing. The secondary color sequence is a little faster and repeats seven times before giving way to the primary colored gems again."

"I would bet if we could time them more precisely, the longer sequence would clock in just over 3.14 seconds, while the shorter one just a bit longer than 2.71 seconds," Kolchak said.

Tom raised his eyebrow. "You're thinking Pi and Euler's number?"

"Yes, mathematics and mysticism have a lot in common."

"I've heard of Pi, but what's Euler's number?" Sharon asked.

Tom spoke up. "Like Pi, Euler's number is an irrational number that cannot be represented by the ratio of any integers. It's the base number for the natural logarithm and appears in the solutions to many probability and number series problems. For example, it's part of the solution for the continuous compound interest problem."

When several of the others gave him strange looks, he smirked. "I was a double major; archeology and math."

"That's all nice, but it doesn't help us figure out what's going on or what we should do for the Sachem," the professor said.

Before anyone could answer, there was a blinding flash of light and a bone-numbing sensation of cold. Both lasted for little more than an instant which culminated in a blood-curdling scream from Sachem Cornplanter.

**THE DIM AND DISTANT PAST, IN WHAT WOULD
BECOME UPSTATE NEW YORK**

"THOSE DARK CLOUDS TO THE WEST LOOK TO BE COMING THIS way, and they don't look very inviting," Iosheka said.

"Yeah, I see them, too. We've only got an hour of daylight left, and I haven't seen anything but these rugged, tree-covered hills. What do you make of that dark area just over the next ridge?" Ataensic asked.

"Uh, I can't quite tell from here because it's in the shadow of the ridge, but it looks flat. I don't see any trees. If I had to guess, I'd say some type of water. Maybe a river or a narrow lake."

"That's what I thought, too. How well can you swim?" she asked.

"You're not thinking of landing in the water, are you?"

Ataensic turned her face from the aerodyne's dials and flashed him with her beaming smile.

"You're serious, aren't you?"

"Those clouds are the leading edge of a storm front, and based on the headwinds we've been fighting, a very powerful one."

A bright streak of lightning flashed from the distant dark cloud down to the ground. Seconds later, the entire aerodyne shook violently as they passed through the thunder's shockwave. Before the Onatha recovered from the initial blast, echoes from the powerful boom bounced off the nearby ridges, sending more shudders through the airship.

"Can't we just fly around it?"

"I'm afraid not. The front extends across the entire horizon." Ataensic motioned across the windscreen with her hand.

Iosheka followed her gesture; there was no way to fly around the oncoming storm.

"How about flying over it, you know, like we did with that rain-storm at sea?"

"If these were normal clouds, we might be able to climb over them. Unfortunately, the convection from the front and the influence of the ridges has driven the clouds very high into the atmosphere, higher than the Onatha is capable of flying. Even if we could safely get the Onatha up that high, we'd never survive the flight. The air's very thin at that altitude. If we didn't freeze to death, we'd certainly suffocate in the ultra-thin atmosphere."

"Could we hunker down somewhere, maybe on the leeward side of one of those ridges?" he asked desperately, pointing out the window.

"Only if you know where we can find an overhang big enough to hide the Onatha from the swirling winds and powerful downdrafts; aerodynes are designed for clear weather flying. If we expose the Onatha to the violence of the coming storm, we'll be knocked out of the sky. So, unless you relish the thought of uncontrollably plummeting to the ground in a driving thunderstorm, I suggest you get ready to swim."

Iosheka conceded defeat. "All right, what do you need me to do?"

"At the moment, it would be very helpful if you could keep one eye on that storm and the other looking for a better landing spot than the water."

"Do you think we'll find one?"

"Well, we sure won't if we don't look, and I'm going to be busy. That headwind we've been fighting for the last few hours forced us to use our energy reserves faster than I expected."

"Do we have enough to land . . . safely?"

"If we don't hit anything unexpected, we should be fine, but we're only going to get one shot at this. And . . ." she paused.

"And you've never landed an aerodyne before," he finished for her.

"Yeah, but first we need to get to the landing site."

"How long will that take?"

"Assuming you don't find a better option that's closer, probably fifteen minutes before we cross the last ridge. At that point, we'll have to commit. Once we begin our descent, we won't have enough energy to reverse course and climb back out."

It took more than twenty minutes to reach the ridge, but even with the extra time, Iosheka hadn't found a better landing site.

"Well, the good news is our landing site's a lake and not a river. So, at least we won't have to deal with a flowing current," Ataensic said.

"That implies there's some bad news."

"The ridge on this side of the lake has a slope that we can follow down to the water, but the other side's vertical; more of a cliff than a hillside. Given the narrowness of the valley, we could experience some nasty swirling winds and a pretty rough ride down to the water."

Iosheka's stomach involuntarily retched, raising the partially digested remnants of his dinner. Without the energy to properly cook it, the meal hadn't been particularly tasty the *first* time he'd eaten it. Several hours of churning in his stomach hadn't improved its taste. He swallowed hard and forced the unpleasant mixture back down his throat and wiped his mouth with his hand.

Ataensic gazed back at him. "We've cleared the ridge top. I'm going to pitch the nose down to match the slope."

ON THE FAR SIDE OF THE LAKE

LIGHTNING FLASHED ACROSS THE SKY, FOLLOWED SECONDS LATER by a deep booming thunder that echoed ominously off the cliff face.

"Sosondo, hurry up! The storm's getting closer!" Genwitha yelled.

"I've got to pull the fishing traps in, or the Sachem will have my head. Why don't you come down here and help me?" he yelled while hauling on the trap line.

Genwitha hesitated for a moment. Then the first drop of rain splashed on her face. She reached up to wipe it away and felt several more drops strike her skin. The storm was descending on them faster than she expected. If she wanted to leave, she'd missed her chance. Even a brief shower would fill the dry streambed that served as their path through the cliff face with a torrent of rushing water; a storm as powerful as this one would turn the path into a rapidly raging river very quickly. There was no point in continuing.

She walked back to the narrow rocky shore toward Sosondo, who was knee-deep in the water, fighting to pull on the trap's retrieval line. He had the first hoop of the bag-shaped net out of the water but was struggling to bring any more of the trap to the surface.

"I think it's caught on something. I'm going to have to swim down and free it. Could you come here and hold the line for me?"

"I'm coming!" She walked through the cold water and took the line from him, wrapping it securely around her wrists.

"We're right at the edge of the deep water. The bottom drops off quickly, so be careful. If you stand over here, there's a big rock you can wedge your feet against, which will keep you from falling." Seeing her hesitate, he motioned her toward the rock. "I'll only be down for a minute. I can't hold my breath much longer than that. Besides, the storm's coming in fast, and we don't want to be on the lake when it gets here."

She moved her feet around the lake's bottom and found the rock. Then she braced herself against it.

"Are you ready?"

"As ready as I'll ever be."

"Good, now I'm going to follow the line down to the traps. If you have any trouble, give the line two sharp tugs, and I'll come back up."

She nodded, and he disappeared under the water.

The storm continued to intensify.

After Sosondo had been underwater for half a minute, a powerful bolt of lightning struck the top of the cliff face. A concussive clap of thunder followed almost immediately on its heels. Instinctively, Genwitha raised her hands to protect her ears from the deafening boom. As she wrenched her hands free from the line, she yanked it several times. When echoes from the thunder passed, she opened her eyes and was surprised to see Sosondo treading water in front of her.

"What happened?" he yelled.

Before she could respond, an earsplitting sound raced down the cliffside.

"Quick, get out of the water!"

Sosondo stood motionless. She grabbed his hand and pulled him toward the rocky shore.

"What are you doing? What about the fish traps?" he screamed.

"Lightning struck the top of the cliff, and I think it's triggered a rockslide!"

Small pieces of debris began to splash into the water around them.

Holding each other's hands, they ran as fast as they could through the water toward the shore, as bigger and bigger pieces of rock fell from the sky.

OTHER THAN A FEW BUMPS AND BUFFETS, ATAENSIC PILOTED THE Onatha down the eastern slope of the valley as if she'd done it a thousand times.

Iosheka patted her on the shoulder. "That wasn't so bad."

"Thanks, but that was the easy part. We're almost at the lake. When we cross the shoreline, I'm going to pull the nose up and level us out about twenty feet above the surface."

"Why are you leveling off so high?"

"Because I don't fancy jumping from any higher."

"Jumping? I thought we were going to land." Iosheka paused, wondering if land was the right word for touching down on the water. He decided it wasn't. "I definitely heard you say we were going to set down on the water."

"I . . . *lied*," Ataensic said.

"What do you mean, you lied?"

"I told a deliberate falsehood." She flashed her brightest smile.

"I know what a lie is. And don't think you can smile your way out of this one."

"Look, I'm sorry, but it was for your own good. I always knew we were going to have to ditch the Onatha, but as soon as we crested that last ridge, I knew it was going to be more difficult than I thought. My original plan was to turn the ship along the length of the lake and settle her gently near the surface using the magneto drive to hold our position while we swam away, but that option's off the table."

"Because of the storm?"

"Yeah, between our low energy reserves and the powerful swirling winds hitting us broadside, I'd never be able to hold us in a stable position."

"If the problem's the crosswinds, why not skip the turn and lower the ship perpendicular to the lake?"

"The lake's too narrow. One strong gust and we could be smashed into the cliff face or driven down into the water. Even an experienced aerodyne pilot would be crazy to try it, and you may have noticed that we don't have one of those."

Iosheka bit his lip as he looked down and saw the green canopy of trees give way to the rocky shoreline of the lake. "All right, what do you need me to do?"

"I knew I could count on you to come around. Make sure the supply bag is tightly sealed and that the line is securely tied to you. When I tell you to jump, throw out the bag first, then jump."

"What about you? I'm not leaving you behind."

"Don't worry. You can't get rid of me that easily. I'll be right behind you. I just need to set the Onatha's controls to make sure she doesn't come crashing down on top of us."

"How are you going to do that?"

"I'm going raise her nose and set her throttles at full."

GASPING FOR BREATH, GENWITHA AND SOSONDO STUMBLED through the rocks at the edge of the lake's shoreline. As soon as they cleared the water, they heard a thunderous crash of the rockslide smashing into the lake where moments before, Sosondo had been looking for the fish trap.

Sosondo collapsed onto the rocky beach with his head in his hands, oblivious to the intensifying storm.

"Come on, let's get out of the rain. There's a small lean-to just off the shore where we can wait it out." Genwitha took several steps away from the shore before she noticed that Sosondo hadn't followed her. She turned back and shook his shoulders.

"Come on. There's nothing you can do about the fish trap now. After the storm passes, I'll help you look for it."

"It won't be there. Even if the storm doesn't wash it away, it'll have been crushed by that rockslide. I should've left when the other boys did. I've not only lost the catch for the day, but I've also lost the fish trap. The Sachem's going to kill me."

"He won't be happy, but I doubt he'll kill you." Genwitha patted him on the shoulder again. "You won't be allowed to fish for a while, but that's probably the worst of it."

Sosondo looked up. "You think so?"

"Yeah, now come on. Let's get to the lean-to." She offered him her hand.

He reached up to take it, but before he grabbed it, she dropped it back to her side.

Angrily, he started to protest, but then he noticed Genwitha's face. Silently, she stared past him, her mouth gaping and her eyes wide open. "Genwitha, what's wrong?"

Unable to speak, she lifted her hand and pointed a finger into the sky over the lake. Sosondo turned and looked out over the water. Though he was unable to comprehend what he saw flying through the air, he *was* able to summon his voice. At the top of his lungs, he screamed, "Aiyee!"

THE ONATHA'S WINDOWS AMPLIFIED THE BEATING RAIN CREATING a cacophonous chorus of pings that echoed throughout the bridge. Ataensic yelled over the storm's assault.

"We're almost where we need to be . . . are you ready?"

"As ready as I'll ever be!"

"It's raining too hard for me to see the lake surface, but according to our instruments, we should be fine. On my signal, open the emergency exit door and throw out the supply bag. Count to three, then jump. Got it?"

Iosheka nodded. He checked the seal on the supply bag one more time and made sure the tether was securely tied around his waist. In addition to a change of clothes and the last of their food, the bag also contained the Sekhem and the Gaol. They were counting on its buoyancy to keep them from drowning in the rough storm-driven lake waters.

"We're almost there. Just a few more seconds . . . All right. Three, two, one, jump!"

Iosheka found the two latches and turned them simultaneously to release the restraining bolts. Without the bolts, there was nothing holding the panel in place, and it should've fallen into the lake, but it didn't.

"What's happening? Why are you still here, and why isn't the door open?" asked Ataensic.

"I don't know. I turned the latches, but nothing happened."

"Try it again!"

Iosheka reset the latches and turned them again; still, nothing happened.

"It's no good." He risked a quick look out of the front window and saw the cliff face rapidly approaching. In frustration, he kicked the door. It moved a little but then quickly resealed itself. He kicked it again, as hard as he could; again, it moved fractionally but quickly slammed back into place.

"We're running out of time!" Ataensic said.

While the bridge wasn't airtight, it was close enough that the pressure combined with the wind made it nearly impossible to open the exit. Iosheka needed to equalize the pressure. He remembered there was a toolbox in the sleeping cabin. He raced up the ladder into the dark room, trailing the supply bag behind him.

"Iosheka, where are you going?"

He found the box underneath one of the bunks, opened it, and removed a heavy metal prying bar. He fell more than climbed down the ladder into the bridge room.

Ignoring Ataensic's frantic screams, he swung the prying bar into the glass of the emergency exit. The thick glass spiderwebbed but did not break. He swung again and again. On the third swing, the glass shattered and blew into the cabin. He dropped the bar and easily kicked the remains of the emergency exit panel away.

The wind blew rain into the bridge room. Iosheka reached down to his waist, found the tether, and used it to pull the supply bag to his chest. He stepped to the open exit, tossed the bag down into the lake, and began counting. At the count of two, something slammed into him from behind, knocking him through the exit. As he tumbled toward the lake, wet and stringy strands struck his face. He grabbed them and yanked them away. At the same time, he heard Ataensic's voice cry out. He turned . . . through the wind-driven rain, he briefly saw her face staring back at him.

Then they splashed into the cold lake water. He lost sight of her. Tossed like so much flotsam, he bobbed up and down in the storm-churned waters. Each time he surfaced, he struggled to breathe. With each outgoing breath, he screamed into the howling winds. "Ataensic! Ataensic!"

Only the sounds of the storm replied.

He strained against the water, kicking furiously to keep his head above the surface. Something bit into his leg. He slipped underwater. He reached down to his leg. The tether line for the supply bag was twisted around his calf. It cut into his skin.

He tugged on the line. It went taut. Fearing it was snagged on something, Iosheka pulled as hard as he could. The line went slack momentarily before going taut again. Either he'd caught an awfully big fish or someone was pulling on the other end of the line.

A large wave rose over his head. The crest curled in on itself. It crashed onto him. He swallowed water. The wave drove him deep underwater. The supply bag's rope remained slack. He kicked upward. He breached the surface. He took in a single breath. Before he could exhale, an earsplitting screech overwhelmed him.

He looked up just in time to see the Onatha smash into the cliff. Driven by its powerful magneto drives, the nose of the aerodyne hit the rock face with awesome speed. The Onatha shuddered on impact. The aerodyne's superstructure defied the thrust of the engines, but the resistance was futile.

Caught between the hammer of its still churning magneto drives and the immovable anvil of the cliff face, the Onatha crumpled like an accordion. The buoyancy balloon ripped apart, spilling the flammable gas into the air. The bridge and passenger gondola continued to accelerate into the cliff. Upon impact, the thick safety glass windows shattered, spilling the craft's controls into the lake. Moments later, the magneto drives rammed into the cliff. Their spinning metal harnesses grated against each other, sending showers of sparks into the night. One of the sparks met the expanding bouncy gas. The resulting explosion swallowed the remains of the Onatha and bathed the entire lake in the glow of an immense fireball.

Iosheka turned away from the intense heat and glare of the Onatha's death and found the supply bag floating next to him. Draped across it was Ataensic, tears running down her cheeks.

22

PRESENT DAY, IN PIPER FALLS

Penny and Duncan walked into the school auditorium where Ms. Parsons had moved their social studies class for the week. They hurried down and sat in the third row with the rest of their gang.

"Hey, where are Grace and Mary?" Duncan asked.

"They're behind the curtain. They wanted to get it over with, so they volunteered to go first," Mark said.

"They've been super quiet about their Pyramid project. Has Mary said anything to you, Gene?"

"Nah, she won't tell me anything. I accidentally walked in on her and Grace talking with their dad about movie special effects, and they went quiet as soon as they realized I was there."

"Yeah, if their dad helped 'em, this oughta be totally awesome. I mean, remember that show he put on at the Halloween party? It was wicked cool," Mark said.

Without thinking, Duncan turned quickly toward Penny and raised his eyebrows. She gently shook her head from side to side. While the entire town thought Mr. Anderson's special effects had been behind the fantastic events at the party, they both knew that it was really a powerful time fold and the *Grimalkin's* battle with Simon.

Misunderstanding their exchange, Mark said, "I'm sorry, I forgot about Simon getting attacked that night. Did you ever figure out what attacked him?"

Duncan shrugged. "We don't know, but the vet speculated that it was some type of cat; maybe even a bobcat."

"Yeah, I remember reading something about chickens and house cats disappearing around that time," Mark replied.

Before Penny or Duncan could respond, Ms. Parsons stepped out onto the stage.

"Okay, class . . . as you know, we're finishing up our Egyptian unit this week with your team projects. Mary and Grace Anderson have graciously volunteered to go first with their presentation on the Pyramids."

Ms. Parsons stepped to the side of the stage and raised the curtain, revealing Mary Anderson sitting behind a large desk. There was an empty chair next to it.

"Good evening, ladies and gentlemen, and welcome to another exciting episode of Archeology Today. I am your host, Mary Anderson. Today, we're fortunate to have the renowned Egyptologist Dr. Ida Builder who's going to preview the new Egyptian exhibit at the Metropolitan Museum. Let's give a warm A.T. welcome to Dr. Ida Builder!"

Ms. Parsons held up a placard with the word "Applause" written on it.

Everyone applauded as Grace Anderson, dressed in khaki pants and a shirt with high-top leather boots and a pith helmet, walked across the stage and sat down next to her sister.

"So, Dr. Builder, tell me something about the pyramids that most people wouldn't know."

"Most people think that the pyramids were built with slave labor, but that's not true."

"You mean those Hollywood movies got it all *wrong*?"

"I'm afraid so. While there were close to one hundred thousand people working on Khufu's pyramid at Giza, they only worked during the three months of the Nile's annual flood. During those months, they couldn't work the land. While they labored on the pyramid, Khufu provided them with food and clothing."

"Okay, that was certainly interesting, but let's get back to your new exhibit. I've been told that it's going to be aimed at a younger audience. How do you plan to reach them?"

"While the pyramids are strongly connected to Egyptian spiritual beliefs, they were built by people using science and engineering principles that we still use today."

"Don't tell me you're going to have kids building pyramids out of sugar cubes? That's going to be a lot of sugar cubes."

"No, no, we'll leave the sugar cube pyramids to the elementary school science fairs. To reach today's kids, you need something with action. We call it, 'The Pyramids: A Stone's Perspective.' It's an animated movie that follows the journey of a stone block from its creation at the quarry to its final placement on the pyramid."

"You made a movie about a stone block?"

"Yes, would you like to see it?"

Throwing her hands up and rolling her eyes, Mary replied, "Sure, why not?"

As the auditorium's movie screen slid down from the ceiling, Grace pulled something out of her pocket and handed it to Mary. "To get the full effect, you'll need these."

"What're these?" Mary unfolded the cardboard to reveal a pair of glasses with one blue and one red lens.

"Oh, did I forget to mention that the movie's in 3D?"

Mary put her glasses on and stepped off the stage with a bag, which she handed to Lisa Giambi. "Everyone, please take a pair of glasses and pass along the rest."

Mark took a pair of glasses from the bag. As he passed it to Duncan, he whispered, "3D's cool, but a movie about rocks? I don't mean to be harsh, but it sounds, uh, lame."

Duncan chose a pair and whispered back, "Yeah, I don't know about this either."

Penny accepted the bag from Duncan. "Don't be so negative. I think it's going to be cool."

The lights dimmed. The movie began with a scene in a quarry filled with hundreds of workers. A gravelly-sounding voice narrated the scene.

"You are about to witness the birth of limestone block number 2,000,083. That's a bit of a mouthful, so we'll just call him 'Eighty-three' for short. The workers are using copper chisels to separate Eighty-three from the rock face. It's the same process they'll use to make all of the nearly 2,300,000 blocks needed to build Khufu's pyramid. Let's take a closer look."

The camera zoomed in behind and slightly above a single worker who was using a wooden mallet to drive a copper chisel into the stone. When he raised his mallet to strike the chisel, it leapt off the screen right at everyone's face. Several people jumped out of their seats and a few, including Mark, actually screamed.

The gravelly voice returned. "With a square cross section measuring a little less than three feet and a length of five feet, our newly born Eighty-three tips the scales at two and a half tons. While he might look large, Eighty-three is a typical block used in the construction of Khufu's pyramid. The largest blocks weighed as much as 16 tons.

Without knowledge of the wheel or the pulley, the early Egyptians relied on wooden levers and sleds to move blocks from the quarry to the pyramid. Let's watch as a team of seven men uses three levers to flip Eighty-three onto the sled."

Once again, the camera zoomed in close to the action, and most of the students were caught off guard as one of the workers thrust his lever out from the screen.

The rest of the movie was more of the same as the gravelly voice narrated the block's trip on the sled, up a ramp, and into its final position on the pyramid. During each phase of the trip, there was at least one 3D surprise as ropes, pebbles, and even elbows poked the audience from the screen. Finally, when block Eighty-three fell into position, a cloud of dust seemed to spread out from the screen over the audience.

As the dust settled, the gravelly voice closed the movie by reciting a few facts about the great pyramid.

"The corners of Khufu's pyramid were aligned with the cardinal compass points. Its sides measured 755 feet, and at 481 feet, it was the tallest man-made structure in the world. It held that title until 1311 when the Lincoln Cathedral reached 525 feet. Using basic principles of science and engineering, the builders of Khufu's pyramid helped create a unified Egyptian identity."

As the voice faded, the film ended, and the house lights came up to the applause of everyone in the audience, including Ms. Parsons, who walked back to center stage.

"Well, what a great way to start our presentations!"

"Next up, Eddie and Steve will enlighten us about the Egyptian practice of *mummification*."

Eddie and Steve walked out onto the stage. "Hey, I hear you're an expert on mummification. Is that true?" Eddie asked Steve.

"I don't know if I'd say that, but I have watched quite a few internet videos and flipped through a few presentations. I even read a book about it."

"Well, that sounds like an expert to me. So, tell us, Steve, why did the Egyptians practice mummification?"

"Their observations of nature—the sun falling in the west each evening and emerging reborn in the east the next morning; the waxing and waning of the moon; and new life sprouting from a seed planted in the earth—taught the Egyptians that life was a cycle of death and rebirth. After death, they believed they would journey to another world and lead a new life that required their old bodies. To ensure their bodies would be available, they preserved them using mummification."

"Okay, but what exactly is the mummification process? I mean, can you just wrap something in a sheet and create a mummy?"

"No, wrapping the body in linen is one of the steps, but there's a lot more to it than that. The first step is to remove the brain and the other soft organs."

"That sounds interesting. Can you describe it for us?"

"Sure. To preserve the body for later use, they tried to remove the organs with as little damage as possible. They reached the brain through the nose and broke into the braincase through the nasal passages. Since they couldn't pull the brain out intact, they used a metal tool to scramble it inside the skull," Steve made a jabbing and swirling motion with his hand. "After thoroughly mixing it, they'd tilt the head up and pour the scrambled brain out the nose into a bowl."

"Kind of like pouring a milkshake out of a blender?" Eddie offered.

Steve nodded. "Yeah, a gray milkshake with streaks of red."

"Ewws" and "Yucks" and the sound of at least one person retching echoed through the auditorium.

Ignoring the audience, Steve continued. "Next, a special person known as 'the splitter' came into the tent and used an obsidian knife to make a three- to four-inch incision on the lower left side of the body. After he made the cut, the others threw stones at him."

"Why'd they do that?" asked Eddie.

"Defiling a dead body was a serious taboo to the ancient Egyptians. So even though they needed the incision to preserve the body, they couldn't condone the act."

"So, they weren't trying to hurt the splitter?" Eddie asked.

"No, it was a symbolic act meant to show their rejection of the defilement. The stones were never more than pebbles.

"Once the splitter left, they reached into the body with various probes and hooks, removing all of the organs except the heart which the Egyptians believed was the center of intelligence."

"What did they do with the removed organs?"

"They stored them in Canopic jars representing each of the god Horus's four sons. Imsety, the human jar, protected the liver; the baboon Hapy, watched the lungs; Duamutef, the jackal, defended the stomach; and the falcon, Qebehsenuef, safeguarded the intestines. The scrambled brains were deemed unimportant and discarded."

"What about the linen wrappings, the shriveled heads, and the dark colors of the mummies?" Eddie asked.

"After removing the organs, they preserved the bodies by covering them with a mixture of baking soda and salt known as Natron. The combination of Natron and the hot dry air took thirty-five days to remove most of the body's moisture. Next, they cleaned the body, rubbed it with perfumes and oils, and wrapped it in multiple layers of linen held in place with a glue-like resin. The resin is what gives mummies their dark color. Finally, they wrapped the body in a linen shroud, which often included protection symbols and sometimes the name of the person."

"That's amazing, but given that the Egyptians stopped making mummies more than a thousand years ago, how do you know so much about the process?"

"Dr. Robert Brier and a team of his students created a modern mummy using a cadaver that was donated to science. A crew from National Geographic filmed the process, and I've brought a few excerpts from the film to demonstrate some of the techniques we discussed."

As the other students reacted to the scenes of ritual disembowelment with sounds of disgust, Penny fought an altogether different and unseen battle. At the exact moment, the boys dimmed the lights and started their video, freezing tentacles of blue extra-dimensional power shot down from the ceiling of the auditorium.

Without thinking, Penny extended her arms upward and summoned a shimmering shield of blue extra-dimensional energy. The tentacles crashed into the shield. Their advance halted, and they pulled back toward the ceiling. More extra-dimensional energy flowed throw the rift into the tentacles. Recharged, they launched a second assault on the shield. Seven glowing blue arms of extra-dimensional power thrashed wildly against Penny's protection. With each blow, sparks of blue power flashed across the higher planes. Beads of sweat formed on Penny's forehead, but her shield held.

Once again, the tentacles retreated toward the ceiling, but this time they disappeared. An instant later, they returned, but they were no longer blue. Now, each one represented a different color of the rainbow. The multi-colored tentacles smashed into the shield.

Sweat dripped down Penny's cheeks along her jawline to her chin. She could feel her heart beating in her temples, but her shield held. Then the red, yellow, and orange colored tentacles struck a simultaneous blow. The shield buckled, shimmered, then collapsed. Before Penny could summon another defense, the tentacles wrapped themselves around her body.

Enveloped in a rainbow-colored cocoon, Penny felt her consciousness separate from her body. Leaving her body below in a trance-like state, the tentacles pulled Penny into the rift opening in the auditorium ceiling. As soon as she passed through it, everything vanished, even the tentacles. Time lost all meaning as Penny floated through a dark miasma of nothingness. Then a trail of silver energy appeared on the horizon. Without any thought or effort, Penny joined the trail. An instant later, she was back in Piper Falls, in spirit if not in body. Her non-corporeal essence floated in the air above the stage of the town library's auditorium. A filament of the silver trail connected her to the podium.

On the stage, several people, including Deputy Barnes and his friend Kolchak, stood in a circle around another man. He stood in the center of an intense field of pulsating trans-dimensional energy, precisely where the silver filament ended. While she didn't recognize the man, she did recognize the glowing object in his hands; it was the *Teyrnwialen o Saith*. It was not only the nexus of her trans-dimensional energy trail but nearly a dozen other trails as well.

The other trails also led up toward the ceiling of the auditorium. At the far end of each one, she perceived something, or someone, connected to the filament. Most, like her, were stationary, but on one trail, a figure struggled. The filament connecting the struggling figure pulsated with a rainbow of trans-dimensional energy. The gems on the head of the *Teyrnwialen o Saith* flashed on and off in patterns that matched the pulsating colors. Each flash brought the beleaguered figure closer and closer to the energy nexus.

The flashing lights formed a mesmerizing pattern that reminded her of the lights in Master Poe's eyes when he'd hypnotized her all those months ago. For a brief moment, the memory brought a smile to her lips. An instant later, a shriek of unbridled fear echoed across the dimensions. The struggling figure finally succumbed. Its essence touched the central gem of the *Teyrnwialen o Saith*, and in a flash of blackness, it ceased to exist.

The silver filaments of higher-dimensional energy vanished, replaced by the deep, penetrating cold of extra-dimensional space. An instant later, Penny found herself back in her body in the school auditorium. She filled her lungs with air and screamed with all her might.

A PIERCING JOLT OF ENERGY SHOT THROUGH THE *COCH COBLYN*, jarring him out of his semi-hibernative state. Groggily, he rubbed his eyes and shook his head. The same energy that had just shot through him was wrapping itself around him like tendrils of ivy climbing a tree. Gently at first, but ever more strongly, the tendrils tugged and pulled on him until he began to move along a path of higher-dimensional energy.

"What's this mischief?" he asked.

Reaching down into his inner core, he touched the essence of his true self. Carefully, he withdrew a diaphanous thread of his being and sent it ahead, down the stream of energy. Along the way, it detected *more* filaments of energy, each bearing entrapped creatures, and all converging toward the center of this ill-mannered village he'd been cursed to land in. At the nexus of all the streams, his thread revealed something he no longer dared to even hope for. Something he'd long since given up hope of ever finding.

One of the weaker trapped creatures lost its will to fight and succumbed to the current; it was consumed in a vanishing flash of darkness. Scarcely an instant later, the energy streams and their nexus vanished, and he was once again ensconced in his thicket of holly bushes.

"It's here, Farsyl, it's really here. Finally, ya can return home."

23

A S THE LAST ECHOES OF THE SACHEM'S SCREAM DIED, KOLCHAK was the first to speak.

"The scepter . . . it's gone!"

Everyone wheeled about and stared at the Sachem's empty hands. Both the scepter and the oak box had vanished.

The Sachem remained standing silently still; only his eyes, blinking away tears, indicated that he had returned from his trance.

Tom asked, "Sachem, are you all right? You seemed to be in some kind of trance."

Fresh tears rolled down the Sachem's cheek. "I suppose that's as good a description as any other. I remember reaching into the box for the scepter. Its shaft was cool, even cold. But when I pulled it out of the box, it immediately began to warm. I felt a tingling feeling spread from my fingertips into my hand and up my arm."

"Was it a numb feelin', you know, like when you hit your funny bone?" Deputy Barnes asked.

"No, it was pleasant and quickly moved throughout my entire body. From the tips of my toes to the ends of my hair; I've never felt so alive before."

"It almost sounds like a religious experience," the professor said.

"Yes, I think you may be on to something. Like your story of Adam and Eve, our people also have a creation story. The people lived as hunters and gatherers in small family clans. They had no permanent homes and wandered the land following game. They feared the nature spirits and trusted no one outside their own clan. If they encountered a rival clan, they wouldn't hesitate to attack them, killing the males and capturing the women and children."

"That sounds like a pretty standard description of many hunter-gatherer societies," Tom said.

"Yes, the people were little more than bands of savages roaming the land . . . until Iosheka and Ataensic descended from the sky in a fiery cloud. They appeared as a normal man and woman, but the people knew them as personifications of the spirits. They taught the people about the spirits of nature, how to live in harmony with them, and how to grow corn to ease the hunger of Gohone's cruel winters."

"Pardon me, Sachem, but that sounds like a myth used to explain the evolution of your people into farmers and villagers," Tom said.

"Yes, that's what I used to believe until I touched the scepter."

"Why's that?" Deputy Barnes asked.

"Iosheka and Ataensic used the Rod of Life to heal the sick and drive away evil spirits, uniting the clans into the People."

"You think the Butterfly Scepter is the Rod of Life?" Tom asked.

"I am *certain* it's the Rod of Life . . . and now it is lost."

Kolchak spoke up. "To all of us, it just seemed to vanish into thin air, but you were in communion with the rod. Perhaps you sensed something we couldn't. Something that might help us figure out what happened."

"Let me see . . ." the Sachem closed his eyes. "After the warm presence filled my body, I felt an odd floating sensation."

"Like you were traveling outside your body?" Kolchak asked.

"No, I wouldn't describe it that way. I was still connected with my body, but I was also more than myself. I felt part of a greater existence."

"What can you tell me about this greater existence?" Kolchak asked.

"I can remember it clearly. It's just that, well . . . if English has words to describe what I experienced, I don't know them. I don't mean to sound crazy."

"I know exactly what you mean. We run up against problems like this in archeology all the time. You know, situations where modern language or culture just doesn't have the right context for something," Tom said.

"How do you handle it?" Sharon asked.

"If we're looking to explain relationships, we'll use a cultural analogy," he replied.

The Sachem raised his hand to his chin and cocked his head for a moment. "It's not perfect, but it was like being inside one of those drawings that doesn't make sense."

"Whaddya mean a drawing that doesn't make sense?" Deputy Barnes said.

"You mean one of M. C. Escher's prints? Like the one with the waterwheel that's powered by a waterfall that's fed from the outflow of the waterwheel, so it looks like the water flows uphill," Kolchak said.

"Yes, only it was much more subtle and also more alien than that . . . although now that I think about it, there was something familiar, too. Before the Rod of Life disappeared, I sensed another presence. It was faint, almost as if it was a shadow of someone or something. It hovered at the very edge of my perception and . . ."

"And what?" Sharon asked.

"It had a distinctive femaleness to it," the Sachem replied.

"Well, now we're getting somewhere," Kolchak said. "But to be sure, I'll need to get the K-IIs to check for residual paranormal energy."

Professor Richards snorted. "Hmmpf, that's ridiculous! Surely you're not suggesting some supernatural phenomenon is at the heart of this."

"That's exactly what I'm suggesting," Kolchak replied.

"You can't be serious."

"I believe the Sachem used the Rod of Life to create an opening to an alternate space-time reality, but instead of entering the other reality, he was caught somewhere in the middle."

"Like a no man's land?" Deputy Barnes asked.

"Something like that," Kolchak said.

"What about the female presence I felt?" the Sachem asked.

Kolchak paused for a moment. "She could be an inhabitant of our reality somehow caught in the vortex you created, or maybe someone from the alternative one. Either way, I don't think it's a coincidence that she showed up shortly before the scepter disappeared."

The professor vigorously shook his head. "That's preposterous! It's nothing but a bunch of superstitious nonsense and conjecture. You haven't got a shred of scientific evidence to support anything you've claimed."

"I've got years of tracking paranormal and unexplained phenomena, not to mention the Sachem's eye-witness testimony," Kolchak answered calmly.

"With all due respect to the Sachem, he was scarcely himself during the incident, and past experience hardly qualifies as evidence." The professor turned from Kolchak to Tom. "As a man of science, you must agree that this is a colossal waste of time."

Tom glanced back and forth between Kolchak and the professor before responding.

"I agree that Kolchak's theory is just speculation . . ." The professor beamed. ". . . but I'll also admit that I don't have a more *rational* explanation for what happened here, and . . ." Tom paused.

"And *what*?" asked the professor.

"And as long as Deputy Barnes and the Sachem don't object, I can't see any harm in letting Kolchak survey the crime scene with his equipment. After all, Sachem Cornplanter is the victim, and Deputy Barnes is the senior law officer on the scene."

"I agree. If the deputy thinks it will help with his investigation, I have no objection to Kolchak taking his measurements," the Sachem said.

"What do you say, Freddy?" Kolchak patted his friend on the back.

"Go get the K-IIs before everything fades away."

Kolchak turned to leave, but the Sachem stopped him. "Before we start, I have one more request for everyone. The loss of the rod under such, shall we say, strange circumstances, is a serious and sensitive matter. If everyone else agrees, I propose that we keep the investigation out of the press. If that happens, I won't be able to guarantee the funding you've requested. Can I have everyone's cooperation on this?"

Everyone nodded their agreement.

24

P ENNY OPENED HER EYES TO A BLURRY VISAGE OF GRAY SUR-
rounding two pinpricks of blue. She squeezed her eyes tightly
shut and blinked several times.

The room brightened, and the gray resolved into strands of
unruly hair; the pinpricks into two pale blue eyes separated by an
overly large nose.

The face was familiar, but it didn't belong. Groggily, she asked,
"Mr. Myrdin, what are you doing in the auditorium, and why am I
lying down?"

"Relax, Penny, you're in the nurse's office."

As her peripheral vision cleared, she was able to see her
surroundings. She was lying on a green vinyl-covered couch . . . no,

it wasn't a couch . . . it was a table in a small, brightly lit room. A white cabinet with a large red cross emblazoned on each of its doors stood next to a medical scale on one wall, while a stainless-steel sink and countertop adorned the other.

"Why am I in the nurse's office? How did I get here?"

Mr. Myrdin grinned. "As usual, I'll answer the second question first. The nurse and Ms. Parsons brought you here from the auditorium. You fainted during a rather graphic video presentation about mummification."

"Fainted? I don't remember that, and I don't remember a video, but I do remember being grabbed by powerful tentacles of extra-dimensional energy—"

Mr. Myrdin cut her off mid-sentence.

"Yes, Master Poe detected something as well, but this is not the place to talk about such things. Ms. Parsons and Nurse Robertson are convinced you fainted because of the video. I see no reason to disabuse them of their error. Now, here she comes; just follow my lead."

"Ah, Miss Preston, it's good to see you're awake. How are you feeling?" asked the kindly, old school nurse.

"Uh, other than my stomach being a little queasy, I feel fine."

"Yes, well, I suspect watching that video right after lunch wasn't the best thing for you. You've got nothing to be ashamed of; the same thing happens to some of the high school kids in biology class. Even now that they let them opt out of actually dissecting the frogs and watch a video instead." Nurse Robertson waved her hand in front of her face and rolled her eyes. "It still bothers some kids. Anyway, I suspect you'll be fine, but I'll need to take your vitals before I can release you to the counselor. Now, Mr. Myrdin, if you wouldn't mind giving us a little privacy?"

"Oh no, of course not, I'll be outside in the waiting room if you need me." He opened the door. Before stepping out, he looked back at Penny and gave her a barely detectable nod of his head.

PENNY AND MR. MYRDIN ARRIVED IN HIS OFFICE A BIT LATER TO find Master Poe perched on the inbox waiting for them.

"What took you so long?" he asked.

"Oddly enough, the school system frowns on taking students out of class, so we needed to establish our cover story," replied Mr. Myrdin.

"Someone has activated the *Teyrnwialen o Saith* which, if my theory is correct, is not only the most powerful talisman ever created but also the *Bodach's Conglfaen*, and you're worried about getting in trouble with the principal?" Master Poe responded derisively.

"That's easy for you to say; she's not your boss."

Master Poe bobbed his beak. "True enough."

"I'm sorry, but what did Master Poe say about the *Teyrnwialen o Saith* being activated? Is that what sent me on a trans-dimensional trip to the library? And what's the *Bodach's Conglfaen*?"

Master Poe replied, "Yes, I think someone activated the *Teyrnwialen o Saith*, but I've never seen that before, so it's hard to be sure. It might shed some light on a few things if you gave us some details about your experience."

After Penny finished explaining, Mr. Myrdin stroked his chin. "Hmm, very interesting. Can you tell us more about what you saw from our dimension at the library?"

"Yeah. There were six people on the auditorium stage. One was holding the *Teyrnwialen o Saith*, and the other five were standing in a circle talking."

"Did you recognize any of them? Could you tell what they were doing or make out what they were saying?" Mr. Myrdin asked.

"I recognized two of them—Deputy Barnes and his friend Kolchak. I couldn't hear what they were saying, but it looked like Kolchak and another man, who I think someone called 'professor,' were arguing about what was happening. There was also another man and a woman there."

"Was the woman rather tall, blonde, and well-dressed and one of the men dark-haired, thin, and wearing glasses?" Mr. Myrdin asked.

"The man was also wearing a tie, but yeah, how'd you know?"

"They're former colleagues of mine at the Monroe. Sharon's in PR and specializes in putting together press conferences with top donors to the institute. Tom's the head of the archeology group that called me in to decipher the writing on the *Teyrnwialen o Saith*. I'll bet the guy arguing with Kolchak was Professor Richards, the dig director over in Byron, and the man holding the *Teyrnwialen o Saith* is probably a representative of the Seneca tribe."

"Why have a press conference with the *Teyrnwialen o Saith*, and why invite someone from the Seneca?" Penny asked.

"Money. In these tough budgetary times, even the Monroe has to reach out for money. I've known Tom for some time, and he only wears ties for weddings, funerals, and fundraisers. I'll bet Sharon pulled some strings with her press friends and made a few calls to local tribal leaders. Finding the *Teyrnwialen o Saith* would be very interesting to them."

"Do you think any of them could have activated the *Teyrnwialen o Saith*?" Master Poe asked.

Mr. Myrdin shook his head. "I've met four of those people, and none of them are *misaligned*. I haven't met the Deputy's friend

Kolchak, but from what Penny tells me, he's one of those paranormal investigators. He may be slightly *misaligned*; that may even be why he got into the paranormal business, but probably not enough to activate the *Teyrnwialen o Saith*. That leaves us with the Seneca representative. He's undoubtedly one of the local clan Sachem."

"Is that a hereditary office?" Master Poe asked.

"It used to be, but not anymore. However, the local populations are pretty small, and they tend to marry within their communities, so there's a good chance he's descended from one of the old Shaman lines. Do you think he activated the *Teyrnwialen*?"

"We've eliminated everyone else."

"True enough, but why would he do it?" Mr. Myrdin asked.

"I doubt he did it intentionally. The thing's been asleep for six thousand years. I doubt anyone alive knows how to use it. Maybe he initiated some ritual that has been passed down through the generations that contained the activation sequence. In the end, it doesn't matter. Somehow it was activated, and someone or probably something, sensed it and seized it."

"I've got to give it to Sharon for getting things done so quickly. A bit too quickly for us, though. If only I'd been there, maybe I could've prevented the loss of the *Teyrnwialen o Saith*."

"Don't beat yourself up, old friend. If my theory is correct, I doubt you could've done anything to save the scepter."

"Okay, maybe now's a good time to clue me in to this theory of yours," Penny said.

Master Poe and Mr. Myrdin looked at each other for a few moments as if they were silently communicating, the way Penny did with Simon, before Mr. Myrdin shrugged his shoulder and said, "It is your theory."

Master Poe nodded his beak up and down.

"It's always bothered me that my entry into your universe robbed the *Bodach* of their powers and trapped them here."

Penny raised the eyebrow above her brown eye. "Really?"

"Oh, I don't mean that I was sorry to see their exploitation of your universe end; quite the contrary. My code of ethics forbids that kind of thing. As you know, my refusal to break that code is why I'm an exile. What I've always regretted is leaving them stranded here with no means to return home. Some might call it justice, but as someone who's been exiled from his own home, it seemed a bit cruel. It also annoyed me from a theoretical perspective."

"A theoretical perspective?" Penny asked.

"I built my portal as a window into your universe so that I could study it. To give me the best data, I insulated it against interference from all the dimensions between yours and mine. That should have prevented any interaction between my work and the *Bodach* universe, but it didn't. For the longest time, I convinced myself that when I hastily converted it from a window to a door, I weakened the insulation. After all, I was under a *lot* of stress at the time." Master Poe paused for a moment.

Mr. Myrdin and Penny both nodded their heads. "So, I reasoned that as I made my escape, some of the energy from my enemies' attacks leaked through and closed the *Bodach's* portal."

"But now you think something else happened?"

"Yes. After you told me about my former apprentice," Master Poe's voice crackled at the mention of his betrayer, "sending energy down the *gwysio sianel*, it occurred to me that maybe the *Bodach's* connection wasn't a portal from their dimension into yours, but rather a *channel* from yours *up* to theirs."

"It matters where the connection originates from?" Penny asked.

"Yes, it matters a great deal. I won't bore you with the mathematical details, but the asymmetry in the conservation of energy flows is different. If the connection originated in your dimension, then that asymmetry would be enough for my hastily converted door to destabilize it."

"Okay, but for your explanation to work, someone in our dimension would've had to initiate the connection, right?" Master Poe bobbed his beak up and down. "But that requires extra-dimensional energy, even for someone who's as *misaligned* as me. The only way to get it is through the trans-dimensional stones which we didn't have until the *Bodach* brought them here."

"Kind of the multi-dimensional version of which came first, the chicken or the egg," Mr. Myrdin said.

"Exactly," Penny agreed.

"Indeed, I reached the same roadblock. But then I thought, what if the *Teyrnwialen o Saith* slipped into this dimension through a seam in the dimensional fabric, say during a natural confluence?"

"I know the fabric's weaker during a confluence, but could they slip a talisman through?" Penny asked.

"Not a *regular* talisman," Master Poe said.

"You mean, there's more than one kind?" asked Penny.

"One of my colleagues proposed that the confluences were the multiverse's way of alleviating the stresses created by the imperfect, asymmetrical dimensional fabric structure. Without them, the whole multiverse would collapse in upon itself."

"Kind of a multiverse Big Bang," Penny said.

"More like a Big Crunch, but you've got the idea. However, as we know, the confluences create new instabilities, which create additional problems. My colleague's solution to that was the existence of a special type of talisman which he called a *Conglfaen* talisman."

"He spoke Welsh?" Penny asked.

"No, of course not. I've simplified his name for it, and following the Druid's convention, translated it to Welsh. The English term is Keystone. In addition to the normal powers of a trans-dimensional talisman, during a confluence, a *Conglfaen* can slip between dimensions without the need for a trans-dimensional portal."

"So how can we tell if the *Teyrnwialen o Saith* is a Keystone talisman?"

"Rifts created with it would be particularly intense. The calculations suggest they might even act as whirlpools for extra-dimensional energy, drawing it into the *Conglfaen*."

"Like the tentacles and energy streams I saw flowing into the library."

Mr. Myrdin joined in. "Your story not only supports Master Poe's theory but with the *Coch Coblyn's* arrival, we may have underestimated the danger."

"Underestimated the danger . . . how is that possible? I mean, seriously, what could be worse than having a homicidal, violence-loving, all-powerful, over-sized Celtic garden gnome with two thousand years of resentment toward the human race running loose in the world?"

"How about hundreds of them?" replied Master Poe.

25

THE PRESENT

SOBEK CLUTCHED THE OAKEN BOX TO HIS CHEST AND WRAPPED himself in a blanket to ward off the lingering chill from his trip through the spirit realm. Grabbing the Sekhem had been a calculated risk. While in their keeping, the Amun-Ra had taken great care to feed the scepter with the essence of captured spirits and occasionally, the souls of those gifted with second sight. After millennia without nourishment, he knew the scepter would seek to replenish itself.

Once the Sekhem woke, even Sobek could not resist the lure of its feeding call, and he was pulled through the spirit world. Fortunately, one of the weaker native creatures from the spirit world succumbed to the Sekhem first. Once the Sekhem devoured the creature's essence, Sobek seized the scepter from the local who had unwittingly awakened it.

Now that it was fed, he could safely wield the Sekhem to perform routine Amun-Ra's rites, but not the restricted First Acolyte rituals. For those, the Sekhem would require a blood sacrifice. Not just any blood, but blood from one gifted with the second sight. Without a ready supply of first-year acolytes to tap, he needed another source. Fortunately, there was the girl he'd met in Caleb's shop. It would be sad to lose one with her potential, but the needs of the people outweighed the needs of the individual. She would no doubt resist, but it would be futile. He bared his crocodilian teeth in a smile. With the power of the Sekhem, he would overcome her, travel back in time, and alter the timeline to restore what should never have been lost.

BACK IN THE LIBRARY

"HEY, FREDDY, WOULD YOU HELP ME GET THE K-IIS FROM THE truck?" asked Kolchak. He discretely patted his right hand into his left three times and hoped that his friend remembered their signal that they needed to talk . . . in private.

Fred raised his eyebrows. "Uh, will you folks please excuse me? I'm going to help Kolchak with his equipment. I'll be right back. Please don't leave the auditorium until I've had a chance to talk with each of you. Thanks." He hustled off the stage to join Kolchak.

As they reached the exit doors, he asked, "Okay, so what's the big secret?"

"Let's get into the truck first."

Deputy Barnes hustled out the doors and into the truck's cab ahead of his friend. Much to his chagrin, he found the front seat occupied by Kolchak's powder blue parakeet, Pandora, who greeted him with, "You have entered . . . The Twilight Zone."

Kolchak opened the driver's side door to the sounds of Pandora mimicking the theme to the classic TV show. Unable to control himself at his friend's discomfort, he laughed.

"I'm sorry, Freddy, there was a *Twilight Zone* marathon on last night, and I guess she picked up a few things."

Pandora stopped singing and said, "Mr. Chambers, don't get on that ship! The *rest* of the book *To Serve Man*, it's . . . it's a cookbook!"

"Does she have to talk all the time? Can't she just be quiet for once?"

"Don't have a cow, man!" Pandora said.

"Pandora, please be quiet. Why don't you have a snack?" He filled a small dish in Pandora's cage with fresh seeds.

Pandora hopped down to the dish and began eating.

"You know that's just rewarding her for bad behavior. You're just encouraging her."

"Yes, yes, I know, but you really shouldn't let her get under your skin. She's just mimicking things she's heard. She doesn't know what any of it means."

"I know, I know, but you gotta admit it's uncanny, it's just uncanny."

Kolchak nodded.

"Now, enough about your crazy bird . . . what's so doggone important that you needed me to come out here? Them K-IIs don't require both of us."

"You're not going to believe it. You're just not going to believe it."

"Well of course I'm not. How can I not believe it if you don't tell me what it is?" Fred threw his hands up in exasperation.

"I think the Butterfly Scepter," Kolchak paused and looked around to make sure no one was listening, "might just be an Atlantean Key."

Fred's shoulders slumped in disappointment. "Uh, I'm sorry, but what exactly is that?"

"Don't you remember Dr. Sellers' Ancient Technology seminar? It was part of the Paranormal Conference in Atlantic City two years ago."

"I had the flu that year and didn't make it, remember? I spent the weekend at my mother's place recovering. There's nothing like my mom's chicken noodle soup to set your system back to right." Fred rubbed his belly.

"Uh, yeah, right . . . well anyway, you missed a great lecture. Dr. Sellers is miles ahead of the conventional scientists in understanding ancient technological capabilities. By correlating myths and legends from pre-Columbian American cultures with newly discovered ancient texts from Egyptian temples, he was able to extrapolate a common cultural source which he believes is Atlantis. The data suggest that the source disappeared six thousand years ago."

Fred's jaw dropped open. "That's the exact same time when the Butterfly Scepter was lost. That can't be a coincidence, can it?"

"I certainly don't think so. Each of the legends he examined mentions capabilities more advanced than ours. While conventional researchers dismiss them as proto-religious ideas, Dr. Sellers believes they refer to the holy grail of advanced technology . . ."

"Don't leave me hangin' here; what are we talkin' about, fusion, nano-lasers, or what?"

"Direct, quantum-level electromagnetic field manipulation. Do you know what that means Freddy?"

"Are you saying that someone or something used a *Star Trek*-like transporter to beam the Butterfly Scepter away?"

Kolchak sighed. "The transporter does work on the sub-atomic level, but it translates objects within our space-time reference. No, what we saw was outside the boundaries of our normal space-time."

"Like a wormhole?" Freddy said.

"Exactly! Wormhole pathways exist between every location; it's just a matter of unlocking them. To someone in our space-time reference, a person using such a pathway would seem to vanish . . . or if you're observing at the destination location, appear out of thin air."

"Amazing, but how do you unlock the pathways?"

"With a device that Dr. Sellers called an Atlantean key. That's what I think we saw on the library stage. The Butterfly Scepter is some sort of Atlantean key, which was activated and transported away."

"What should we do?"

"First we need to get back there with the K-IIs and take some measurements. If my suspicion is correct, we'll find very strong residual electromagnetic energy signatures where the scepter vanished."

"Should we tell the others?"

"No. One of them may be involved in the disappearance. We'll continue playing up the paranormal activity angle. The Sachem's certainly open to that, so it'll make a great cover story. After we've collected the data, I'll bring it back to the truck and run it through some analysis. We'll let the data drive our next move."

"Makes sense to me."

"If we can recover an actual Atlantean key . . ." Kolchak paused and shook his head, "it would be the greatest discovery in history."

26

P ENNY ENTERED THE SCHOOL LIBRARY AND LOOKED OVER THE
tables in the study section for a sign of Duncan. Before she'd
"fainted," they'd planned to meet after school and polish up their
presentation on Hatshepsut. Between recovering in the nurse's office
and meeting with Mr. Myrdin and Master Poe, she'd missed the rest
of her classes, so this was her first opportunity to catch Duncan up
on what had happened.

She spied him at the far end of the library and was impressed
to see that he was dutifully buried behind a stack of books. So
many that she'd passed over him several times before recognizing
his tousled hair sticking out over the top. She made her way over
to him as unobtrusively as she could but still managed to garner a

few hushed comments and covert stares from her fellow students. It wasn't every day that someone passed out in school. She did her best to ignore them.

Her stealthy approach went unmarked by Duncan whose head remained firmly locked on whatever tome he was reading. She peered over the stack of books on ancient history, Egypt, Pharaohs, and other relevant topics to discover that he wasn't reading a book but rather playing something on his new e-toy that he'd gotten for Christmas.

"Ahem," she said, clearing her throat.

Startled, Duncan looked up from his screen.

"Oh, uh, hey, Penny. I thought they sent you home from school. I was going to drop by after I finished working on our project. Are you okay?"

"I'm fine. I spent some time with the nurse and had an interesting conversation with Mr. Myrdin, and . . ." realizing others were listening in, she caught herself just before she added Master Poe.

"And what?" Duncan asked.

"And I thought I'd come here to help you out, only I find you playing *Angry Birds* on your e-thingy."

"It's a tablet, and I was just taking a break from working on our Hatshepsut project. Besides, I wasn't playing Angry Birds."

"Oh?" Penny raised the brow above her brown eye.

"If you must know, I was playing Stick Wars 2, and I was just about to defeat Lord Maelnik when you interrupted me. Now I'll have to start the level over again."

Penny rolled her eyes. "Whatever."

"I *really* was working on our project. Look, I even marked several pages in these books for new information to use in our presentation." Duncan picked up several books and opened them to his marked pages. "You know, your dad was right . . . Hatshepsut was pretty cool. She wasn't the first female ruler of Egypt, but she did rule longer than any of her predecessors. Did you know that during her reign, she re-established Egypt's trading networks with the Kingdom of Punt?"

Penny shook her head.

"Yeah, I'm not kidding; there was a land called Punt. Not only did Hatshepsut's trading mission bring back giraffes and gold, but it also brought back an even more valuable treasure—thirty-one myrrh trees."

"Myrrh, as in the gifts of the three wise men?"

Duncan nodded.

"It's one of the most expensive ingredients in the mummification process. She was so successful that her heirs tried to erase her from the records by chiseling out her pictures, and some even claimed her building projects as their own. I mean, our presentation is fine, but we've got no chance to win the bonus points. Heck, we might not even be in the top three." He sighed.

Penny patted him on the shoulder. "No doubt, but we've got bigger problems."

"Oh right, how are you feeling? I've never seen anyone faint before."

"I'm just fine, and before you ask, I heard you . . . we're not going to win. We need to talk about what happened today. Preferably somewhere private," she whispered the last part.

"Uh, okay. You're sure we don't need to beef up our project?"

"Positive," she replied with a crisp nod. Picking up several of the books, she added, "I'll help you return these, and we can talk on our way to swim practice."

THEY CAME OUT OF THE LIBRARY, AND PENNY MADE A LEFT TURN while Duncan made a right one.

"Hey, where are you going? The pool's this way. Are you sure you're okay?" Duncan asked.

"I know which way the pool is, but those halls are crowded. If we go outside, we'll have more privacy."

Duncan shrugged and followed Penny toward the exit. She paused to let him pass, and as he did, she punched him in the shoulder. Not with all of her might, but a little more strongly than her usual playful punch.

"Hey, what was that for?"

"That was to prove to you that I'm fine."

"All right, all right, so what really happened to you?"

As they stepped outside into the cold winter air, Penny told Duncan about her extra-dimensional trip to the library, then about Master Poe's theory of the *Teyrnwialen o Saith* being a *Conglfaen* talisman.

Duncan whistled. "So, who do they think stole the scepter?"

"They didn't say exactly, but I think they're still focused on the *Coch Coblyn*."

"Who could blame them? I mean, if it was bad news for him to get a normal seven-stone talisman, it's got to be even worse for him to have a keystone talisman. Besides, who else could it be?"

Penny looked at Duncan but didn't say anything.

"I know that look. What are you *not* saying?"

Penny raised the brow over her blue eye, shrugged, and let out a sigh.

"Come on, Preston, out with it."

"Well, if the *Coch Coblyn* took the *Teyrnwialen*, why hasn't he used it already? With a talisman that powerful, he should've been able to reenergize all the *Bodach*, or at least the ones in Piper Falls. Have you noticed anything different about the *Bodach*?"

Duncan shook his head and rather lamely offered, "Maybe he doesn't know how to use it or he's missing something to use it properly."

Penny gave him a sidelong glance.

"All right, then what do you think?"

"I think we may be wrong about the *Coch Coblyn*."

Before she could explain herself, a familiar, yet somewhat out of place voice yelled, "Hey, why are you two sitting outside in the cold?"

Penny and Duncan turned to see Coach Harlow and Katie Duley getting out of the coach's minivan.

"Penny, since you're here early, why don't you and Katie go on in and work on your crossover turn for the 200 IM. Since I've lost Katie's help, Duncan, you come over and help me unload. I've got the new sweatpants and shirts for the state meet as well as some new toys for us to use in practice."

DEPUTY BARNES COMPLETED THE LAST OF HIS INTERVIEWS WITH the witnesses and headed out to join Kolchak. Dreading another encounter with Pandora, he was happy to see that the rear liftgate was unlatched. He walked to the back of the truck and carefully opened the gate to find his friend sitting in front of a 40-inch flat-screen.

"Hey, whatcha doing watchin' TV?" he asked, taking the second seat in the paranormal processing center that occupied Kolchak's revamped U-Haul.

"Well, there were a couple of strange readings in the K-II data from the auditorium. I'm running a deep analysis algorithm to filter out the noise from the real data. It's going to take a while for the computer to correlate everything, so I thought I'd work on our other problem."

"What other problem?"

"The pranks . . . you know, the stolen laundry and the hanging cats. I can't shake this feeling that there's a connection between them."

"Well, both victims were women, and both reported seeing a strange, little red man asking to be let into their homes not long before the incidents occurred."

"I'm sorry; you misunderstand me. What I meant is that I think there's a connection between the pranks and what happened in the auditorium."

"What makes you say that? I mean sure, there's evidence of a paranormal connection to the pranks, at least with Ms. Johnson's suspended cats . . . and the K-IIs were going crazy down there in the auditorium. But that doesn't mean the two cases are connected. Like I've been trying to tell ya for months, there's all kinds of paranormal activity here in Piper Falls. We had the ghosts at the Bluebird's Halloween party and all of those Celtic artifacts that Ms. Morgan had in her possession when she was caught."

"What types of artifacts?" asked Kolchak.

"There was lots of stuff. Two really old Welsh books, a silver mortar and pestle, and a tripod with a silver bowl that had strange designs on it."

"Spell books and a summoning bowl!"

"You think Ms. Morgan was a witch?"

Kolchak tilted his head and raised his eyebrows.

Deputy Barnes shook his head. "Well, she can't be the connection."

"Oh, and why is that?"

"She's been gone since before Christmas. The FBI and that special agent from London took her and all them things back to the UK."

"Maybe she cast a curse on the town or summoned something before she was captured," Kolchak suggested.

"I don't know, maybe, but even if yer right, that don't connect the auditorium to the pranks."

"No, I guess it doesn't." Kolchak nodded slightly. "I was just thinking that maybe this Ms. Morgan was the female presence the Sachem felt when he was in his trance."

"That's just your untrained mind jumpin' to conclusions that ain't based on facts. Take it from me, as a seasoned lawman, these incidents ain't connected in any way, shape, or form."

27

THE RED MAN'S EXCITEMENT AT SENSING THE PRESENCE OF the *Conglfaen* lasted only a few short-lived moments. Just as quickly as its familiar essence had appeared, it had vanished. He twisted his gnarled fingers in the air, spoke the ancient words, and redirected the gossamer thread of his life force to search for the vanished talisman. Slowly and deliberately, he guided the thread through the tangled nexus of residual energy from the *Conglfaen's* feeding streams.

His greatest fear was that it had been taken by the dark fiend, so he concentrated his initial search on looking for traces of his nemesis but found none. Many of the streams had bourn fellow entities from his home plane. To himself, he said, "Perhaps one of our cousins had the strength to take the *Conglfaen*." He carefully searched through the remnants of those streams and found no hint of the powerful talisman.

"If neither the dark fiend nor my erstwhile relatives took the *Conglfaen*, what happened to it, eh Farsyl? Surely I'm not so far gone that I imagined its return."

Pondering his dilemma, he lost track of his probing essence thread which floated aimlessly through the residual energy currents of the room and directly into the scan of Kolchak's K-II where it registered as a barely perceptible spike of paranormal energy. Simultaneously, the energy of the K-II's scan harmonized with the essence thread and sent a resonating wave of energy back along the connection to its owner.

"*Diafol Fragu!*" he cursed in what he'd come to think of as his native tongue as the returning energy seared through his adopted flesh in a blazing jet of agonizing pain. Instinctively, he recalled his probing essence. The thread snapped back through the emptiness of trans-dimensional space and rejoined his inner core. The pain immediately ceased.

Pausing for a few seconds to regain his thoughts, Farsyl remembered the last time he'd felt such intense pain. The details were sketchy, but he remembered his first summoner throwing him into the void, where he'd drifted for uncounted years. The void was a terrifyingly empty existence, but it was preferable to enslavement by the inhabitants of this lower dimension.

When he was summoned again, he resisted the calling, but his summoners, a band of powerful Druids, were very persuasive. Through their *gwysio sianel*, they sent blazing streams of *derwyddon tân*, the Druids' fire. Unable to resist the searing heat, he'd succumbed. He savored their deaths only briefly before understanding that without them, he could not be released from their summons.

Had the Druids returned? If so, could they have taken the *Conglfaen*? Sending energy back along his thread was just the type of thing one of them would do. If a Druid did steal the *Conglfaen*, they would, of course, hide it from him until they could master its powers. That no doubt meant using an oak tree.

Yes, the more he thought about it, the more he convinced himself that recent events were no coincidence. The return of the *Conglfaen*, the dark fiend, large numbers of his weakened cousins, and now the Druids . . . the circle was nearly complete. Only a small opening remained, and with the coming of night, he would close that last gap.

"HOW'D YOUR TUTORING ON THE CROSSOVER TURN GO?" DUNCAN asked as Penny met him outside the pool.

"It started out rather rough."

"Let me guess, you either got water up your nose or had to breathe before you finished your breaststroke pullout."

Penny nodded.

"The same thing happened to me, too."

"I've seen your crossover turn; it's great."

"Thanks, but it wasn't always so good."

"How do you go so far and keep water out of your nose?"

"I make sure to take a deep breath right as I touch the wall."

"I tried that, but I still blow too much air out when I flip."

"Yeah, you have to get used to holding your breath through the turn. I also plug my nose."

"I've never seen you using nose plugs."

"I tried nose plugs, but I had to clip them on too tight to keep them from coming off during my start. I couldn't stand them, so I gave up on them."

"Okay, so how do you plug your nose? Using your hand would ruin your streamline, wouldn't it?"

"Yeah, that's why I don't use my hand. I use my upper lip."

Penny raised the brown eye's brow. "Your lip?"

"Like this," he replied, curling his upper lip toward his nose to block his nostrils.

Penny tried but couldn't manage anything more than a rather sad fish impression.

Duncan shrugged. "I guess you'll just have to work on your breath control and lung capacity. Now how about coming over to my house for a snack and a final run-through on our project?"

"Sure, but first we need to go to Caleb's."

"Why, did you find another gold coin?"

"No, something's bugging me about our last visit there."

"You mean that creepy Mr. Sobek?"

"Partly, but there's something else. I can't put my finger on it, but I felt like I was being watched."

"Maybe Mr. Cowling has security cameras," Duncan suggested.

"No, I sensed a presence . . . from outside our world." Penny shivered.

"Great, so we're just going to go into Mr. Cowling's shop and tell him you've got a hunch that something in his shop just might save our universe from a deranged, nearly omnipotent gargoyle?"

"Of course not. We're going to look for a present for your uncle's birthday."

"It's not my uncle's birthday."

"No, but Mr. Cowling doesn't know that."

"Fair enough, but what's our plan?"

"I'm not really sure. I think I just need some time in the shop to look around."

"Extra-dimensionally?" Duncan asked.

"Yeah," replied Penny.

BELLS CLANGED AGAINST THE DOOR ANNOUNCING DUNCAN AND Penny's arrival in Caleb's Collectibles.

"Hi, Penny... Duncan," Mr. Cowling said from behind the counter. "What can I help you with? Have you found another rare coin for me?"

"Hi, Mr. Cowling. No, I'm looking to buy something for my Uncle Gavin. He's my confirmation sponsor. We're supposed to get them a small gift, and I want to get him something cool."

"You've come to the right place. What type of cool thing are you looking for?"

"Well, I'm not sure, he's a big audio guy, but he only listens to vinyl records. He says digitization makes everything sound too crisp and clean. He likes to hear the pings and pops."

"Oh, he sounds like a real music aficionado."

"Yeah, my dad thinks he's a nut."

Mr. Cowling nodded. "Well, what were you looking to get him? I have a rather limited vinyl collection, but I do have some accessories he might be interested in. Why don't you come with me into the back of the shop where I keep my less popular items." Mr. Cowling motioned Duncan around the counter.

As Duncan walked into the back, Mr. Cowling smiled at Penny. "That commemorative Nixon tea set is gone, but you're welcome to come into the back too, Penny."

"Oh no, if it's all right with you I'd just like to browse around out here," she replied.

"Sure, sure, just let me know if you see anything you like. We'll only be a few minutes," he said, and he disappeared into the back.

Without the distraction of the others, Penny concentrated on her surroundings. Everything in the normal dimensions seemed fine. To be sure, Caleb's shop was filled with bizarre and eclectic items; an entire wall featuring taxidermy, several shelves of old power tools, and strange mechanical implements whose functions she couldn't fathom, but nothing gave her that eerie sense of being watched.

She hadn't expected to find it that easily, but she wanted to be sure whatever she'd sensed earlier didn't have an ordinary explanation. She extended her awareness into the higher dimensions and immediately detected two sources of energy.

"Now we're getting somewhere," she whispered.

The stronger of the two was coming from the aisle near the taxidermy wall. Reluctantly, she crossed the shop and started walking down the aisle. The blank-eyed stares of the stuffed creatures—three deer, several fish, two foxes, and one bear—made her uneasy, but not in the same way she'd felt before. She carefully probed each one with her mind but found nothing unusual.

Slowly, she extended her senses beyond the aisle itself and into the walls and floor of the shop. The floors were clear, but there was something fuzzy in the wall behind the mounted bear's head. Carefully, she narrowed the focus of her attention onto the shadowy area behind the bear.

Despite her increased concentration, it remained an ill-defined, amorphous blob, but it was clearly made of higher-dimensional energy.

Frustrated, she gathered her will and poked the nebulous patch.

The fuzzy patch of energy immediately shot itself into the bear head and released a booming roar.

Caught off guard by the sudden animation of the bear, Penny lost her extra-dimensional focus and screamed, "Aiyee!"

From the back of the shop, Mr. Cowling called out, "Penny, is everything all right out there?"

"Yeah, sorry about that . . . I think I saw a mouse, and it startled me," she answered as convincingly as she could.

"Yes, yes, ever since I lost Roscoe in the fall, I've had a little problem with them coming into the shop. As much as I hate to do it, I think I'll talk to Ms. Johnson and see if I can borrow one of her cats for a few days."

In the moments it took her to refocus herself, the depleted *Bodach*, which had been hiding in the walls of Caleb's Collectibles, made its getaway. Penny followed its energy trail outside the shop for a hundred yards or so before deciding it was gone.

While the hidden *Bodach* was probably the source of her earlier unease, there was still the second weaker energy signature to examine. It emanated from a half-open cardboard box sitting on a counter across the store. Penny walked across the shop to the counter and cautiously opened the box's lid, half expecting something to jump out at her. When nothing did, she peered inside to find a collection of what could best be described as junk. Penny reached into the box and began digging through its contents.

The items included numerous old action figures, ranging from Star Wars to GI Joe and everything in between. Most of the figures were missing hands, arms, and in the case of one Darth Vader figure, its head. There were also two puzzle boxes with writing on them. One said, "23 pieces missing" and the other, "puzzle doesn't match the picture." She found several chipped plastic tea cups and saucers with characters from Cinderella drawn on them and a dozen or so Christmas decorations in varying stages of disrepair, but none of the items gave off any extra-dimensional energy.

As with every search, it was the last thing she found that turned out to be what she was looking for. It was a small painted ceramic figurine a little larger than her thumb. A bearded dwarf, wearing a red vest, long pointed shoes, and a comical hat. His eyes were set with red gems. Despite never having seen the *Coch Coblyn*, she instantly knew it was a depiction of him. The figure's eyes emitted a faint glow visible only in the higher dimensions. The figurine was a talisman!

Holding it in her hands, she stared into the eyes of the miniature *Coch Coblyn*. She knew this was the source of her sense of being watched. Unsure of what to do, she reached out with her multi-dimensional senses and wrapped them around the figurine.

A spike of trans-dimensional energy shot back along her senses and reached into her mind. In the few seconds of contact, the alien energy combed through her memories. It called up images and sensations in no discernible pattern of time or reference: visions of her parents smiling down on her in her crib; the soft fur of her favorite stuffed Eeyore rubbing against her cheek while she slept; the taste of her dad's cinnamon and vanilla waffles smothered in maple syrup; the sharp pain of her arm fracturing as she fell off the swing; the joy of winning her first swim race . . . all of them and countless others flashed through her mind faster than she could digest.

They ended just as abruptly as they'd begun, with her cradling Simon in her arms in the snow-covered glade where they'd defeated Ms. Morgan and the apprentice.

The trans-dimensional presence weakened. In its final lingering moments, Penny half-imagined that she heard a muffled cry echo through her mind, an unmistakable cry for help.

While she stared at the miniature replica of the *Coch Coblyn*, Duncan and Mr. Cowling returned from the back room. Duncan placed a small velvet cinch sack on the counter.

Before he rang it up, Mr. Cowling called out to Penny. "Did you find anything interesting? Besides the mouse, of course."

Startled out of her concentration, she replied, "Maybe. How long have you had this box? I don't remember it being here before."

"Oh, never mind that box, it's just junk that I cleaned out from my Christmas and toy section over the last few weeks."

"Is any of it for sale? I didn't see prices on anything."

"Most of that stuff's been in here for months, or in some cases, years. I've been meaning to throw it away. Why? What have you found?"

"This." She held out the miniature *Coch Coblyn*.

"What is it?" Duncan asked.

"Let me see." Mr. Cowling said, taking the ceramic figurine from Penny's hand. "It's a Christmas ornament . . . see the loop for a hook or string." He pointed to the top of the hat. "Ugliest elf I ever saw. You'd think they'd make Santa's elves a little happier."

"Maybe someone got him confused with Grumpy from Snow White," Duncan offered.

"Could be, could be. Anyway, I couldn't find any of the other elements from the set, and there's not much of a market for individual elf ornaments, especially ugly ones."

The eyes of the figurine seemed to glow a little brighter at the last comment, enough that even Duncan noticed them.

Penny ignored his quick questioning glance. "Do you remember where you got it?"

"Funny you should ask. About a week or two after Christmas, I was in the back, and I heard the bells clang on the door. I called out to whoever it was that I'd be out in a minute. When I came up to the counter, no one was there, and this was sitting on the counter."

"Maybe whoever came in didn't hear you and just left the shop," Duncan suggested.

"If they did, they were awfully impatient and quiet about it. I wasn't in the back for more than another minute before I came out, and I didn't hear the bells clang when they left. Anyway, I was exhausted, so I just figured I'd imagined the whole thing."

"But what about the ornament?" Penny asked. "You didn't imagine that."

"No, no, I must've found it in the back, brought it up here, and forgotten about it. I tried to find the rest of the set several times, but I never did." He handed the figurine back to Penny. "If you want it, you can have it."

"How much do you want for it?"

"Seeing how it was halfway to the trash bin and I pay to have the trash hauled away, how about you keep it and we call it even?"

"Thanks."

"No problem. Now, Duncan do you still want that record cleaning kit?" Duncan nodded. "That'll be seven dollars."

28

**IN THE DIM AND DISTANT PAST, MONTHS AFTER
THE CRASH OF THE ONATHA**

G ENWITHA AND SOSONDO STOOD WITH THEIR BACKS TO THE
skunk's den and stared out at Gohone's two Jogah and the
pack of snarling dogs.

"Look, that was a nice trick, getting the skunks to spray you
two. Can't say I would've done it myself, but it probably saved you
from the dogs," the taller man said.

"Not for long, they're already getting over their fear. In a few
more minutes, I probably won't be able to hold 'em off even if I
wanted to," said the shorter man with a grin, making it clear that
he didn't.

"For now, you're safe as long as you stay near the skunks' den,
but if you get more than a few paces from the entrance, the dogs will

rip you to shreds. That stench may protect you from the dogs, but other hunting parties are on the way, and some of them have bows."

"You won't kill us," Genwitha said.

"Oh, and why is that, little girl?" the taller man asked.

"Because even if we took this box you're looking for, which we didn't, we clearly don't have it now. You've been chasing us for more than an hour; the box could be anywhere on our trail. If you kill us, you might never find it. What will Gohone do to you when he learns you killed the only people who knew how to find the box?"

"Shut up, girl!" yelled the shorter man.

"No, no, she's right. We can't kill them, but we can make them wish they were dead." He paused as if in thought. Then a wicked smile crossed his face. "How tough are you, little girl?"

"She's tougher than you!" Sosondo shouted.

"Oh, I don't doubt it, little man. I'm sure she's prepared to take any torture we could think of, but that's not what we have in mind. Is she tough enough to watch as we disembowel you and let the dogs feast on your entrails . . . while you're still alive?" He finished with a throaty cackle that passed for laughter.

The dog-master started to laugh with his taller companion. Several of the dogs added their baying to their master's evil chortle, creating a cacophonous chorus of malevolence.

The tall man made a horizontal motion with his hand, which the short dog-master copied, and the sounds quickly ceased. "I'll give you five minutes to reconsider your situation before we feed the hounds."

To emphasize his point, he held up a finely sharpened obsidian knife.

Sosondo huddled close to Genwitha and whispered, "We're not going to tell them anything, are we?"

"No, of course not," she whispered back.

"Do you think Gohone got to Iosheka and Ataensic?"

"I don't know, but if he did, we're in for an unpleasant end."

"I've been thinking about that, and I don't plan to let them slice me open without a fight."

"The tall one's almost twice your size, and the dog master's arms are as thick as your body. No offense, but you couldn't take one of them, much less both."

"Yeah, that's what I'm counting on." Genwitha gave him a confused look. "Overconfidence. They think I'm such an easy mark. I should be able to surprise them. I might even get lucky and take one of them out with my staff." He emphasized his point by banging the staff into the ground.

"Maybe, but what about the other one?"

"He'll have to deal with me, which will give you time to climb up that steep rock face—"

"No," she said in her regular voice, earning them a wave from their captors. "I'm not leaving you here alone."

"Look, these guys don't have bows, and the dogs can't climb that rock face, so if I can buy you enough time to reach the top, you might escape. It's your only chance."

"You've got one more minute before we see how tough you are, little girl. If you don't want to save yourself, at least think of your boyfriend. He's far too young to meet such a tragic ending," the taller man said.

"The box for our freedom?" Genwitha asked.

"Once we have the box, you can go on your way, and we'll tell the other searchers that you drowned in the river."

"How do I know I can trust you?"

"I give you my word."

Sosondo said, "Your word? You can't be serious. You're one of Gohone's trained killers. How can you possibly think we're gullible enough to accept your word?"

"Watch your mouth, boy!" the dog master growled.

The tall Jogah placed his hand on his companion's shoulder. "You're correct that we work for Gohone and that our customers may not always enjoy the fruits of our labor." He paused to pat his shorter companion, who laughed. "However, we Jogah live by a strict code. Our word is our bond, and we hold our bond unbreakable. All we want is the box. I cannot guarantee you will escape, but we will do our best to give you time."

The dog master grunted and nodded his agreement.

"Besides, what choice do you have?"

"You make a strong point," Genwitha said.

"No! Genwitha, no!" Sosondo yelled.

"It's the only way, Sosondo. We're beaten. Iosheka's not coming. There's no reason to die a horrible death for a lost cause." Grabbing him by the shoulders, she looked him squarely in the eye. "You've got to trust me on this." Then she winked at him and added, "It's what Iosheka wants us to do. Understand?" She gave him several exaggerated nods of her head.

Sosondo nodded back. "Uh, yeah, I think I understand."

"Time's up, little girl. What's it going to be? Are you going to give us the box, or is your boyfriend dinner for the dogs?"

"The box is in the skunks' den."

"I knew it!" the dog master said.

"All right, why don't you send your boyfriend in to get it?" the tall man suggested.

Genwitha turned to Sosondo. "You heard the man . . . go get the box."

Sosondo turned toward the den, paused, and looked over his shoulder to Genwitha, who nodded her head toward the entrance. He approached the den and cautiously crept inside the entrance. The baying of the dogs must have driven the skunks deeper into the cave. They ignored Sosondo. After fumbling around in the dark for what seemed like an eternity, he found the hidden box. With both hands, he carefully removed it and left the cave.

"Very good, boy," the taller man said. "Now bring the box to me and I'll let you and your girlfriend go."

Sosondo looked at Genwitha. She met his gaze and gave him a slight nod of her head.

"There's been a slight change in plans," he said. He opened the box. The gems of the Sekhem flashed brilliantly.

"Release the hounds!" the taller Jogah said to the dog master.

Before his companion had a chance to comply, seven large wild cats with a single distinctive patch of fur on their bodies materialized between the dogs and their quarry.

THE PRESENT

IT WAS EARLY EVENING, AND PENNY HADN'T COME HOME YET, so Simon extended his senses. He found her several blocks away walking with Duncan toward his house. She hadn't told him anything about visiting Duncan, but then she often kept him in the dark about her plans. He considered heading over to Duncan's, then decided against it. Partly because he knew she was safe, and partly to avoid the old woman who lived there.

It wasn't that he was afraid of her, but something about her ability to see him as more than a large domestic cat unnerved him.

Even the gray man and the black bird couldn't see as deep inside him as the old woman. He knew she meant no harm to him—or more importantly, to Penny—but he was a cat, and stealth and secrecy were second nature to him. Anything that robbed him of those traits was something or someone to be treated with caution.

Besides, when he'd reached out with his senses, he detected something unusual at the edge of town, something that extended into what Penny and her friends called the higher dimensions. It seemed a strange name to him: they were no higher or lower than anywhere else, they were just different. In any event, it was probably nothing more than one of the *Bodach* conserving its energy, he told himself. The town was full of them, and for the most part, they were completely harmless. Nothing to worry Penny about, and he enjoyed solving problems on his own.

He thought about teleporting to the disturbance but decided against it. If it was something dangerous lurking in the higher dimensions, teleportation might give him away. So, despite the chill, he chose to walk through the town. True to his cautious nature, he stuck to the side streets, occasionally detouring a block or more off the most direct path to maintain his inconspicuous approach. On the few occasions when he had to break concealment, he darted between cover, seeming to be nothing more than a silent shadow. The one or two people who managed to catch a glimpse of him out of the corner of their eye never suspected his supernatural origins.

He was *Cait Sith*, and his curiosity had gotten the better of him.

29

"AH, THE SUN IS FINALLY GOING DOWN, FARSYL, MY BOY. 'TIS time for us to escape this cursed domain and finally return home." With a few gestures of his knobby fingers and some words in the ancient tongue, the *Coch Coblyn* lifted the fog of his concealment. Carefully looking about and seeing no one, he stepped out from the holly bushes and into Piper Falls.

He still couldn't sense the *Conglfaen*, but that did not surprise him. Until they mastered its powers, the Druids would keep it hidden. The Druids were a wicked distrustful lot; they even hid their talismans of power from each other. His summoners, including the original Farsyl, used oak staffs to contain him while they crafted the bounds of their summons. But they had other devices of power, too:

rings, amulets, and scepters containing trans-dimensional gems bound in energy-conducting silver, which they jealously guarded.

Since all of them possessed a higher-dimensional awareness, the best way to conceal their treasures from each other was to use oak. Small boxes hidden in abandoned animal dens or secret oaken compartments in walls were the most common arrangements. In a pinch, even oak leaves could conceal the presence of a talisman, allowing druids to veil their powers from one another.

For truly powerful items, a living oak tree provided the best hiding place. He'd seen his namesake pull a powerful talisman from inside a giant, old oak. One moment, there was nothing in the higher planes, and in the next, all five planes were filled with the radiant glow of a five-stoned ring.

"If the Druid who had seized the *Conglfaen* was anything like his predecessors, then he'd hide it in an oak tree; the larger the better." The *Coch Coblyn* stroked his beard. Luckily for him, the previous centuries' logging and farming industries had removed the oldest and largest trees from the surrounding forests. The only section of large old-growth trees left was where he'd arrived in Schoen Park.

Of course, that was only half the battle. Even after he found the right tree, there was still the matter of how to retrieve the *Conglfaen* from it. Oak's strong resistance to extra-dimensional energy meant that he couldn't use his primary powers, at least not without exhausting all his energy. Fortunately, there was another way, a much simpler way, one that he had used many times before. He would need to use some of his energy reserves to move things along, just like he'd done in Rome, Amsterdam, and London, but if he was successful in getting home, he wouldn't need an energy reserve.

The *Coch Coblyn* shook his head from side to side and rubbed his hands together. "A truly despicable bunch, the Druids. This plane is none the better for their return. Perhaps a little of my fire will teach them a lesson." He snapped his gnarled fingers, and a bright red flame sprang from the tip of his thumb. Lest anyone see, he quickly extinguished the flame by closing it in his fist. At the slight hissing sound of the flame's death, the *Coch Coblyn* chuckled and continued his walk to Schoen Park.

PROCESSING THE DATA WAS TAKING LONGER THAN KOLCHAK expected which gave him more time to look over the video he'd shot of the hanging cats at Ms. Johnson's house. Despite Freddy's trained opinion to the contrary, he was convinced there was a connection between the pranks and the disappearance of the scepter. He must've missed something. If he could just watch the video one more time, he was sure he'd find the connection.

His third time through and he still couldn't find anything. Disgusted, he let the video continue rolling to the scene where Sofie, Ms. Johnson's overly large, white Persian cat, fell claws-first onto Freddy's chest. Try as he might, Kolchak couldn't suppress a laugh at his friend's misfortune.

His high-pitched chortle disturbed the snoozing deputy, who groggily asked, "Hey, what's so funny?"

"Did I disturb your sleep, Freddy?"

"I wasn't asleep. I was just restin' my eyes. It's part of my training."

Kolchak rolled his eyes just enough for his friend to notice.

"When you're on a stakeout, you learn to rest your eyes without fallin' asleep. The trick is to dial up your other senses, so you don't miss nothin.'"

"Is snoring part of that *training*?" Kolchak asked.

Fred shook his head. "Oh, very funny. You laymen just don't understand the intricacies of being a lawman."

"Sorry, old friend. You didn't miss much anyway. I've just been watching the video of the hanging cats, looking for clues."

"And what's so funny about that?"

Kolchak pointed to the screen, which showed Fred removing the last of Sofie's claws from his shirt and handing the big white furball to Ms. Johnson.

Fred turned several shades of red and mumbled something that Kolchak ignored.

"Anyway, I've seen it three times, and other than no cats hanging from the oak tree and the scepter's box being made of oak, I can't find any connection."

"I told you there wasn't any connection. Now, why don't you turn that off; all you're gettin' now are the spectators."

"You're probably right." Kolchak reached for the off button, but something on the screen caught his attention. Two people were hiding behind a large tree. The camera panned by them once, then came back to them again . . . and he recognized them as children. Kolchak stopped the video and backed it up to the beginning of the sequence.

"Do you recognize these two kids?" he asked Fred.

"Uh, yeah, that's Duncan O'Brien and Penny Preston."

"Is there any chance they might be involved with the pranks?"

"Nah, they're good kids, never been in trouble with the law. What makes you ask about 'em? There was lots of people at the crime scene. I mean, it's not every day you find thirteen cats hangin' from trees, especially in Piper Falls."

"I hear you, but do you notice how everyone else is looking at the cats?"

"Yeah, so?"

"Well, do you notice that these two aren't?" He backed up the video again. "And look at how they turn away when the camera pans toward them. What does that suggest to your expertly trained eyes?"

"It sure looks like they're tryin' to avoid bein' seen by the camera."

"Maybe, but I doubt they noticed the camera. It looks more like they were listening in on our conversation and didn't want us to catch them."

"Why would they do that?"

A loud *ding-ding* echoed throughout the back of the U-Haul.

"What the heck was that; have you got a microwave in here, too?" Fred asked.

"The microwave's in the front cab. That's the computer telling us it's finished crunching the data from the auditorium." Kolchak slid his chair along the tracks and began looking at the output on a second screen. He clicked through several screens before returning to the first one. He cocked his head to the side, took in a deep breath, and slowly let it out.

Fred sat up, excited. "Well? What's it say?"

"Here, why don't you take this chair." Kolchak got up and motioned for his friend to take a seat.

After exchanging places, Fred stared at an LCD screen filled with undulating colored lines. "What am I lookin' at?"

"That's a graphical representation of the paranormal energy reading from the auditorium."

"Why's it got different colors?"

"Paranormal energy comes in different wavelengths or frequencies. The program uses different colors to represent them.

The height of each colored line indicates the strength of the residual paranormal energy in a given frequency."

"Okay, but why are they moving up and down like that? It looks like there's a pattern. When the red, blue, and yellow lines go up, the purple, green, and orange ones go down . . . and vice versa," Fred said.

"You're right, they are moving relative to each other. Did you notice anything strange or familiar about the pattern?"

"Wait a minute, let me think on it." A moment later, Fred snapped his fingers. "I got it . . . that's the same color groups that the scepter was flashing!"

Kolchak patted his friend on the back. "That it is, Freddy my boy. Now take a look at this." He clicked the mouse, and more than a dozen smaller colored lines were added to the graph.

"What's that?"

"These are much smaller pulses of energy. See how they start after the scepter pulses but drop-off immediately after the scepter pulses end? All except for this smallest one . . . it repeats with the others every time . . . except it misses the last beat."

"Yeah, I see it. What's it mean?"

"I'm not sure, but look at this. I'm going to overlay the auditorium graph with the readings from Ms. Johnson's house." Kolchak made a few clicks with the mouse.

"Hey, nothin' changed."

"That's what I thought too . . . at first. Then I turned down the intensity of the auditorium data and raised it for the Johnson data." Again, Kolchak clicked the mouse a few times.

"Well, I'll be," said Fred. "The Johnson data matches up with some of the smaller pulses from the library!"

"Yes, and paranormal energy signatures are unique."

"Right, like fingerprints."

"Exactly. According to the computer, there are two distinct signatures in the Johnson data; one that seems to be from the incident, and a second that only shows up *after* the incident. Those same two signatures appear among the smaller patterns in the auditorium data."

"So, the pranks and the scepter's disappearance are connected."

IN THE DIM AND DISTANT PAST, IN FRONT OF THE SKUNK'S DEN

THE SEVEN FEROCIOUS FELINES SPRANG INTO ACTION BEFORE THE hounds knew what hit them. Two black cats, one with a white patch on its back and the other with one on top of its head, took out the two nearest dogs with powerful slashes to their throats. Three brown cats, also with single white patches on their bodies, like their smaller *Cait Sith* descendants, crippled their quarry with strikes to the haunches.

The remaining dogs never recovered from their initial surprise. Despite outnumbering the wild cats, they were no match for the lightning-quick felines. Three more dogs were wounded before the survivors turned and fled. While the brown and black cats dealt with the dogs, the others turned on the Jogah. A gray cat with a black diamond-shaped patch of fur on its chest went after the dog master. The powerfully built man was deceptively quick, but not quite quick enough. He dodged what would have been a death blow to his throat, but the great cat's paw raked his face, leaving four deep red furrows across his right cheek. The second paw also missed his throat but struck with such force, that it snapped the dog master's neck. His lifeless body crumpled to the ground.

Balanced lightly on the balls of his feet, the tall Jogah established a strong defensive position, wielding a staff in one hand and his obsidian knife in the other. From his calm expressionless visage, Genwitha knew that he was no ordinary henchman, but one of Gohone's elite weapons-masters.

A large white cat with a triangular brown patch on one side cautiously closed to about ten paces from the weapons-master. It stopped and stood motionless, studying its prey.

The weapons-master continued to lightly shift his weight from one foot to the other. With his right hand, he began to spin the staff in slow circles, while with his left, he kept the obsidian blade's point aimed at the chest of the great cat.

While it seemed longer, the stand-off lasted little more than a few seconds. Whether it grew impatient or it perceived a weakness in the weapons master's defense, the great cat ended the stalemate with a tremendous leap.

The weapons-master responded by swinging his staff down at the white cat's head and simultaneously thrusting his black blade at its chest. The attack was executed with precise timing and unerring skill. The flying feline could not twist to avoid the staff's strike without impaling itself on the blade, and turning from the blade ensured a crushing blow from the staff. Either outcome spelled certain death.

Perhaps sensing the futility of either maneuver, the cat did neither and continued on its flight path into the weapons-master. In the split second, before the staff met its skull and the black blade pierced its heart, the cat shimmered into a ghostly shape. The staff and the knife passed harmlessly through the ethereal cat.

Having braced for the impact, the weapons-master momentarily lost his balance. In that instant, the cat returned to solid form and drove the weapons-master to the ground. No longer able to defend himself, he was quickly dispatched by the powerful jaws of the white feline.

AT THE SAME TIME, NEARLY A DOZEN MILES AWAY

IOSHEKA WOKE WITH HIS FACE IN THE DIRT AND A PAINFUL throbbing in his head. Without getting up, he brought his left hand to his temple, where the throbbing seemed to be centered. He winced as he examined the sticky, egg-sized lump with his fingers. He recognized the dark red, sticky substance as partially congealed blood. Had he hit his head falling, or had someone struck him? He couldn't remember.

He sat up, a little too quickly, and the image of the forest clearing around him began to spin. He closed his eyes and rubbed them gently with his fingers. When he opened them again, the spinning stopped, and he was able to take in his surroundings.

He took a deep breath and surveyed the clearing. Two dead bodies were sprawled on the ground. He couldn't see any of their faces, but from their dress, he recognized them as Gohone's Jogah. Broken spears, flint knives, and several clubs littered the clearing, which was covered with tracks from men and beasts. There'd been a battle here, and he had been a participant, but the throbbing pain in his temple kept him from recalling any of the details.

Feeling too weak to stand, he found a nearby spear shaft and levered himself off the ground. Leaning on the headless weapon, he took in the full scope of the carnage. A third man, not one of the Jogah, lay on the far side of the clearing. Even through his throbbing vision, Iosheka could see the shallow rise and fall of the man's chest.

He was still alive. Using the spear as a make-shift crutch, he worked his way across the clearing toward the fallen man.

He'd only managed a few halting steps when he heard a familiar voice call out from behind him. "Iosheka!"

He turned slowly to see Ataensic and several men enter the clearing, accompanied by two very large wild cats. Both cats were brown. One had a white patch on his chest, and the other had a similar patch on her neck. The female cat walked with a limp, and Iosheka saw a dark red streak flowing down her front leg from her shoulder.

Ataensic ran to Iosheka and wrapped him in her arms. He returned her embrace, leaning on her for support. "You're alive!" The relief in her voice was palpable.

"Yes, although based on the drums pounding on my temples, I'm not sure it's preferable to the alternative."

His droll attempt at humor earned him a grimace from Ataensic, who turned her attention to his wound. She gently probed the area, causing him to involuntarily wince a few times. "It *looks* worse than it is. I suspect you'll have that pounding headache for a while, but you should be fine." Ataensic rewarded him with one of her heart-warming smiles.

"Thanks. My memory's a bit scrambled right now. Could you tell me what happened?"

"After capturing the Sachem, Gohone and a few of his Jogah warriors came to the village and demanded we give them the Sekhem. Naturally, we refused."

"I gather Gohone didn't accept our refusal gracefully."

"No, he didn't. He was quite unhappy. I'm sure he wanted to kill us right then and there, but he hadn't figured on the townsfolk supporting us."

"If there's one thing Gohone dislikes more than resistance, it's a fair fight."

"Indeed, but he wasn't going to give up so easily. He summoned more of his Jogah henchmen, and they brought a large number of their fighting dogs."

"And the result was this little brouhaha?"

Ataensic nodded. "But first, you sent the Sekhem away with Genwitha and Sosondo."

"I don't know how we'd have survived without those two helping us. We were very lucky Sosondo didn't pull his fishing traps at the first sign of that big storm."

"True, although I'm not sure his Sachem would agree."

Iosheka nodded. "What happened next?"

"Somehow, Gohone figured out we didn't have the Sekhem. He ordered these men to kill us and sent the rest of his Jogah warriors out to search for the Sekhem. When the killers attacked, we formed a protective ring around you. We held our own, even after Adeka went down," she indicated the third fallen man, who was now being attended to by two of her companions, "but then seven of the wild cats suddenly disappeared. Right after that, he . . ." she pointed to one of the dead Jogah, "threw a war club and hit you in the head. You fell and well . . ." She paused."

"You thought I was dead?"

"Yes, so we went on the attack. We killed these two, and the rest of them split up and fled through the forest toward the village. We'd left only a few men to guard it. We formed into two teams, each taking two cats and followed them through the forest. We were just returning from taking out our group when I saw you. I'm so happy you're alive!" She hugged him even more fiercely than before.

"You and me both." He returned her hug as best he could.

"What were you doing before you went down, and what happened to the other wild cats? They just vanished."

"It's coming back to me now. I know it's going to sound strange, but I used mind-speech to communicate with Genwitha."

"I thought only those in the Amun-Ra could do that," Ataensic said.

"Mind-speech does require second sight, but it doesn't require Amun-Ra training."

"But if you had second sight, you'd have been recruited by the Amun-Ra. They tested every child," Ataensic said.

"True, they tested me, and I didn't have the power, but now I do. When I used the Sekhem to create the wild cats and give them the ability to teleport, something happened to me. It's hard to explain, but I could see and sense things that others couldn't. At first, I thought it was just one of the effects of using the Sekhem. Now I understand that the Sekhem didn't change me, but its power roused my dormant second sight ability."

"So, you sent the wild cats to rescue Genwitha and used mind-speech to let her know they were coming?"

"Yes, I also told her to hide the Sekhem where none of our people will ever find it."

"I don't understand why we couldn't keep it here. Surely now that you have the second sight you could use its power to help our new people."

"Yes, and initially we'd use the Sekhem's power wisely, but over time, it would corrupt the people. Maybe not in our lifetime or even our children's." Ataensic beamed at the mention of their yet to be born children. ". . . but at some point in the future, wars would be fought to control its power. Eventually, someone like Gohone, or even worse than him, would gain its power. And they'd use it to create another cult."

"Like the Amun-Ra?"

"Yes, and I can't be responsible for unleashing that type of evil on our new family. It destroyed our old home, and I will not let it poison our new one."

"Then why not destroy it?"

"My second sight tells me that someone in the distant future may need its power."

30

THE PRESENT

B EFORE THE BELLS ON THE CLOSING DOOR OF CALEB'S COLLECT-
ibles stopped jingling, Duncan turned to Penny with a wide-
eyed look and asked, "Is that what I think it is?"

"Yeah, it's a talisman shaped like the *Coch Coblyn*."

"Are you sure? I mean, we've never seen the *Coch Coblyn*."

"We haven't, but I'm sure. You saw the extra-dimensional glow
when Mr. Cowling called it ugly?" Duncan nodded. "It's also the
source of whatever was giving me that watched-over feeling."

"That can't be a coincidence."

"No, it can't. There's something more."

She told him about the statue reaching out to her and sifting
through her memories. She even told him about its muffled cry for

help. When she finished, she asked, "Have you ever felt a presence through your necklace?"

"No, I've never felt anything like that! I did feel the *Crom Dubh* through Ms. Morgan's triquetra, but that wasn't quite the same thing."

"No emotions or feelings?"

"Oh no, there was plenty of anger, but it wasn't directed specifically at me. More generalized, kind of like a grumpy old man being woken up from a nap to do something he doesn't like, only much nastier."

"Hmm . . . maybe Ms. Morgan's summoning incantation protected you," suggested Penny.

Duncan shrugged. "Maybe, but don't you think this is the kind of thing we should talk to Mr. Myrdin and Master Poe about?"

"Probably." Penny turned toward Duncan's house.

"But Mr. Myrdin's house is the other way," Duncan said and hoisted his thumb over his shoulder.

"Yeah, but your grandmother is this way."

Duncan put his hand on Penny's shoulder and turned her toward him. "Okay, what's going on? A talisman that bears an uncanny resemblance to a crazy two thousand-year-old *Bodach*, whose idea of a prank is burning down cities, reaches into your mind, flashes through your memories, and you want to talk to my *grandma*? Am I missing something here?"

"No, you've got the gist of it." Penny removed Duncan's hand and continued toward his house.

"That's just crazy talk. What can my grandma possibly tell you that Master Poe and Mr. Myrdin can't?"

"I don't know, but I've just got this feeling that I need to talk to someone but that it can't be Master Poe or Mr. Myrdin. The only other person I could think of is your grandmother."

"Are you sure that whatever entered your mind didn't somehow, uh . . . you know . . . mess with you, like Master Poe did with me?"

Penny faced Duncan and pursed her lips. "Oh, it messed with my mind. You can't watch scenes from your life, half of which you've forgotten, flash through your consciousness without some sort of impact."

Duncan returned her stare but remained silent.

"Look, I can't explain it in words, but I know that something . . . something with a connection to the higher planes . . . used this statue." She raised the statue to eye level and shook it from side to side. "And they used it to communicate with me. I don't know if it was the *Coch Coblyn* or not, but whatever it was, it wasn't evil."

Duncan skeptically raised an eyebrow. "What would you call something rifling through your memories?"

"I think it was trying to understand me, you know, to get to know me."

"Like some sort of mental background check?"

"In a way, but without the sketchy implications. Whatever it was, I sensed a great deal of fear, almost terror."

"Of what?"

"Of Master Poe, and I'm afraid of what'll happen if we bring it to Mr. Myrdin and Master Poe."

"Wait, so you trust some unknown entity more than Mr. Myrdin and Master Poe?"

"No, it's not that. I just have the sense that this is what I must do."

"So, you're going to show it to my grandma and hope for the best?"

Penny nodded her head. "That's my plan."

"Well, she did know about the *Coch Coblyn*, but if she doesn't know anything, we go right to Mr. Myrdin's. Agreed?"

"Agreed."

Penny and Duncan arrived at the O'Brien's house just as the last of Duncan's siblings, the twins Sean and Patrick, came racing out the front door.

"Hey, Duncan, you missed dinner," Sean said.

"Yeah, your favorite; homemade mac and cheese with chunks of ham in it," Patrick added.

"Before mom and dad went out, they made us promise to save enough for you, but we didn't save enough for Penny," added Sean, shaking his head with an all too knowing smile.

"Yeah, you really should keep us up to date on your social life, little bro," Patrick said with a wink.

Sean tousled Duncan's hair. "Yeah, and where's your hat? Didn't you hear? The groundhog saw his shadow this morning. We've got six more weeks of winter."

The twins looked at Duncan and Penny, then back at each other before breaking into laughter and continuing on their way.

Duncan straightened his hair and turned to Penny. "Sorry about that."

"About what?" Penny asked as they crossed the porch and entered the O'Brien's living room.

"About the twins; they can be real jerks sometimes."

"Oh, don't worry about it, that's nothing compared to some of the stories Eddie tells about his older brothers."

"Yeah, I guess you're right. Let's go see how much mac and cheese my mother managed to save. We can share it."

Penny smiled. "Okay." The truth was that no matter how obnoxious Duncan's brothers were, she was always a bit envious of his family. Her parents were great, but sometimes she wished she had a younger sister or even a brother.

While it may not have been very much by the twins' standards, there was more than enough mac for both Duncan and Penny.

As they were cleaning up the dishes, Duncan's grandmother came into the kitchen.

"Duncan, you know better than to ask a guest to help you clean up the dishes," she scolded. Then she turned to Penny. "Hello, Penny."

"Hello, Mrs. Cadogan. I don't mind helping with the dishes. I did drop in unexpectedly."

"Yeah, we were lucky mom saved enough mac and cheese for her."

"Oh, luck had nothing to do with it, dearie. I had a feeling you wouldn't be coming home alone. I thought Penny might be coming over. I held back a little extra from the twins' plates."

"What kind of feeling, Grandma?"

"Oh, you'll probably think I'm crazy, but this afternoon I . . . well, I don't know how to explain it, but I felt compelled to go to the library."

"Did you have an overdue book?" Duncan asked.

"No, and before you ask, I didn't want to check one out either. It was like I was being tugged there, but not with a rope or anything. Just with every step I took toward the library, I felt better. I'm sure you think I'm just a crazy old lady." She looked back and forth between Duncan and Penny.

"No, no, Mrs. Cadogan, we don't think that at all . . . do we, Duncan?"

"Uh, no, not at all, Grandma."

"Why did you tell us about it if you thought we wouldn't believe you?" asked Penny.

"Well, dearie, you see, when I got to the library . . ." she paused, looking back and forth between the two children.

"Yes, when you got to the library?" repeated Penny.

"I saw a bunch of ghosts, and . . ." she paused again, "and one of them looked just like Penny, right down to the clothes she's wearing."

———◆———

IN THE BACK OF KOLCHAK'S U-HAUL

"SO, WHAT'S THE CONNECTION BETWEEN THE PRANKS AND THE library auditorium?" asked Fred.

"I was thinking about that while you were, eh, practicing your surveillance techniques." Fred knotted his brow but remained silent. "First of all, we've only got data for one of the pranks, but I think it's safe to assume that all of them are connected. Would you agree?"

"Sure, witnesses in each case stated they saw a small, gnarled man dressed in red before each incident."

"Yes, and I'd bet that if we had data for those other cases, we'd find this same red energy line," he pointed to the screen, "at each prank scene."

"Okay, but what about the other line? Nobody reported anything blue at any of the scenes."

"That's where things get a bit fuzzier. In previous cases with multiple apparitions, there's always been an identifiable pattern in their appearances. I had the computer run a correlation analysis between all the lines in both the Johnson and auditorium data, and these are the only two with positive identifications at both scenes. There are a few odd signatures that might be present in both data sets, but their probabilities and relative strengths are several orders of magnitude lower."

"Huh?"

"Basically, the computer couldn't distinguish them, with any certainty, from the general background noise in the Johnson data."

"Oh, did the analysis tell you anything else?"

"In the Johnson data, this one . . ." Kolchak pointed to a red-colored line, "appears first, and this one . . ." he pointed to the bluish line, "comes second. In the auditorium data, they're closer together, but it's the other way around."

"Is that important?"

"Honestly, with only two incidents, I can't tell. If the relationship was constant, we'd have something, but given that it's not, we really can't draw any conclusions. The lines might represent entangled entities, or they might not."

"What you're sayin' is that we need another few pranks if we're going to learn anything."

"I wouldn't say we *need* them, but they would certainly help with the data."

"I ASSURE YOU, I'M QUITE ALIVE AND WELL," PENNY SAID.

Mrs. Cadogan placed her hand on Penny's. "Oh, I know, dearie. It wasn't your ghost, but as we used to say in the old country, your *enaid,* or soul, that I saw."

"My soul?"

"That's the direct translation, but essence is probably a better word. It was only for a few moments. Then everything disappeared."

"How did that tell you that Penny was coming over to visit?" Duncan asked.

"I've always been sensitive to the spirit world, dearie. One of my grandmother's friends—a red-headed fortune-teller named Mrs.

Gough—told me I was a *dawnus* or one of the gifted people. She wanted to train me to become a seer, but my mum wouldn't allow it. She thought the old ways were a bunch of superstitious nonsense that held us back. Despite my mum, I did sneak in a few lessons before Mrs. Gough died. I never became a true seer, but I learned enough to recognize signs. I can sense troubles and dangers from the spirit world and even have some premonitions."

"You had a premonition that I was coming?"

"Yes and that somehow you were in danger."

"Can you tell me anything about this?" Penny reached into her pocket and pulled out the figurine of the *Coch Coblyn*.

Mrs. Cadogan's eyes widened at the sight of the diminutive depiction of the red leprechaun. "Where did you get this?"

"I found it in a box of junk at Caleb's Collectibles."

"Did Mr. Cowling tell you what it is?"

"He said it was an old Christmas ornament."

"Oh, dearie, if that's an old Christmas ornament, then I'm the queen of the faeries." Mrs. Cadogan laughed and shook her head. "Cowling . . . a good Welsh name . . . his mother must've frowned on the old ways, too. It's a shame so much of the old knowledge has been lost to modern ways. That's a *carchar enaid*, or in English, a soul prison."

"You mean someone's soul is trapped in there?" Duncan asked.

"That's certainly possible. The Druids would use a *carchar enaid* to capture the power of their enemies, but they also used them to control the *hysbrydion* or spirits."

"Can you tell who or what's inside?" asked Penny.

"No, dearie, that's beyond me. All I can tell you is that it contains something. Something very powerful . . . and extremely old."

"Do you think this is what's behind the recent sightings of the red leprechaun and all of the pranks?" Penny asked.

"It would be a strange coincidence if the *carchar enaid* is not somehow involved."

"Should we destroy it, or would that let its prisoner out?" Duncan asked.

"It may look fragile, but I doubt you could break it without a Druid's power. As for what would happen if you did, well, I don't know, but I wouldn't try it."

Penny felt the friendly presence of Simon enter her mind.

Penny, the red man is out and causing more mischief.

Where?

He's in the park with the big trees. He's lighting a fire!

Watch him but keep a safe distance. Don't let him see you. He's very dangerous.

He will not see me. I am Cait Sith.

"I'm sorry, Mrs. Cadogan, but we've got to leave . . . right now."

"What are you talking about?" Duncan said.

"Simon's found the *Coch Coblyn*. He's in Schoen Park, and he's starting a fire!"

"Sorry, Grandma, I'll try and explain later."

"I understand, dearie, your friend Penny's a *dawnus*, and Simon is her familiar."

Penny and Duncan just stared at his grandmother.

After a moment, Mrs. Cadogan placed a hand on each of their shoulders. "Don't worry, your secret's safe with me. Now, please be careful, dearies."

THE CLAXON'S WARBLING "EEEEEEOOOOO EEEEEEOOOOO" SCREECH synchronized perfectly with the flashing blue and white strobe light in the back of the U-Haul. The combination nearly knocked Fred Barnes out of his seat. He scrambled to maintain his balance while simultaneously trying to cover his ears with his hands.

"What in blazes is that?"

"An alarm." Kolchak leaned over to the console and flipped several switches, silencing the claxon but leaving the strobe light on.

"I know it's an alarm, but what's it an alarm for?" The sound of the claxon still echoed in Fred's ears even though the warbling had stopped.

"Did you notice the curved roof over the back of the truck?"

Fred pulled his hands off his ears and aggressively worked his jaw. "Yeah, I just figured it was for aerodynamics. You know, to improve yer gas mileage."

"I suppose it might do that, too, but that's not its main purpose. It's a protective cover for an antenna that detects paranormal energy waves."

"Cool, but why the annoying alarm and flashing light?"

"I usually turn the antenna on as a background process while I'm doing something else. I use the strobe and alarm to let me know if the computer's detected something. I only turn on the claxon when I'm resting in the front cab. I must've forgotten to turn it off this time. Sorry about that."

"Why's it so loud? Are ya goin' deaf? 'Cause if ya aren't, then just a few seconds of that thing and ya will be."

"That's another feature I should've thought more about. See, the antenna's pretty sensitive, and sometimes it misreads everyday things as paranormal."

"Okay, but that still doesn't explain why it's got to be so loud."

"Because it's sensitive; stuff like Wi-Fi hotspots, low flying aircraft, and even changing traffic lights can set it off. In this town, there's an awful lot of background noise, so I set the detection point at the highest level. Unfortunately, the alarm's tied into the detector on a proportional basis, so the higher the detected energy, the louder the alarm."

Fred rolled his eyes.

"Again, I'm sorry, but don't you know what this means?"

Fred shook his head.

"It means we've probably got our third interaction!"

"Well, what are we sitting around for?"

"Just because we've detected the energy, doesn't mean we know where to find the source."

"That's a fine how-do-ya-do. All that racket and we don't even know where to go."

"Normally I'd move the truck to several locations, take new readings, and use triangulation to find the epicenter of the activity. Unfortunately, that takes time."

"Isn't there a faster way?"

"Maybe. You'd have to stay back here and watch the monitors while I drive. We could open the cabin window, and you could tell me which way to go."

"Kinda like that old kids' game where you hide somethin' and you say 'warmer' or 'colder' as the person moves around the room?"

"That's right."

"Sounds like a plan to me."

Kolchak quickly showed Fred how to track the signal strength with the computer and took his place in the truck's cabin. After buckling up, he opened the sliding window between the cab and the back. "Make sure you secure yourself before we get moving," he yelled back to his friend.

"Will do."

Turning back to the front, Kolchak turned on the engine and hit the gas to accelerate out of the library parking lot onto Elm Street. As he did, he heard, "Aiyee!" from the back of the truck, followed closely by a loud thump and a lower-pitched grunt. Turning back toward the open window, Kolchak yelled, "Hey Fred, there's a locking screw on the bottom of the chair that'll keep it from sliding along the track while we're driving."

"Uh, yeah . . . uh, I found it . . . thanks," Fred said breathlessly.

"Sorry about that, Chief," Pandora said in a perfect imitation of Maxwell Smart.

"Can't you just shush that bird!"

Switching to the German accent of Kaos Agent Siegfried, Pandora replied, "Zis is Kaos! Vee dun't 'shush' here!"

Doing his best to suppress a laugh, Kolchak shouted back through the window, "We're coming up on Sycamore . . . which way do we turn?"

31

CONCEALED WITHIN A DENSE THICKET, SIMON WATCHED AS THE strange, little red man carried bundles of sticks from the forest and stacked them against the largest oak tree in the park. Careful not to touch it, he piled the sticks at the base of the giant tree until it was completely encircled with kindling. The red man stepped back from the trunk, wriggled his fingers, and spoke some words in a language Simon recognized as Welsh. He didn't understand them, but he didn't need to.

The red man cupped his palms and spoke a few more words. As soon as the last word escaped his lips, a bright red ball of flame sprang to life between his palms. Through its glow, Simon saw a twisted smile cross the red man's face.

While Simon contacted Penny to update her, the red man sent the ball of flame through the air toward the tree. With a gentleness belying the malevolence of its purpose, the super-heated ball danced around the kindling circle, igniting the tinder in several places before returning to the red man. There, it settled in the cup of his palms. With a soft puff of his breath, the red man dismissed the ball of fire which dutifully winked out of existence.

"I CAN SEE A REDDISH GLOW OFF TO OUR LEFT!" KOLCHAK SHOUTED through the sliding window.

From the back, Fred yelled back, "Okay, take a left at the next street . . . the epicenter oughta be almost immediately to our right."

The truck turned sharply left and continued for a few seconds before coming to a complete stop.

"Hey Fred, would you pass me one of the K-IIs?" Kolchak yelled through the window.

Fred unstrapped himself from the chair and looked around the back of the truck.

"Well, what do ya see?" he shouted.

Ignoring his friend's question, Kolchak shoved his hand through the window into the back of the truck and barked, "I'm not sure, but can you hurry up with that K-II? I don't want to miss any of this."

Fred found the portable electromagnetic field meter and placed it in Kolchak's hand.

Unable to wait for his friend to open the liftgate, Fred poked his head through the window into the front cabin. A dim reddish glow filled the cabin. Fred saw the source—a raging column of dark red flames engulfed a towering oak tree in the park. He immediately recognized the tree. "That's the Founder's Oak! Someone's set fire to the Founder's Oak!"

"Don't you think you're overreacting, Fred?"

"No, no you don't understand! That's the Founder's tree! PJ Piper and Walter Schoen settled their feud over this valley right under that tree. It's got a commemorative plaque and everythin'."

"Now calm down, Fred. Take a closer look at the fire. Does anything look funny to you?" Kolchak asked.

"What could possibly be funny about the town's heritage goin' up in flames? That's the problem with you big city folks . . . you've got no respect for traditions."

"Sorry, Fred, bad choice of words. I meant strange, not humorous. Notice how the flames are all red? Flames normally contain reds, yellows, and oranges, but other than some small bits around the trunk, that fire's mostly red."

"Who cares what color the flames are. Why are we arguin' while the Founder's Oak's goin' up in smoke?"

"If the tree's on fire, where's the smoke? A normal fire consumes the wood, leaving ash and embers. A fire big enough to consume that tree should be throwing up all kinds of smoke and sparks, but there's hardly any. I bet when we step outside, we won't hear anything either. There's something different about that fire."

"Hey, yer right!" Fred nodded. "There ain't enough smoke. Why do you suppose that is?"

"I don't know, but according to the K-II, the area's flooded with paranormal energy."

"Let me guess, it matches the signature from the auditorium and Ms. Johnson's."

Kolchak pointed his index finger at Fred. "Give that man a prize."

"Whadda we gonna do?"

"You call in some back-up, and while it's on the way, we'll collect some more data."

"Right-o."

AS PENNY AND DUNCAN LEFT HIS HOUSE FOR SCHOEN PARK, PENNY felt the familiar touch of Simon's thoughts in her mind.

The little red man has ignited the kindling, but the flames are not burning the big oak tree.

What do you mean, they're not burning the tree? That's what flames do; they burn things.

There are two kinds of flames in the fire. The smaller ones are like the flames that your father makes in the brick box with glass doors in your house. They are concentrated around the base of the tree. The bigger ones are like the flames that the lady in black made on top of the cold rock in the glade, and they are spreading throughout the tree.

You mean the flames from the summoning fire that Ms. Morgan used to wake the Crom Dubh?

Yes, but instead of including three colors, these are only red.

"I think we should run," Penny said out loud.

"Why? What's happening?" Duncan asked.

"The *Coch Coblyn's* set a summoning fire at the base of the Founder's Oak."

Even at a drop-dead run, it still took several minutes to reach the entrance gate to Schoen Park. Before they entered, Simon contacted Penny again.

The man with the small blue bird and his friend with the metal badge on his shirt have just arrived near the tree.

What are they doing?

They're carrying boxes with lights. They're pointing them at the tree and around the . . . Reaow! screeched Simon telepathically . . . and physically.

Simon! Simon, are you all right? Simon, where are you?

Penny searched her mind for some trace of her guardian and friend but found none.

"What was that screech?" asked Duncan.

"I think it was Simon. One moment we were sharing thoughts, and the next he was gone!" she cried.

"I can't sense him. Can you?" Duncan asked.

Penny shook her head.

"Okay, maybe he's hiding from something. What was the last thing he said?"

"He said Deputy Barnes and Kolchak were at the Founder's Oak using some of their high-tech gear."

"Nothing about the *Coch Coblyn*?"

"No. Do you think the *Coch Coblyn* attacked him? Maybe we can't sense him because it did something to him!" she screamed.

Penny turned to rush into the park, but Duncan grabbed her shoulder and held her back.

"Let go of me! Simon's in there, and he needs our help!"

Grabbing both her shoulders now, he looked her straight in the eye.

"Listen to me. We're going to help him, but we won't do him any good if we get ourselves into trouble, too."

"Okay, okay, you're right. You can let go of me. Now, what's your plan?"

"HEY, DID YOU HEAR THAT INHUMAN SCREECH?" KOLCHAK ASKED.

"Oh, it's probably just a rabbit," Fred said.

"A rabbit, are you *sure*?"

"Yeah, park's full of 'em. Local cats come in here and hunt 'em all the time. A screamin' rabbit'll make a sound like a person. Civilians mistake 'em for people gettin' attacked all the time. If I had a dime for every rabbit false alarm . . ."

"You'd what?"

Fred shrugged. "Well, I'd have an awful lot of dimes."

"How are your readings?" Kolchak asked.

Fred looked down at his scanner. "I'm still gettin' a strong red reading from near the tree. I had a yellow one from somewhere deeper in the park, but it disappeared just after that screech."

"Are you suggesting a demonically possessed rabbit?" Kolchak asked and smiled at his friend.

Faking a British accent, Fred replied, "Aye, ever hear of the Killer Rabbit of Caerbannog, a foul-tempered, nasty rodent with big pointy teeth." Fred placed his right hand on his chin and flexed his fingers like giant teeth.

Kolchak laughed. "*Monty Python and the Holy Grail*, what a classic movie. It cracks me up just thinking about it. By the way, that's got to be the worst British accent I've ever heard."

"Well, I don't get much time to practice here in Piper Falls. Now, how 'bout your readings?"

Kolchak stifled his laughter and looked down at his K-II which was sweeping the park in the opposite direction of Fred's. "I think you should take a look at this." He pointed to the scanner's screen.

"Hey, that looks like the same blue color from Ms. Johnson's and the auditorium."

Putting his finger to his lips, Kolchak whispered, "You're right, Freddy my boy, and just like Ms. Johnson's, it's coming late to the scene."

"Can you tell where it is?"

"Well, it keeps popping in and out of the screen, but each time it reappears, it gets a little closer. Right now, I'd say it's roughly fifty yards that way." Kolchak pointed away from the path.

"That's the thickest part of the forest in the park."

"No trails?"

"Some of the more adventurous Nordic skiers bushwhack in there, but there's no groomed paths. Is that important?"

"Well, unless our blue visitor's a Nordic skier out for a little night training, I'd say it's a good bet that whatever's moving toward us through there is up to no good."

PENNY'S BOOT SNAGGED ON A ROOT BURIED UNDER THE SNOW. She only avoided a frozen face-plant by grabbing onto a small tree. Unfortunately, the tree she grabbed was barely up to the task. Bending under her weight, it smacked into the boughs of an evergreen in front of her. Shaken by the tree, the evergreen released its accumulated snow right on top of Duncan's head.

"Hey, what's the big idea?" Duncan whispered. He shook the snow off his head trying, with mixed success, to keep it from sliding inside his coat and down his back.

"Sorry." She hoped he didn't see the laughter in her smile. "How much further?"

"Well, the glow of the summoning fire's getting pretty bright; if we just get around these trees, we ought to be able to see what's going on. Have you been able to sense Simon?"

Penny extended her senses again, but she couldn't find her *Cait Sith* guardian.

Telepathically, she called out to him but received no reply. She turned to Duncan and shook her head.

"Okay, let's get closer to the summoning fire; maybe it's interfering with the link between you two."

Before they took another step, a voice from behind called out, "Don't move! I'm with the Sheriff's department! Keep your hands where I can see them!"

Penny and Duncan both froze and raised their hands into the air. Penny heard the crackle of an exchange over the police radio but couldn't make out any of the words from the far end.

"Okay, you two, keep your hands up, and turn around . . . slowly."

As Penny and Duncan followed the instructions, Deputy Barnes and his friend Kolchak entered the scene. "Good work, Volunteer Deputy Pyle! Why don't you head back to the Founder's Oak and see if the fire crew needs any help." Deputy Barnes said.

"Are you sure you don't need me here?"

Fred walked closer to him and said in a quiet voice, "Nah, we got reason ta believe that this incident may be connected to a string of vandalism and crimes that me and Kolchak have been workin' on as a special detail for the Sheriff."

"Really? You think these two kids are connected to the recent pranks around town?"

"Shush, we don't know fer sure. They're probably not acting alone, and we don't want other suspects to know what we know. Get my meanin'?"

The volunteer deputy nodded. "I got it, Deputy Barnes. My lips are sealed." He pulled his thumb and forefinger across his lips to emphasize the point. "You need anything else from me?"

"Yeah, can you give me the keys to the squad car?" He accepted the keys from the volunteer deputy. "Now remember, mum's the word." For emphasis, he brought his fingers to his closed lips and twisted a pretend key, which he promptly threw over his shoulder.

The young man nodded and left the scene.

Fred turned to Kolchak. "Pyle's a good kid, just a bit green. With a little seasonin', he'll make a fine lawman." He turned back to Penny and Duncan and took a good look at them for the first time. "What are you two doin' here?"

"You know these two?" asked Kolchak.

"Yeah, that's Penny Preston and Duncan O'Brien."

"Aren't they the same kids from the Johnson video?" Kolchak asked. Fred nodded.

"Mighty big coincidence finding them at both incidents, don't you think, Fred?"

"You know, come to think of it, they was also involved in the capture of Ms. Morgan."

"You mean the woman found with the ancient Druid texts?"

"Well, now that I remember it, she wasn't found with the books or the ritualistic stuff. The FBI and the British detective found the stolen goods with these kids and their teacher."

"Is *that* so? Well, things are getting curiouser and curiouser." Motioning Fred to come closer, he whispered, "I think we should take them in for questioning."

Careful to keep his eye on Duncan and Penny, Fred said, "But they're just kids."

"True, but we did find them acting suspiciously at a crime scene, and we have evidence of their presence at an earlier incident that's likely related to this one. I'm not saying they're involved, but it sure seems like they must know something."

"You may be able to take kids to jail on such flimsy evidence in the big city, but not here in Piper Falls."

Kolchak shook his head. "I'm not suggesting we throw them in jail."

"Just what are you suggesting then?"

"We did find them in a potentially dangerous situation, right?"

"Yeah."

"Okay, so why not take them home in the patrol car? It's for their own safety. I mean, look at them, the boy's covered in snow, and the girl looks like her dog just died."

"So, you don't think Penny and Duncan are involved?"

Kolchak shrugged. "They might be, but only as witnesses. I just checked my K-II, and the paranormal energy has dropped back down to residual levels. We've got all the data we're going to get. Whatever's going on here is no longer a paranormal event."

"Yer right, Pyle and the fire crew should be able to handle the clean-up. The sooner we get back to the truck, the sooner we can analyze the data."

"Sounds like a plan to me, Deputy." Kolchak nodded and slapped his friend playfully on the back.

While Deputy Barnes and Kolchak were trying to decide what to do, Penny slid her foot over and tapped Duncan's. "What should we do?"

"I don't know."

"What about Simon? He's in there, and he's in trouble," Penny said.

Duncan shrugged, "I know, but we can't just run away from the police. Maybe we can learn something from Kolchak."

"How can he help us?"

"He's got one of his paranormal detectors; maybe he found something."

Before Penny could respond, Deputy Barnes turned back to Penny and Duncan, who still had their hands up. "Okay, uh, Miss

Preston and Mr. O'Brien . . . you can put your hands down now . . .
I'm sorry for keepin' you waitin' . . . but it's been a strange night.
Why don't you come with me, and I'll give you a ride home in the
patrol car?"

"Are we in some kind of trouble?" Penny asked.

"No, no, of course not. It's just that there's been another prank.
Someone set a fire at the base of the Founder's Oak. But don't worry,
it's under control. We're just gatherin' up the evidence."

"What's Mr. Kolchak doing with that ghost detector?" Duncan
pointed to the K-II. "Do you think ghosts were involved?" Duncan
asked.

Without thinking, Fred glanced at his friend.

"Let's just say that we've got reason to believe that recent strange
events, including this fire, might have a paranormal connection.
Did either of you two notice anything strange on your way here?"

Both shook their heads vigorously.

They reached the patrol car and took their places in the back
seat. Deputy Barnes opened the driver's-side door and was about to
get in when a loud whirring sound came from Kolchak's K-II.

"What is it?" Fred asked.

"I don't know," Kolchak replied, checking his instruments. "I've
never seen anything like it. It's coming from near the Founder's
Oak. Why don't you give Pyle a call and see what's going on."

"Sheriff Two to Volunteer One, Sheriff Two to Volunteer One,"
Barnes said into the radio. His call was greeted with nothing but
static. He repeated the call but again, received static as a response.
"I'm not gettin' any reply. Do you think somethin's happened?"

"If it was only the K-II or just the radio, I'd say it was just a
glitch, but with both of them going crazy, that's just too much of a
coincidence for me."

"Yer right; we'd better get over there."

"What about them?" Kolchak asked.

"They'll be safest if we leave them in the patrol car. I'll lock the doors, just in case." Deputy Barnes leaned down and ducked his head into the car. "Somethin's come up back at the Founder's Oak. It's probably nothin', but we need to check it out. Just sit tight in the patrol car." Without waiting for a response, he closed the door.

Penny heard the click of the doors being locked and saw the deputy and Kolchak run into the park.

32

DUNCAN RAN HIS HAND ALONG THE SMOOTH INSIDE OF THE rear door.

"Hey, there's no door handle!"

"Of course, there isn't. We're in the back of a police car, where they put the *bad guys*."

"Oh yeah, do you think they left us back here on purpose?"

Penny furrowed her brow and looked at Duncan. "They may not know what's going on here, but they're suspicious. Deputy Barnes hasn't connected the dots, but his friend Kolchak's a little too close to the truth for me."

Just then, a shadow settled on the hood of the patrol car and began tapping the windshield with its beak. Having gotten their attention, it cackled, "This is a fine mess you've gotten yourselves into."

"Great to see you too, Master Poe. Give me a moment, and I'll get us out of here. I was waiting to make sure Deputy Barnes and Kolchak were far enough away so that we could make a clean getaway." Penny opened a small rift, reached through, and opened the patrol car door from the outside.

"Good, now that you're free we need to get moving. I created an energy yo-yo that will flicker in and out of the lower five dimensions for another few minutes before it winks out. I doubt we've got more than five minutes before the deputy gets back."

"We can leave after we find Simon," Penny said.

"I don't think that will be necessary," Master Poe responded.

"Look, I know you're in a hurry to leave before Deputy Barnes and Kolchak get back, but I don't really care. We came here because the *Coch Coblyn* created a summoning fire at the Founder's Oak. Simon was watching him. Then something happened, and we haven't heard from Simon since. We're not leaving until we find him," Penny said.

"I think you misunderstand me," Master Poe replied.

Before she could launch into her retort, Penny felt a familiar presence in her mind.

"Simon!" she screamed vocally before switching to telepathic communication. *Simon, you're here! Are you okay? We thought something had happened to you.*

Yes, I am fine. I am sorry to have worried you, but when the two men point the boxes with lights at me, I burn without flames. Simon arched his back and rubbed up against Penny's legs.

"What's he saying? What happened?" Duncan asked.

"The K-IIs hurt him."

"Ah, yes, the paranormal energy detection devices can interfere with the trans-dimensional energy flows of entities from the higher planes," Master Poe said.

"Then why don't they bother you, or Penny?" Duncan asked.

"The devices are calibrated to pick up energy from the *Bodach*, who, as I've mentioned, are from the fifth dimension, while I'm from the seventh. That difference enables me to avoid their interference. As for Penny, even though she's misaligned, she's a native of this dimension and should be immune to their interference. They can probably detect her if she's working in the higher dimensions, but that should be the extent of it."

"All right, don't take this the wrong way, but just exactly why did you show up here?" Penny asked.

"I've always liked the way you cut right to it, my dear, so I'll do the same. Myrdin has disappeared."

"What do you mean, disappeared?" Duncan asked.

"I mean that one minute he was there, and the next I couldn't find him. Whatever else would I mean?" cackled the raven. "By the way, the trans-dimensional yo-yo is winding down. How about we get moving, and I'll fill you in as we go."

"Sounds like a plan, but where are we going?" Penny asked.

"There's an old barn just outside of town."

"The Austin farm; it's been abandoned for years. What of it?"

"In addition to the summoning fire, we also detected the opening of a trans-dimensional rift just outside of town. It didn't last very long, but while it was open, we detected the *Teyrnwialen o Saith*."

"Are you sure?" Penny asked. "I didn't sense anything."

"As I said, it was very brief, and its signature was obscured by some sort of energy cloak. It was pure chance that I was flying close enough to notice it when it happened. We were going to investigate it together when the summoning fire flared up. Since we were closer to the barn and I can fly faster than Myrdin can walk, he continued on to the rift while I flew to the summoning fire."

MYRDIN AWOKE TO BLACKNESS AND A THROBBING HEADACHE. The incessant pounding in his head gave him a new appreciation for horseshoes, nails, or any other piece of iron caught between the blacksmith's hammer and the anvil. As his mind gradually awakened, he recognized that he was sitting on the ground leaning against a wooden post. He tried to bring his hands up to his temples to massage away the pulsing pain but couldn't. His hands were bound behind his back. He twisted and wriggled his wrists against their bindings, but other than chafing his skin, he achieved nothing. He opened his eyes and quickly squeezed them shut against the gauzy brightness of the room.

Keeping his eyes shut, he turned his head from side to side and listened. At first, he heard nothing, but gradually, he made out a muffled rhythmic sound. It seemed familiar, but the throbbing in his temples made it difficult to concentrate. He took a deep breath and let it out very slowly. He repeated the process, pushing the pain further and further into the background until it was little more than a dull ache at the edge of his consciousness. With his pain conquered, he focused on the rhythmic noise and quickly identified it as the sound of someone breathing. It was only one person, but was it another prisoner or his jailer?

Taking one more deep breath, he cautiously opened his eyes, letting them slowly adjust to the brightness of the room. As the yellow glow subsided, he identified several other large wooden posts, a dirt floor, and beams connecting the tops of the posts. The last thing he remembered was being outside the old Austin barn; it was obvious he was now inside it.

Near the center of the barn, surrounded by five burning candles, he found the source of the breathing sounds . . . and from the look of things, his captor. He was a rather nondescript man dressed in faded brown corduroy pants with a heavy plaid flannel shirt. He focused more closely on the man's face; the first thing Myrdin noticed was the man's eyes . . . one brown and one blue . . . just like Penny's!

Foreboding gripped Myrdin's heart even more tightly when he recognized the scepter in the man's hand. It was the *Teyrnwialen o Saith*.

The man spoke.

"Ah, it is good to see that you are coming around so quickly. I feared you might not awaken in time for the ritual. Not that it would change things, but an artisan such as myself does appreciate an audience."

"Who are you?" Myrdin asked.

"Yes, you're right. A proper introduction is in order. My name is Sobek. I'm the First Acolyte of the Amun-Ra."

"Who or what are the Amun-Ra?"

"Excuse my bluntness, but I have introduced myself, and I believe good manners require that you do the same."

"My name is Myrdin."

"Much better." Sobek smiled, exposing the crocodilian points of his teeth between his stretched lips. "I believe it is also customary in this culture to offer a hand at such times. Please forgive my slip in protocol, but I am afraid that will not be possible."

"You're standing in a pentagram." Myrdin only now noticed that the candles marked the points of a five-pointed star inscribed within a circle on the dirt floor.

"Yes, I see that some of the ancient learning has survived into these uncouth times, but then, I expected as much when I saw your ring."

Myrdin said nothing but felt for the ring with his fingers.

"Do not fear; I let you keep the ring. Five stones, that's very powerful. We did not make very many of those. Would you mind telling me how you came by it?"

Myrdin had no desire to feed the ego of his captor, but he needed more information if he hoped to escape. Whoever Sobek was, he was supremely confident, and over-confident people often disclose more than they should.

"My master gave it to me just before he was killed."

Sobek shook his head from side to side. "I am sorry to hear about your master's death, although judging by your age, that must have been a long time ago."

"Yes, I was just thirteen. May I ask you a question?"

"Of course."

"You said, 'we did not make very many of those.' Who did you mean by we?"

"I and my colleagues in the Amun-Ra."

His answer fed Myrdin's suspicion that Sobek was a time traveler, but from when? He pressed on for more information. "I don't mean to question your integrity, but how is that possible? My master received the ring when he finished his apprenticeship, as did his master before him, who in turn got it from his master, and so on, back many generations. Yet you appear younger than me."

Sobek smiled his crocodilian grin. "Would it surprise you to learn that I have lived nearly two of your centuries?"

Myrdin's eyes widened with genuine surprise, but he quickly recovered. "That still wouldn't make you old enough to have made the ring."

"You are correct, but what if I told you I was born more than six thousand years ago?"

This time, Myrdin's jaw dropped open.

"Yes, when your ancestors were nothing more than filth-covered, mud-hut dwelling, uncouth savages, my people had unlocked the secrets of the spirit world and built a fantastic civilization beyond your possible comprehension. Our crowning achievement was our unlocking of the Sekhem's power." He waved the *Teyrnwialen o Saith*. "With it, we created the lesser artifacts and devices, such as your ring. Using their power, we were not only masters of our domain but that of the spirits as well." Sobek's eyes glowed with the recollection of past glories.

"What happened?"

Sobek spat out a single word. "Scientists."

"It's been my experience that scientists have greatly improved the lot of mankind," Myrdin said.

"Improved the lot of mankind? And here I thought you might be an informed soul, but you're just another uncouth conjuror, aren't you."

"Perhaps you could enlighten me."

Sobek bobbed his head from side to side and shrugged.

"Secure in our mastery of the spirit universe, our people wandered from the straight path prescribed by the Amun-Ra. Their scientific heresy created the magneto drives which destabilized the balance and harmony of the universe. When they tried to correct their folly with the power of the Sekhem, the universe revolted at their sacrilege."

Sobek paused, his joy-filled recollection of his home was supplanted with a growing rage. His eyes narrowed, and his nostrils flared.

"The conveniences of the scientific heresy held the people in their steadfast grip. Even the leadership of the Amun-Ra failed to see the danger. We tried to warn them. We tried to protect them from themselves, but they could not hear our message."

Several tears rolled down his cheek and dripped onto the dirt floor of the barn as Sobek's emotions drove him from rage to anguish.

Ignoring his tears, he continued. "The earth itself rose up against our folly and cleared its surface of the indecency we had become. First, the ground shook and turned our buildings into piles of rubble. Then the earth belched forth its purifying fire, burning and burying the ruins. Finally, the sea rose up and scoured the land clean of the last remnants of our arrogance."

It was clear that Sobek was mad and near, if not already past, his breaking point. Myrdin still had no idea what was really going on or how to stop it. He needed to pull Sobek back from the brink. He needed to stall for time. "Yet you survived."

"Yes, I survived. I hoped that the people had learned their lesson, that they would repent their heresy, but I was wrong. They were unwilling to make the hard choices and sacrifices necessary to revitalize and preserve our culture. They not only continued with their science, but they chose to actively mingle with your uncouth ancestors. Everything that you are—your knowledge, your achievements, your very culture—has its roots in that repugnant intermingling of our scientific heresy with your crude forebears.

"I have spent the better part of three lifetimes traveling through time, fighting in vain to stem the tide of science. I was not entirely unsuccessful, but for every victory over the likes of Galileo or Darwin, there were dozens of defeats at the hands of Newton, da Vinci, Tesla, Curie, and countless others.

"However, just as Elpis, the spirit of hope, remained at the bottom of Pandora's jar, so too did my hope persist. It was small and weak, but it survived. And while it lived, I continued my relentless search for the only thing that could raise my hope to reality and stem the tide of scientific abomination." Sobek raised the Sekhem to eye level and pointed it at Myrdin. "And now I've finally found it. With the Sekhem's power, I will fix everything. I will finally be able to rid the world of science!"

"Inconceivable! You can no more erase science than Pandora could return evil to the jar."

"That's where you're mistaken, my uncouth friend. With the Sekhem's power, I will travel back to a time before the cataclysm destroyed my people. I will eliminate Tarhuya and her closest disciples and assume leadership of the Amun-Ra. Without the temptation of science, and with a revitalized Amun-Ra to guide the people, our civilization will not only survive, but we will also cleanse the earth of your uncouth ancestors. Nothing will stand in the way of our blissful reign!"

Myrdin took solace in knowing that his plan could never succeed.

He hadn't understood all the math, but when he'd wanted to go back and save Abigail, Master Poe had proven to him that it was impossible.

No longer concerned with sending the clearly mad Sobek over the edge of sanity, Myrdin said, "Your plan will never work. Without an open portal to the higher dimensions, time travel into the past is impossible!"

Sobek smiled his toothy grin and shook his head from side to side. "Ah, my uncouth friend, you're forgetting about the unique power of the Sekhem. With the right sacrifice, the Sekhem can channel the proper energy from the spirit world!"

Master Poe was right! The Sekhem was a *Conglfaen*, but even a *Conglfaen* only worked during one of the eight natural confluences . . . at the beginning of the seasons and their mid-points.

Suddenly, Myrdin remembered a snippet from the morning news. A groundhog in Pennsylvania had seen his shadow, so there'd be six more weeks of winter or some such nonsense. That didn't matter. What did matter was that today was the mid-point of winter, or Imbolc, as the Celts called it. How could things possibly get worse?

"I must prepare for the sacrifice," Sobek said.

Myrdin gulped. "What do you mean . . . sacrifice?"

"To safely use the power of the Sekhem to invoke the ritual, I must feed it the life essence of someone gifted with the second sight. It has been a long time since the last feeding, and the Sekhem demands a powerful sacrifice. Fortunately, I have found just such a person. Even now, she approaches us."

"She?!" screamed Myrdin. "You're going to feed Penny to that, that, thing?"

"Yes, I believe that was her name. I must prepare for her and her friends' arrival."

Sobek began chanting in a language that Myrdin didn't understand.

Myrdin's mind raced through what he'd just heard. Friends, Sobek had said.

At least Penny wasn't coming alone. Of course! Master Poe must've found her and led her here. No doubt Simon and Duncan were coming, too. The Sekhem might reach into the upper planes, but even with that, Sobek would be no match for Master Poe. Myrdin's fear subsided. He even managed to smile.

Finished with his chant, Sobek looked down on the smiling Myrdin.

"You do not think I can handle the bird spirit, do you?"

"Even with the Sekhem, he's more than a match for you. I'm going to enjoy watching him scatter your atoms across the universe!"

"You are probably right . . . if I planned to fight him. But of course, I do not. You see, this old barn is made of solid oak. I know what you are thinking. He could come in through the dirt floor or one of the many gaps in the walls. A very good point, but not likely since I reinforced the building with three loops of silver wire backed by an exclusion incantation. No, the only person entering the barn will be the sacrifice." Sobek laughed and barred his teeth in a crocodilian smile.

"You're insane!"

"THERE'S THE BARN. WHAT'S THE PLAN?" DUNCAN ASKED.
Hovering a few feet overhead, Master Poe said, "I can't read anything inside the barn. What about you?" he asked Penny.

"There's something there, but it's hazy like I'm looking through a thick fog bank."

"What about Simon? Can he detect anything?" Master Poe asked.

I cannot see through the fog, but I can sense a presence on the other side.

Is it the Coch Coblyn?

I saw the strange, little red man come out of fog earlier today on the far side of town, but it is not his presence I sense. I recognize the five-stoned ring that the gray man wears.

Are you sure Mr. Myrdin's in the barn?

I cannot see the gray man through the fog, but I am certain that his ring is in the wooden building. I am sorry that I cannot tell you more.

Don't be sorry, that's better than either of us could do. She reached down to scratch Simon behind his ears, causing him to purr.

"His vision's better than ours, but it's still a bit blurry. He can't see Mr. Myrdin, but he can see his ring."

"What about the *Coch Coblyn*?" Duncan asked.

"No sign of him, but Simon did see the *Coch Coblyn* emerge from a similar patch of fog earlier today."

"Well, it seems like we've come to the right place," Duncan said.

"You're probably correct, but something about this situation ruffles my feathers the wrong way."

"What do you mean? We know the *Coch Coblyn* created the summoning fire, then left. We can't find him, and the barn is hidden by the same type of fog he hid in earlier. On top of that, it's the same barn that Mr. Myrdin was headed toward, and Simon's sensed his ring inside. It seems like a pretty straightforward case to me," Duncan said.

"All good points . . . that's exactly what worries me," the raven said.

"You think it's a trap?" Penny asked.

"The thought did cross my mind. Don't you find it rather suspicious that we can't detect anything in the barn except Myrdin's ring? We don't even know if he's in there. There's a chance that the ring is an illusion to trick us into trying to rescue him and thus spring the trap."

"I see your point, but what choice do we have?" Penny asked.

Duncan spoke up.

"A friend once reminded me that you never desert a friend. If there's even a small chance to help him, then you do whatever you can until you can't do it anymore."

"I'm sure your friend meant well, but sentimentality's a poor substitute for facts," Master Poe said.

Penny gave Duncan a knowing smile.

"Mr. Myrdin was that friend, and it's what he told us when we thought we'd lost you just over six weeks ago. We followed his advice, and it worked out pretty well." Duncan said.

"Simon's sensing Mr. Myrdin's ring is our best lead. We've got to follow it. If it's a trap, at least we'll go in prepared," Penny said.

"You're both set on this course. Nothing I can say will dissuade you?" Master Poe asked. Penny and Duncan nodded. "Very well, have either of you ever been in this barn?"

"I have, why?" Duncan asked.

"Does it have a dirt floor or a wooden floor?" Master Poe asked.

"Dirt."

"Good," pointing his beak at Penny and Simon, he said, "the three of us will—"

"What do you mean the three of you?" Duncan interrupted.

"That barn is made of oak, that's one of the reasons we can't perceive what's inside. It also means we can't use a multi-dimensional rift to enter through the walls," Master Poe said.

"It's still got a door. Why don't we use it?" Duncan said.

"No doubt that's what our enemy wants us to do, but we're not going to oblige him. The three of us will create a dimensional rift through the ground and enter the barn through the floor."

"Avoiding any trap focused on the door," Penny said.

"Precisely," Master Poe said.

"What about me? I'm not sitting this one out."

"Of course not, once we're safely inside, we'll defuse the trap and let you in through the barn door. Agreed?" the raven said.

Duncan remained silent for a moment. "You promise to let me in as soon as you can?"

Penny punched him playfully in the shoulder. "I wouldn't have it any other way."

Duncan rubbed his shoulder. "All right, I agree."

"Good. Now, it'll be best if we all pop in at once, so if you would be so kind as to give us a count of three, we'll be on our way," Master Poe said.

Duncan nodded. "One, two, three!"

On three, his companions disappeared from our universe. Thanks to his amulet, Duncan saw their shimmering shadowy images before they plunged through the earth toward the barn. Once they were underground, he lost track of them. Sighing, he waited a minute and began to walk toward the barn door.

He hadn't taken more than a few steps when he felt a deep chill on his back. Quickly, he turned around to see Master Poe and Simon reappear on the surface.

"What happened?"

"It appears we were right to expect a trap," Master Poe said.

"Where's Penny?" Duncan asked.

Looking quickly from side to side, the raven replied, "She must be in the barn."

PENNY OPENED HER RIFT AND SHIFTED OUT OF PHASE WITH THE universe. Her companions did the same. The three of them descended into the earth and moved toward the barn. The obscuring fog, which extended into the higher planes, thickened as they neared the barn. Penny's sense of her companions became fuzzier and fuzzier. By the time she was directly below the barn, she'd lost all contact with them. She called out *Simon!* over their shared telepathic link, but her *Cait Sith* protector didn't answer.

Despite a growing foreboding, she continued through the extra-dimensional fog, which gradually began to thin, until she saw a multi-colored star shining overhead. Mr. Myrdin's ring! While she couldn't see him, she did detect the aura of his presence. It was still blurry, but sensing him renewed her spirit and removed her doubts. She accelerated up through the earth and emerged out of the floor into the dim glow of the barn's interior . . . right in front of Mr. Myrdin.

"Ahh!" she gasped. He sat at her feet, leaning against one of the barn's support posts with his hands tied behind his back.

"It's nice to see you too, Penny, but I think you'd better turn around," her mentor said.

She didn't want to turn away. She wanted to help her friend. That's why they came, to save him, but something in Mr. Myrdin's eyes frightened her. Against her strongest desire, she turned around.

"Ah, Miss Preston," Sobek said with a sinister smile, revealing his crocodilian teeth. "I gather you weren't expecting to see me. Well, I've been anticipating our meeting for longer than you can imagine."

Penny glanced to each side and extended her extra-dimensional senses, searching for her friends. Other than Mr. Myrdin, who was in no position to help, she was alone with Sobek, who stood in a candlelit pentagram that had been etched on the barn floor. And he was brandishing the *Teyrnwialen o Saith*.

"Looking for someone?" he asked with a snicker.

Penny remained silent.

She looked toward him and stared directly into his mismatched eyes, the mirror image of her own, trying, but failing, to veil her surprise and her fear.

"No need to confirm it. I know about your feline protector and the spirit-inhabited raven, but I chose not to invite them to our little meeting. Other than your gray-haired friend, who was necessary to encourage your attendance, ours must be an exclusive meeting. If their presence was required, I would have invited them. I thought that even the uncouth had more common courtesy than to come uninvited. I find uninvited guests to be quite tedious. So, I took the precaution of preventing their arrival."

"You're the one who stole the *Teyrnwialen o Saith*," Penny said, her voice sounding stronger than she thought it would.

"I beg to differ. It is impossible to steal what is rightfully yours. As First Acolyte of the Amun-Ra, the Sekhem," Sobek raised the *Teyrnwialen o Saith*, "belongs to me. I alone am entitled to its power, and I shall use that power to eliminate scientific heresy and restore my people to their rightful place. That will, of course, alter your past and eliminate your uncouth civilization, but in all honesty, no one will really miss it." He laughed an evil-filled chortle.

Keeping one eye on Sobek, Penny said over her shoulder, "What's he talking about?"

"He plans to go back in time and change the past," Mr. Myrdin said.

"That's not possible, is it?"

"Normally no, but today is Imbolc, winter's mid-season day, which is a natural confluence. If he sacrifices a strong enough essence to the *Teyrnwialen o Saith*, it could be possible."

"Sacrifice?"

Before Mr. Myrdin could answer, Sobek said, "Sacrifice is such a tainted word. Think of it more as your honorable contribution to the improvement of humanity."

"You're crazy if you think I'll willingly offer you one drop of my life's essence."

"I had hoped you would be more reasonable, but I am not surprised. After all, you are uncouth." Just as he finished, Sobek lowered the *Teyrnwialen o Saith* and a blazing bolt of blue higher-dimensional energy shot across the barn at Penny.

With a flick of her wrist, Penny swatted the bolt out of the air, deflecting it into the floor of the barn. She had no time to savor her victory as Sobek began rapidly firing bolts of higher-dimensional energy from the colored gemstones of the *Teyrnwialen o Saith*. Swinging both arms like a whirling dervish, Penny knocked yellow, green, blue, purple, red, and orange energy bolts aside.

As Sobek sent the bolts faster and faster toward her, Penny opened a small rift and sent the energy into the upper dimensions. Recognizing that she needed to take the offensive, Penny raised her hand and formed a cup with her fingers and palm. A blue energy bolt struck her palm, driving her arm back. Penny curled her fingers around the bolt, shaping its energy into a blue ball of fire. Gripping the ball tightly between her first two fingers and her thumb, she hurled a fastball straight at Sobek's head.

Sobek raised the scepter and uttered a few words in some lost language. A shimmering force field of higher-dimensional energy surrounded him. The energy ball struck the field. Multi-colored fractal patterns raced across the field's spherical surface, harmlessly dissipating the ball's energy.

"Very well done. I commend your teacher." Sobek nodded toward Mr. Myrdin. "It is indeed a shame that there are no other suitable sacrificial candidates at hand. You would have made a superb disciple for my new Amun-Ra."

"I would never join a twisted cult of overzealous nutjobs!"

"Probably not." Sobek moved the scepter to his left hand and made several gestures in the air with his right. At the same time, he began chanting in a language that Penny didn't recognize. He seemed to be repeating a pattern. Penny risked a glance over her shoulder toward Mr. Myrdin.

"It's a summoning incantation."

"For what?" she asked.

Mr. Myrdin shrugged. "I don't know, but we're about to find out."

The extra-dimensional fog streamed into the room, concentrating itself just outside of Sobek's force field. As it continued to coalesce, Sobek changed his chant and altered his gestures. The amorphous fog took on a vaguely humanoid form, its details slowly becoming clear.

It stood more than twelve feet tall and was covered in scales that varied in color from light green on its torso to dark blue on its two stumpy legs. Instead of two arms, a single tentacle-like appendage grew from the center of its chest, like an overly long elephant's trunk with a three-pronged claw at the end. Two curving horns protruded from the top of its reptilian head, which featured a broad mouth and a single eye beneath a bony brow ridge.

"It can't be," Mr. Myrdin said.

"It can't be what?" Penny asked without taking her eyes off the solidifying creature.

"A *Fomoire*; it's a powerful entity from the depths of the nether planes. The only restraint on its power is the control of the summoner."

"How do I fight a *Fomoire*?"

"You don't. You can't defeat it. All you can do is return it to the depths from which it came."

"Okay, how do I do that?"

He shuddered. "Once it enters our universe, the only way to send it back is to feed it a human soul."

Penny heard the loud crackle of higher-dimensional energy discharging into the atmosphere. She turned to see the *Fomoire* throwing itself against Sobek's energy field.

"What's happening? I thought entities had to obey the command of their summoners," she said.

"They do, but only after the summoner establishes control. The *Fomoire* come from one of the most alien aspects of the multiverse and are very hard to control. Being in our dimension causes them great pain; all they want to do is leave. They know they need a soul to return home, and their first instinct is to attack their summoner to get it. If the summoner has any weakness in his defenses, the *Fomoire* will find it and feed on his soul."

"Any chance that Sobek loses?" she asked.

An overwhelming high-pitched wail of anguish filled the barn. The piercing sound reverberated through Penny's entire body so powerfully that she had to lean against a support post to keep from falling.

"I gather that's not the cry of victory?" she said.

"Not ours," replied Mr. Myrdin.

"Any last advice?"

"No doubt Sobek commanded the *Fomoire* to capture you for the promise of my soul. I suggest you offer it my soul without the bother of having to fight you first. If it accepts, you'll still be left with Sobek, but at least the *Fomoire* will be gone."

"Absolutely not; that's out of the question. I came here to rescue you, not sacrifice you!" She said.

"I'm not exactly thrilled about the idea of becoming a martyr either, but I think it's our only chance."

"There's got to be another way," Penny insisted. "If I weaken Sobek's defenses, would the *Fomoire* turn on him?"

"Yes, but if the *Fomoire* couldn't beat them, what makes you think that you can."

"Don't underestimate me," she said with a smile. "Sobek must be pushing his limits to control the *Fomoire* and maintain his defenses. Maybe I can be the straw that breaks the camel's back."

"Perhaps, but promise me that if you're not, you'll sacrifice me." Penny said nothing.

"Promise me!" Mr. Myrdin insisted.

Penny looked away and nodded her head ever so slightly.

"Good, now remember, the *Fomoire* is trying to capture you and deliver you alive, so use that to your advantage."

Penny faced the *Fomoire* which had backed away from Sobek's force field. Using its tentacle, it leaned in a tripod stance toward Sobek. Safe within his pentagram, Sobek continued to gesture and speak in an unintelligible language, but there was no mistaking his final gesture in which he pointed directly at Penny and back at himself.

The *Fomoire* swung its tentacle around and planted its sharp talons into the barn floor. Using the clawed end as a pivot point, it lifted the rest of its body into the air and swung around to one side. It repeated the process to the opposite side for its next step. After just three of the bizarre ground-swinging sidesteps, the *Fomoire* was close enough to attack Penny.

Standing on its small legs, it swung the tentacle along the ground and tried to knock Penny's feet out from under her. She easily leapt over the first pass but was nearly caught by the surprisingly quick backswing. It didn't connect, but she had to leap awkwardly. She fell to the ground.

Faster than she imagined possible, the tentacle rose vertically, but before it could deliver its paralyzing blow, the barn filled with a thunderous explosion. A brilliant blue shockwave of energy spread around the exterior walls of the barn and the poised tentacle paused. The brief hesitation saved Penny. She rolled out of the way and quickly got to her feet as the talon struck the ground where she had just been.

Another swing, this one at her waist level, forced her to drop and roll again. She anticipated this ploy and rolled toward one of the loft's support beams. The *Fomoire's* swing went over her head and struck the beam with a loud thwack. The force of the blow shattered the beam.

Fortunately, Penny wasn't under the loft when the beam snapped. The *Fomoire* wasn't so lucky . . . the loft crashed down on top of it, burying it in heavy debris.

Penny used the opportunity to move away from her attacker and catch her breath. She felt something in her pocket and pulled out the small statue of the *Coch Coblyn*. Its trans-dimensional eyes sparkled, and she thought she heard the word *Help!* in her mind. She looked to the collapsed loft and saw the *Fomoire's* tentacle making steady progress in clearing the pile. She had only a few moments before it freed itself and renewed its attack. She had been lucky to survive this long and knew that eventually, her luck would fail. She looked to Mr. Myrdin and thought of the promise he'd extracted from her just moments before. Would she offer his soul to the *Fomoire*? Could she do it to save the world? Even if she could, how would she defeat Sobek?

She looked down at the figurine. Again, its eyes twinkled, and she distinctly heard the word *Help!* in her mind. With sudden understanding, she realized that it was not a *plea* for help, but an *offer!*

Unsure of what to do, she opened a tiny rift and pumped a bit of extra-dimensional energy into the statue.

The eyes glowed as they received the energy, and she heard in her mind, *Promise ta free me an' I'll save ya from the Fomoire*, the voice said.

How am I to do that? she asked.

Give me 'nother shot of the spirits' fare an' toss me inta Sobek's pentagram, the voice replied.

You want me to give you more extra-dimensional energy?

Aye, yer unnerstandin' my meanin' awright, the voice said.

How can I trust you?

Not meanin' ta be rude, but I dun't see anytin' better on the table.

As if to punctuate his point, Penny heard a loud crash from the debris pile that used to be the barn's loft. The *Fomoire* tossed aside a large rusted tractor wheel and had nearly freed itself from the collapsed debris.

As for trust, I could say the same fer yer kind, but I huv searched yer soul an' if there ever was a creature of this plane I could trust, yer it. Alls I can do is give ya my honor's promise ta do as I huv said. As for my name, I call m'self Farsyl.

The *Fomoire* pulled itself out of the remaining wreckage, found Penny, and quickly moved toward her.

Penny had mere seconds to make the biggest decision of her life. Did she lead the *Fomoire* toward her friend and mentor to feast on his soul, or did she trust the promise of the *Coch Coblyn* to help her defeat Sobek?

Mr. Myrdin mistook her consideration as a hesitation to offer him up to the *Fomoire* and yelled across the barn, "Penny, you must lead him to me!"

In that instant, Penny made her choice. She sent a strong shot of trans-dimensional energy into the statue of the *Coch Coblyn*. Its eyes burned with a bright red fire, and she heard Farsyl's voice in her head, *T'anks, lass, now toss me!*

Penny stepped away from the main support beam she'd been hiding behind and cocked her arm to throw the figurine at Sobek.

The *Fomoire* spotted her and lashed out with its tentacle.

She released the small statue at the same time that the tentacle wrapped itself around her legs.

Mr. Myrdin screamed, "Penny!"

The *Fomoire* pulled her legs out from under her. She hit the barn floor with a resounding thud, and the creature dragged her toward its body.

The figurine flew end over end through the air. Much to Sobek's surprise, it passed cleanly through his energy shield and landed upright inside the pentagram. As soon as it hit the ground, the flames on all five candles at the points of the pentagram's star flared bright red. Then winked out. The energy field flickered and collapsed.

The *Fomoire* reached the inscribed pentagram at the same instant that the energy field vanished. It dropped Penny and shot its tentacle across the previously impenetrable outer circle of the pentagram and wrapped it around Sobek's waist.

Sobek screamed, "No!"

The tentacle lifted him from the ground and brought him before its gaping maw. A forked tongue that flashed iridescently shot out of the *Fomoire's* mouth and struck the First Acolyte of the Amun-Ra right above his heart.

Sobek's eyes widened with horror. He opened his mouth to scream, but no sound escaped. The *Fomoire's* tongue pulsed rapidly, and its single eye blazed with a bright blue fire as it drank the life force from Sobek's body. Within seconds, all that remained of Sobek was a shriveled and desiccated corpse. It reminded Penny of the mummies from Steve and Eddie's presentation.

As soon as the *Fomoire* finished its meal, everything except its blazing blue eye turned instantly into the dense fog from which it had been formed. The fog streamed into the eye, which continued to glow until it swallowed the last of the dimensional mist. Then it too winked into nothingness.

Sobek's body fell to the floor as soon as the *Fomoire* vanished. The corpse crumpled into a pile of fine black dust.

Penny rose from the ground and picked up the small statue of the *Coch Coblyn* which said, *I've held my end of our bargain, now 'tis time fer you to uphold yers.*

I don't know how.

It's really simple, lass. Just declare yer desire ta free me from this realm and smash me statue with the Teyrnwialen o Saith.

That sounds simple enough.

Aye, 'tis, but there be one other thing ya needs ta know. 'Cause me original summoners is no longer here, releasin' me will forever drain the scepter of its powers.

I understand. She found the *Teyrnwialen o Saith* and raised it above the figurine. Before she swung it, she said, *"Goodbye Farsyl. I free you from this realm,"* and just before the scepter smashed the figurine, she swore she heard, *"Da bo ti fy ffrind."*

She couldn't be sure, but it sounded like a goodbye.

34

PENNY AND MR. MYRDIN EMERGED THROUGH THE BARN DOORS
to find Duncan and Master Poe standing over an unconscious
Simon. Penny ran to his side to tend to him.

It was Myrdin who spoke first.

"What happened out here?"

"Some sort of force prevented us from getting into the barn. No
matter which way I turned, I kept returning to where we entered
the ground. After several attempts, I gave up. When I surfaced, I
found Simon but was surprised to not see Penny. What happened
in there?" Master Poe said.

"We tangled with a *Fomoire*," Mr. Myrdin said.

"A *Fomoire*? You must be mistaken," Master Poe exclaimed.

While he rubbed his sore wrists, Mr. Myrdin replied, "No, I'm afraid not."

"Don't take this the wrong way, but how are the two of you here?"

"To be honest, old friend, I'm not sure."

Everyone's attention turned to Penny, who knelt next to the inert body of her *Cait Sith* protector. "What's happened to Simon?"

"When you weren't with us, we immediately realized that the trap had been set for you. Blocked from teleporting, Simon tried to leap into the barn through that opening above the door." Master Poe pointed toward the opening with his wing.

"I didn't think he could jump that high, but he did," Duncan said.

"Unfortunately, instead of flying through the window, he hit some sort of energy field. Probably the same one that kept us from following you in," Master Poe said.

"Yeah, he bounced off the open space, and bright blue sparks raced around the barn. When we got here, he was unconscious and barely breathing," Duncan said.

"He's going to be all right, isn't he? I mean, *Cait Sith* are tougher than regular cats, right?" she asked.

Mr. Myrdin let out a sigh. "His physical condition is not life-threatening."

Penny raised her eyebrows. "But?"

"That barn was protected by a field strong enough to prevent a Master from the seventh dimension from entering."

Tears streamed down Penny's face. She looked at Master Poe. "Isn't there something you can do?"

"The field drained me as well. I'm afraid he's beyond my help."

"No!" Penny leaned over Simon, stroked his fur, and reached out across their telepathic link.

Simon opened his eyes, and she felt his weakened presence in her mind.

Penny, I am glad you are safe. I am sorry that I failed in my duty.

No, you didn't fail me!

I should have been by your side. The blue fire stopped me. A Cait Sith cannot accept failure.

No! You didn't fail. Your impact with the barn's energy field distracted the Fomoire just long enough for me to escape.

After a pause, Simon asked, *You needed my help?*

Yes!

Then I am still Cait Sith. His shallow, irregular breathing stabilized. Simon began to purr.

"He's purring. Does that mean he's going to be okay?" Duncan asked.

"Yes, he's going to be fine," Penny said.

"Good. Now what happened to the *Teyrnwialen o Saith*?" Master Poe asked.

"We left it in the barn," Penny said.

Master Poe released a high-pitched squawk. "You can't be serious. You left a *Conglfaen* in the barn?"

"Not exactly," Mr. Myrdin said.

"Either you did or you didn't, which is it?" Master Poe said.

"We left the *Teyrnwialen o Saith*, but it's no longer a *Conglfaen*. I had to discharge all of its power to defeat Sobek and the *Fomoire*."

"It's powerless?" Master Poe asked.

Mr. Myrdin nodded. "We left it sitting on the floor of the barn next to its oak box. Can you sense any trace of it in the upper dimensions?"

Master Poe paused for a moment, then shook his beak from side to side. "There's not even a spark of energy left in it."

"Still, should we really leave it behind? I mean, couldn't someone recharge it?" Duncan asked.

"Unfortunately, there's no power in this dimension that could bring it back to life," Master Poe said.

"It's nothing more than a jeweled scepter now," Mr. Myrdin added.

"Isn't that a good thing?" Duncan asked.

Master Poe shrugged his wings. "It's hard to say. The loss of such a powerful tool is never without consequences."

"On that cheerful note, what about the *Coch Coblyn*?" Duncan asked.

"I believe he and Sobek were tied together," Mr. Myrdin said.

"So, they were the braided time strand?" Duncan asked.

Mr. Myrdin nodded. "Yes, and now that Sobek is gone, I believe we've seen the last of our charming little red friend. Wouldn't you agree, Penny?"

She nodded.

"Good, I think we need to get moving. Penny and I have been through quite an ordeal, and I could use a spot of Earl Grey."

"I quite agree. With an extra-dimensional event as powerful as this, it won't take the deputy and his friend long to come here to investigate," Master Poe said.

"Right, and we want to be far away when they get here," Duncan said.

MEETING HOUSE OF THE HERON CLAN, SEVERAL WEEKS LATER

"DEPUTY BARNES AND MR. KOLCHAK," JESSE CORNPLANTER SAID. "On behalf of the Heron clan and the Seneca Nation, I want to thank you for not only finding and returning the Rod of Life but for avoiding any undue publicity. Thanks to your efforts, our people are more unified than they've been in generations."

"Aw, it was nothin'." Deputy Barnes looked toward the ground and shuffled his feet.

"We just followed the trail to the biggest spike of paranormal energy and found it in the middle of that wrecked barn," Kolchak said.

"All true heroes are modest, and make no mistake that you two are *true* heroes of the Seneca people. Therefore, as Sachem of the Seneca Tribe, it is my honor to offer you membership in the Heron clan of the Tonawanda Band."

"I don't know what to say," Kolchak said.

"Me neither," added Deputy Barnes.

"I gather you accept?" the Sachem asked. Both men nodded. The Sachem placed his arms around each man's shoulder. "Welcome, brothers."

ACKNOWLEDGMENTS

T O QUOTE THE GRATEFUL DEAD; WHAT A LONG, STRANGE TRIP it's been. From its beginnings as a cure for a sleepless night to the finished tale, innumerable people helped me complete this story. Two of the most important are Rosanne Cornbrooks Catalano and Debi Staples. Without their support and belief, this story would have never made it out of my basement. I would also like to acknowledge Cathy, Nicholas, Anna, and Alex. Your suggestions and enthusiastic requests to read the latest chapters, inspired me through some of the toughest spots. I also appreciate your tolerance for the antics of a grumpy author. Finally, I would like to thank everyone at my publisher, CamCat Books, especially Helga Schier.

ABOUT THE AUTHOR

A RMEN POGHARIAN WAS NOT AN EARLY READER. HE CAN honestly say he didn't voluntarily read a book until he finished *The Hobbit* in sixth grade. He earned a BS in Electrical Engineering from Rensselaer Polytechnic Institute, where he was an Honorable-Mention All-American swimmer. As a USAF officer, he worked on classified 'Area 51' projects—he never saw a single alien (dead or alive). He later earned an MBA from the University of North Carolina in Chapel Hill and spent more than a decade in the high tech and biotech industries. His stories mix elements of science and history with a healthy dose of fantasy. When not writing he enjoys swimming, reading, and the outdoors. He lives outside Rochester, NY with his wife and family.

For more information about upcoming books and the occasional nerdy post about maps, science, and history, visit his Author Facebook page at www.facebook.com/AuthorArmenPogharian.

Armen also maintains a website and blog.

Visit www.armenpogharian.com for information about the Misaligned and Warders book series as well as reviews of similar books. His blog covers history, science, and writing as well as the popular Map Monday posts. The monthly feature shares a different interesting or obscure map on the first Monday of the month.

MORE FROM ARMEN POGHARIAN

PENNY PRESTON AND THE KING'S BLADE
MISALIGNED BOOK 3

PROLOGUE

NEARLY 1,700 YEARS AGO IN THE DEPARTURE CHAMBER
SOMEWHERE IN THE 5TH DIMENSION

T HE NOVICE DESCENDED THE ENDLESS STAIRWAY AND CROSSED the energy threshold that sealed the Departure Chamber from the rest of the 5th dimension. Inside, the chamber was bathed in the blue glow of the spinning orb. Created from eons of labor with convoluted hyper-dimensional constructs, the globe's elegantly simple three-dimensional form belied a sinister nature. The overwhelming awe of being in its presence strained the connections of the novice's synapses. He needed to relax. He focused on the glowing sphere.

The spinning orb was the key to escaping the bounds of the universe's five dimensions, but not in the way the Principals who created it envisioned. Their aim was to reach for the unknown wonders of higher dimensional existence. Despite spending countless ages contemplating their mathematical creation, they overlooked the obvious. In a multiverse, everything is possible, including universes with less than five dimensions. The spinning portal was a gateway to such a universe. Passing through it enabled the Principals and their select friends to enter a three-dimensional universe where they enjoyed god-like powers.

The novice had joined the Association dreaming of the day he would make that journey. His first assignments had been mind-numbingly dull tasks. He spent an age verifying a Principal's latest calculations of irrational mathematical constants. How many digits of π were really necessary?

Then he was assigned to monitor the inter-dimensional portal for incongruities. No one had ever seen an anomaly, but the possibility existed. Other monitors had told him that if you aligned your senses with the energy output of the portal just right, that you could catch a glimpse of the alien three-dimensional universe.

Success required complete synergy with the portal. A single unrelated thought would preclude proper alignment and prevent synchronicity.

He stared blankly into the revolving globe. Slowly he filled every synaptic gap of his aura with its never-changing rotation. He released the last tendrils of his consciousness into the sphere. Its blueness seeped into his being. His essence aligned with the portal's energy. He prepared himself for a treasured glimpse of the bizarre three-dimensional world.

Blinding yellow and red lights flashed across the surface of the spinning orb. Their colors entered his essence mixing with the pure blue. Green, purple, and even a hint of orange saturated his synapses as the unwanted lights continued to mingle. He fought to flush the invading colors from his aura. He failed. Anguish filled his essence. Fear quickly followed.

Novices were forbidden from directly interacting with the portal. Their task was to observe, nothing more. He disengaged his senses from it. He extended them beyond the portal but found no one else in the chamber. He returned his full attention to the portal. The yellow and red flashes were gone, replaced by the deep blue glow of the orb . . . but something was different. It took a fraction of a moment for the novice to recognize . . . the orb had stopped spinning.

PRESENT DAY IN PIPER FALLS

D UNCAN RAN UP BEHIND PENNY AND PLAYFULLY PUNCHED
her in the shoulder.

"Hey, what's the big idea?" she asked.

"Uh, nothing," Duncan replied.

"Why'd you punch me?"

"You're always punching me in the shoulder. I thought it was,
you know, our thing."

"*Me* punching *you* is our thing. You punching me, well, that's
just wrong. Got it?" Penny said.

Duncan broke eye contact, looked down at the ground, and
shrugged.

"Uh, okay, I didn't think it was a big deal."

Penny tried to follow-up with another quip, but instead of saying something witty, she lost her self-control and a squeaky laugh escaped her lips.

Duncan gazed into her mismatched blue and brown eyes and furrowed his brow. "You're just messing with me, aren't you?"

Tilting her head coquettishly to the right, as she'd seen Lisa Giambi do so effectively with other boys, she replied, "Guilty." For good measure, she softly punched Duncan in the shoulder.

Instead of pretending her punch hurt by rubbing his shoulder like he usually did, Duncan narrowed his eyes and shook his head. "Very funny. I hope you're more serious at practice. Coach Harlow said today's target set is the final and most important piece of our preparation for States. After this practice, we start our taper."

Penny didn't respond.

One of the reasons Penny enjoyed swim-ming, besides being good at it and spending time with her friends, was the variety of training. Lots of people thought swimming laps back-and-forth in a pool must be boring. Penny agreed, but swim practice was a lot more than laps.

Besides the four different strokes, there was kicking, pulling, sprinting, innumerable stroke drills, breath control sets, and target time swims.

Penny hated target sets. Oh, she understood the whole point of 'training at your optimal level.' It was impossible not to get it. Coach Harlow rambled on about it almost every day. The woman was obsessed with the concept. Penny was sure that some of the older boys purposely went too fast just to hear Coach Harlow go off on the importance of swimming to pace in the target sets. Sometimes she wondered why boys did what they did. Absentmindedly, she shook her head.

"I wasn't kidding," Duncan said. "She talked to me after practice yesterday and told me if I wanted to beat Charlie Shopp at States, I needed to nail the target set today."

Charlie was the only swimmer who'd beaten Duncan during the season. One of Duncan's goals was to be state champion and to do that he'd have to beat Charlie.

He wouldn't admit it, but Penny knew he was nervous about swimming against Charlie again. "Don't worry about it; you've trained harder than anyone else on the team. I'm sure you'll swim a best time."

"Yeah, but what if that's not good enough to beat Charlie?"

"Then remember what Coach always says."

Duncan let out a long sigh. "Anytime you swim a best time, you've swum a great race."

PENNY TOUCHED THE WALL, LIFTED HER HEAD, AND QUICKLY found the pace clock. It was an older analog model with a sweeping red second hand that was just passing the ten.

"Penny!" Coach Harlow yelled, "what's your target time for this set?"

"Uh, 1:15," she replied.

"You just swam a 1:09. That's more than five seconds too fast. A couple of seconds is okay, but five is not. The point of a target set is to maximize the benefit of your training without swimming too hard. We've only got a few more practices before we leave for the State meet. If you train too hard, you're going to blow your taper. Now, give me one more hundred and bring it in on the 1:15. Leave on the bottom."

Penny nodded and adjusted her goggles.

As the second hand approached the thirty, Coach Harlow called out, "Ready . . ." and when it reached the thirty she yelled, "Go!" Penny pushed off the wall, taking three powerful dolphin kicks while emphasizing her streamline position. She also took three strokes before taking her first breath. At least if she went too fast, she'd do it with great form.

She never finished the 100. She didn't even reach the far wall. As she took her first breath, the lights in the pool flickered several times before going out. The emergency lights failed to click on. Only the wall of glass along the north wall by the deep end kept the pool from becoming pitch black.

Concentrating hard on maintaining her pace, Penny kept swimming toward the deep end of the pool. She didn't hear the lifeguard frantically blowing his whistle or Coach Harlow yelling for her to stop swimming and get out of the water. She continued swimming, thinking only about the timing of her last breath before her flip turn. As she crossed into the red zone (named for the change in color of the lane-lines five yards before the wall), she suddenly stopped moving forward. She increased the turnover rate to a full sprint, but she couldn't get any closer to the wall. Instead, she started to go backward.

If her pull was nearly useless, her kick was even worse. She couldn't move her legs at all. No matter how hard she tried to kick, she couldn't break free from a vice-like grip pinning them together.

In the blink of an eye, she went from going backward to moving downward. With a panicked last stroke Penny grasped for the lane-line. Her fingertips latched onto the outer edges of the wave-suppressing buoys. The line stained against her weight as the force pulled her down. She managed one quick gasp of air before her fingers slipped and she disappeared below the surface.

Fully submerged, she turned to face who or what was pulling her down. She didn't see anything, at least not anything in the normal dimensions. In the upper dimensions, she saw what at first glance appeared to be a mermaid. But this mermaid didn't come out of any Hans Christian Andersen fable.

Instead of a female torso, this one had the well-muscled upper body of a linebacker with two sets of arms on top of his fish-tailed lower body. The longer of the two sets were more like tentacles with suction cup-covered pads at the end. The shorter set ended in powerful bone-crushing claws. The pads wrapped around Penny's lower legs and the long arms pulled her toward the lobster-like claws.

Incapable of speaking underwater, Penny pointed to the surface.

The creature grinned, revealing a mouth full of razor-sharp teeth. He shook his head from side-to-side. In case Penny misunderstood, he snapped his claws open and shut several times while his tentacles continued to pull her down.

Unable to reason with him, Penny quickly went to plan B; she opened a trans-dimensional rift and shifted into the higher dimensions. Since her attacker was *Bodach*, a native of the 5th dimension, her transformation didn't break his grip on her legs, but it did allow her to breathe. Revitalized, Penny seized the opportunity to go on the offensive. Using the creature's grip on her legs as leverage, she executed a flip-turn. The maneuver brought her inside his snapping claws. She stared directly into his dark bottomless eyes. Weaponless and unable to think of anything else, she cupped her hands and smashed them into the monster's ears.

His mouth opened and emitted a high-pitched scream. Ringing pain shot through Penny's ears, bouncing against the inside of her skull. Barely able to think, she struck the creature again and braced for another siren scream.